MURDER SO FESTIVE

MURDER SO FESTIVE

A Merry March Mystery

Eileen Curley Hammond

Twody Press

Cover designed by SelfPubBookCovers.com/ RLSather

Eileen Curley Hammond
Visit my website at www.eileencurleyhammond.com

Printed in the United States of America

First Printing: Oct 2018
Twody Press

ISBN-978-1-7325460-3-5

Library of Congress Control Number: 2018910844

AUTHOR'S NOTE

Thank you to those of you who purchased my debut Merry March mystery, *Murder So Sinful.* I truly appreciate the time readers took to share some lovely comments with me. I hope you enjoy this book just as much. And if you do, please let others know about it through your favorite social media platform or a review on Amazon.

I also appreciate the people who so generously invest their time in making my writing better. In particular, I'd like to thank young adult writer Jenna Grinstead, Eric Henderson, and the Buckeye Crime Writers group (a Sisters in Crime chapter).

Miranda, of Editing Realm, helped me on my journey with her encyclopedic knowledge of punctuation and grammar. She also gave me some great ideas on how to make the ending even more suspenseful.

My family, as always, is a great source of inspiration and support. Specifically, I'd like to thank my sister-in-law Linda who served as an early reader of this book, and my sister-in-law Donna (plus her fabulous assistant and daughter, Allison) for creating such a gorgeous tableau post on Facebook for my first book. It's nice to know I have such a great team surrounding me.

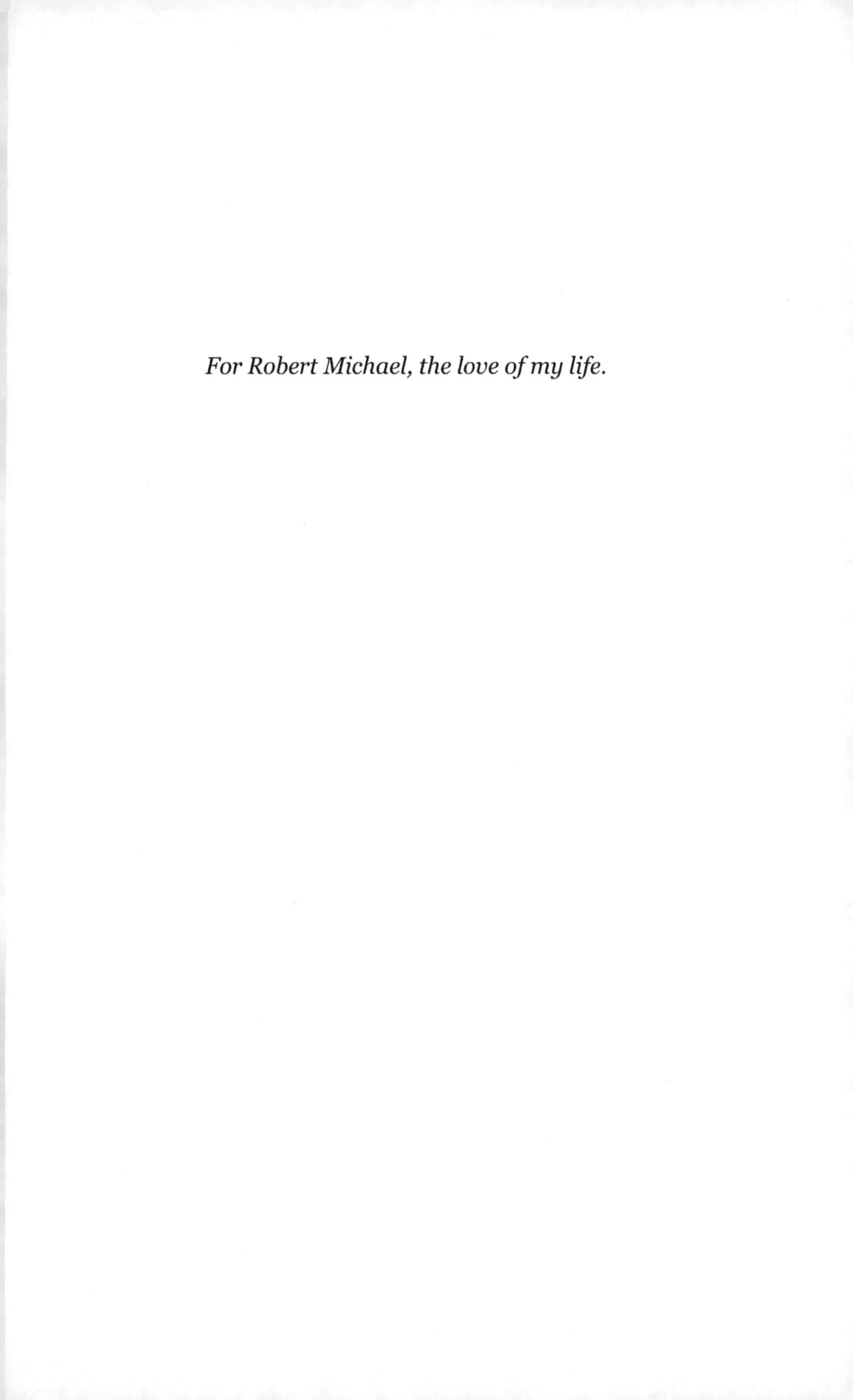

For Robert Michael, the love of my life.

CHAPTER 1

I ran down the stairs, opened the door, and gasped. "Drew, when did you get out?"

Without saying a word, he picked me up and pressed his lips to mine. We careened into the sofa, falling on it. "I've missed you so much," he murmured into my ear as he fumbled with my clothes.

I pushed him away. My hand slid off his shoulder and hit him hard on the nose.

"Ow." He held his nose and slid off the sofa onto one knee. "What did you do that for?"

Scurrying up to stand on the sofa, I pointed at him. "We are divorced. That means we are no longer intimate." I straightened my shirt and wiped my mouth with the back of my hand. Frowning at it, I rubbed my hand on my pants and shuddered.

Rob thundered down the stairs to stand over Drew. "Who the hell do you think you are?"

Drew scrambled up, still holding his nose. "I could ask you the same question."

"Merry's friend. I assume you're the ex-husband." They glared at each other like warring predators. "Now that we've been introduced, you need to leave." He punched his fist into his palm. "Or do you need help?"

Drew studied Rob, appearing to weigh his options. They were both roughly six feet tall and in good shape, but it looked like Drew had been working out in prison. Drew snorted. "I'm leaving, but we're not done here. Merry, I'll call you. I want to see my daughter." He stormed out and slammed the door behind him.

I hurried over, flipped the deadbolt, and leaned against the door to steady myself. "Well, that was unexpected." An uncertain laugh escaped my lips. I picked up one of the throw pillows that had fallen, smoothed it, and put it back where it belonged.

"Are you okay?"

I shook my head. "I can't believe they didn't let me know he was going to be let out of prison. I thought they would tell me so I'd have some time to prepare myself." The clock chimed, making me jump. "And Jenny. I need to tell Jenny."

Rob put his arms around me. "Calm down. We'll break the news to her together."

I hugged him. "No. I need to tell her alone."

His eyes narrowed as he backed away. "Why don't you want me to be there? Is there something you don't want me to hear?"

"Don't be silly. It's just sensitive. Jenny and I have been alone since Drew was convicted four years ago. I want to make sure she feels she can ask me any questions she wants."

Rob's eyebrows rose. "We've been living in the same house together for the last month. Why would you think that my being there would make her uncomfortable? I thought we were a team."

"We are. This is hard. You're just going to have to trust me on this."

His jaw tightened. "I may as well pack up and move back to my place. Now that the murderer is in jail, you and Jenny are no longer in danger." His lovely green eyes searched mine. "There's no reason for me to stay here anymore."

The clock ticked. I didn't say anything, so he turned on his heel and took the stairs two at a time. He moved about in the guest room.

Hangers rattled. After a few minutes, he came back down, zipping his duffel bag closed.

My eyes welling with unshed tears, I stopped him with my hand on his chest. "We knew that life was eventually going to go back to normal, didn't we?"

He lifted my hand. "I guess we did." He kissed my cheek and strode out the door.

I sank down onto the sofa, and my tears spilled over. I picked up Courvoisier, one of my cats, and hugged her. "Why does normal feel so bad?"

As I stroked her gray fur, my heart rate slowed. Sighing, I gave her a few last pets and made my way to the powder room. A look in the mirror confirmed that my mascara wasn't waterproof. I splashed my face with water and toweled off. Squaring my shoulders, I grabbed my purse and headed over to my best friend Patty's house.

My spirits couldn't help but lift as I entered. The noise was deafening. Patty's three boys fenced in the kitchen. Draped in aprons, they pretended that their various spatulas and wooden spoons were light sabers. They completed the look by wearing pots on their heads.

I patted one of the pots. "Where's your mom?"

The youngest used his long wooden spoon to point toward the living room. Saluting the squad, I wandered in that direction.

Patty sat on her sofa reading a magazine and drinking a glass of wine. She raised it to me. "You ran the gauntlet. For that, I salute you. I care not, but how does my kitchen fare?"

I laughed and wagged my finger. "How many glasses of wine have you had? And in response to the question about your kitchen, you don't want to know."

She waved her hand dismissively. "Patrick will be home soon. Let him deal with it." She gestured to her glass. "Would you like to imbibe?"

"I certainly would." I poured myself a glass and sank onto the chair across from her. I took a big gulp. "I needed that."

"Why in particular? You captured the murderer, uncovered insurance fraud, and promoted your business all at the same time. You should be feeling quite accomplished." She smiled and took a sip.

"Drew's out."

Shooting straight up, she plopped her glass on the table, straightening it as it threatened to tip over. "What a buzzkill." She sat next to me and put her arm around my shoulders. "How could he be out? Did they tell you he was going to be released?"

I gave her a death stare. "Don't you think I would have mentioned it?"

She held up her hands. "In my defense, you have been kind of busy."

I hugged her. "You're forgiven. No, they did not give me any kind of notice. I thought they would too. Apparently, we were both mistaken."

"How did you find out? Are you sure?"

"Quite sure. He showed up at the house just as Rob and I were finally going upstairs for some hanky-panky."

She arched her eyebrows. "Talk about bad timing. And something about star-crossed lovers comes to mind." She chuckled. "But that's not quite right because you're not lovers yet, are you?"

I groaned and sank farther into the sofa. "Don't remind me."

"Tell me everything."

I just finished the story when what sounded like a heard of elephants clomped down the stairs. It was our two ballerinas: my daughter, Jenny, along with her sidekick, Patty's daughter, Cindy.

"Mom, Matt Hawkins texted me that he heard from Jenna Bell that someone saw Mr. Jenson fighting with Dad at our house. Is it true? Is Dad out?" Jenny asked, stringing her questions together in a staccato rhythm.

"Oh, great." I glanced at Patty. "Drew left the door open when he came in. Now everyone in town knows he's back."

Jenny stood in front of me, stretching to her full height of five foot ten, her blue eyes blazing. "Answer me, Mom. When did Dad get out? Why didn't you tell me?"

I patted the seat next to me. "Jenny, sit down." She did, and I put my arm around her. "I found out when he showed up at the house. I didn't know either."

"Why was Rob fighting with him?"

"They weren't really fighting. Your dad greeted me a bit too enthusiastically, and Rob took offense."

Leaping off the sofa, she pulled me up and scanned me from head to toe. "Did Dad hurt you?"

I hugged her. "No, I'm fine. I'm just sorry the door was open."

"Where's he going to stay? Where will he live? Is he going to stay in town?"

The overhead light glinted off Jenny's long blond hair. *She's so like Drew.* I sighed. "The answer to all of your questions is I don't know. We really didn't have time to chat." I held her at arm's length, as my green eyes raked hers. "Would you want him to stay in town?"

Jenny frowned. "I don't know. I was so mad at him for so long. He cheated a lot of people in town out of their money. And some of their kids were my friends. They didn't talk to me for like forever. If you hadn't paid everyone back, I don't think they'd ever have forgiven me. I'd probably have no friends at all." Her shoulders slumped, and she looked like she was about to curl up into a ball.

Cindy bounded next to her. "I'd still be your friend." She hugged Jenny hard, and it was like a ray of sunshine erupted when Jenny smiled.

It dimmed a bit as she continued. "He is my dad, though. I remember that he used to read me stories at bedtime and that he'd make up hysterical characters. Mom, do you remember the mouse named Manny? He'd even sing little songs he made up just to get me to smile." She frowned. "Is it wrong for me to miss him?"

"No, honey. He's your dad. He did some very bad things, and he needed to pay for them. If you want to see him, we'll arrange it." I hugged her. "We should probably get home."

"Is Mr. Jenson cooking? Maybe I could charm him into making some pancakes for dinner. What are my chances?"

"Normally they'd be good. You are such a charmer." I tweaked her nose. "But Rob moved back to his house."

"Without saying goodbye? I can't believe he did that. I thought he liked us."

"He does. He's just moving home. We knew it would happen sometime."

Jenny stood and stomped out the door. "I hate change!"

After waving goodbye to Patty and Cindy, I followed her. "Me too."

I squeezed Jenny's hand as we strolled home. "Even though your dad paid his debt to society by finishing his prison term, people are likely to still be angry about it. I just hope it won't get too bad."

CHAPTER 2

Frost was on the window when I woke to do my stretches. My cats, Courvoisier and Drambuie, vied for space as I bent over, hoping an errant pet might come their way. Disappointed when I rose to take a quick shower, they disappeared into the kitchen in hopes that I would soon feed them.

I whispered, "Fair weather friends," as their loping bodies slid through the open doorway.

The house felt empty without Rob in it. Still in my robe, I padded to the guest room, closed my eyes, and slowly pushed the door open. Peeking around it, I held my breath. He wasn't there. *What did you expect? That he crept back in the middle of the night? He's gone.*

I crawled into the bed and cradled the pillow, smelling a mélange of bay leaves, argan oil, and the slightest hint of buttered rum. Tears coursed down my face. I should have told him to stay. Drambuie leapt onto the bed and head butted me, still waiting for her food. I rubbed my face against her side and groaned. Climbing out of bed, I stripped it and threw the sheets down the stairs.

Returning to my room, I splashed my face with cold water. I dressed quickly and knocked on Jenny's door. I stuck my head in. "Time for sleeping beauty to get up."

She flung a pillow at me. "I'm up."

"Doesn't look like it."

She pushed her hair from her face. "I'm up-ish. I'll be in the shower before you even make it downstairs."

"It's a bet. But I should warn you that I stretched already, which means I'm ready to move."

She laughed. "Yes, but I'm seventeen, and you're thirty-nine."

I swung the door shut. "Smart aleck. Let's see if I defrost a muffin for you."

"Sorry!"

I reached the bottom of the stairs. Picking up the sheets, I took them into the laundry room and dumped them in the wash.

Feeding the cats and putting two muffins in the microwave to defrost, I checked my work calendar for the day at my company—the Meredith March Insurance Agency. I groaned, remembering that today was our standing staff meeting. I was sure there would be quite a few questions about Drew.

The shower turned off, so I shouted up the steps, "I'm leaving. Muffin's on the table with some juice."

"Thank you," echoed down the hallway.

Grabbing my briefcase, I headed out only to stop in my tracks halfway through my gate. There was a For Sale sign in the yard next door. Shifting my gaze to the bleak front porch, I sighed. My neighbor and friend, Nancy, had been murdered in her house not long ago. *It's going to be hard to sell that house. But I guess at the right price anything will sell.*

The staff meeting started at eight thirty on the dot. As expected, there were multiple questions about Drew. I shared what little I knew and asked everyone to keep their minds on their jobs. One of my associates, Susan Clime, had invested some of her meager savings with Drew.

She gripped her pencil so hard it snapped. "Four years wasn't long enough for that bastard."

Startled, I stated, "That's what he got, and we can't change it. I know that a lot of people were disappointed they didn't get the returns they were led to expect, but at least they got their principal back."

Susan looked up. "It's not your fault, Merry. People don't blame you, at least not anymore. They know you worked hard to make sure everyone got their money back. It was just that I had plans for that money."

Tempted to say, "If it sounds too good to be true, it usually is," I bit my tongue. *After all, he fooled me too.* "It was a painful time for all of us. Now, if there are no further questions, I would like to move on to Tony's terrific presentation on a new product one of our companies is introducing next month. Tony?"

As I sat, my mind wandered. Where will Drew end up living? How will he make any money? No one around here will hire him, and I depleted his savings making everyone whole. I guess that's his problem now.

Later that day, I was surprised I hadn't heard from Rob. I wasn't sure if we were having dinner together or not. *I'll give it another night. I'm sure he'll call by then.* I packed my things and left the office. It was a very quick trip home, especially now that the weather had turned and the cold seemed to settle into my bones.

As I bustled in the back door, Jenny yelled, "Shut the door. It's freezing out there."

"How do you expect me to get in if I don't open the door?"

"You could have come in the front."

I rolled my eyes. "But how was I supposed to know you were back here instead of in the front?"

"Because I am doing the endless homework that my cruel teachers heap on me and I always do it in the kitchen."

I sighed. "Okay, Miss Grumpypants. Is pizza good for dinner?"

"Is Mr. Jenson bringing it?"

"Not that I know of. I haven't heard from him today."

Jenny's eyebrows rose. "That's different. Did you break up?"

"I think he just needs a bit of space and time. I'll call him tomorrow night if I don't hear from him by then."

The next morning was another rush to get us both out the door on time. The monthly breakfast meeting for the Small Business Association of the chamber of commerce was at eight, and I wasn't looking forward to it. The good news was that the group finally made a decision on Christmas decorations. That meant I wouldn't have to hear Mort Wilson talk about the psychological benefits of round shapes versus peaked ones anymore. The bad news was that everyone would likely be talking about Drew. With a sigh, I pushed myself out the door. I dropped my briefcase when I reached the sidewalk—the For Sale sign was gone from Nancy's yard.

Entering the Iron Skillet, I hurried toward the private room where some of our meetings were held. It was busy for a Tuesday, and it seemed like every head in the restaurant was swiveled toward that room. Someone was shouting. As I neared the door, it became clear there were multiple raised voices. I couldn't make out the words because everyone talked over everyone else. What had stirred them all up so early? I opened the door. The volume dropped so abruptly it sounded like one of those hot summer nights when the crickets stop. Several members looked at me nervously.

Lauren Stamper said, "Merry, we heard Drew is back."

"It's true."

"He's not planning on staying in town, is he? Don't tell me he's staying with you?"

"No. He's not staying with me. I'm not sure what his future plans are."

Amanda Thomas stood. "I'm sure you know this, Merry, but we consider Drew to be an unsavory element in town. Having him back will likely cause trouble. Our expectation is that you will take point on convincing him of the folly in staying here."

I shifted uncomfortably, my coat still in my arms. I hung it on the rack and took a deep breath. "Drew and I are divorced. I suspect I will have very little sway over whether he stays or goes." John Little, Tom Butler, and several others studied the table, signaling that they were uncomfortable with the discussion. However, more than a few people looked on with great interest. "He served his time; it's up to him where he ends up. Needless to say, it would be more comfortable for me if he did not choose to live here."

Amanda frowned. "So you will try to influence him?" Philip Piper, Amanda's boyfriend, pulled on her arm to try to get her to sit. She shrugged off his hand.

"No. But I can assure you I won't encourage him to stay. That's all I'm going to say on this subject, so I suggest that we move on to the topics that were on the agenda." Sitting down, I picked one up and motioned for the association chair, Will Jones, to take charge.

Amanda harrumphed, sat, and glared at Philip. Will picked up the agenda. "If everyone would look at item one. We need to start working on our annual St. Valentine's Day dance." He droned on.

I knew this was going to be bad. What happens if Drew stays? It looks like I will get blamed.

Somehow I made it through the meeting. As I was leaving, Amanda pulled me to the side, her eyes full of anger. "Merry, tensions are running high on Drew. It would be in his best interest to leave." Philip stood next to her.

I wrenched her arm from mine. "I heard you the first time, and my answer stands."

She pivoted, marched straight out the door, and slammed it behind her. Philip stayed behind for a moment. "I'm sorry, Merry. Amanda's been a bit out of sorts ever since Drew was released." He paused, and his gaze skittered about. "I better go."

Tom Butler pulled on his coat. "I'm sorry about Amanda, Merry. Most of us know that you don't have control over this situation. It's just that there's a lot of talk in town. It will get worse the longer he stays. I pray it just stays talk." He nodded at me.

"Thanks, Tom."

Other people picked up their coats and shuffled past without comment.

Andy Perkins stopped and gave me a hug. "It's going to be okay. Don't you worry your pretty head. They're all talk and no bite." I smiled up at him. Andy and his spouse, Ed, lived behind me and ran the antique shop, Tempting Treasures, a block down from my business. "Accompany you to the office?"

I hugged him back. "I'd like that."

As we ambled, I said, "Nancy's For Sale sign was down this morning. Have you heard anything?"

"No. The last time I spoke with her cousin, Melissa, she said she wasn't getting a lot of interest. She had to disclose that the murder happened there, and I think that's scaring off potential buyers. If it doesn't sell soon, she's going to think about renting it to pay the mortgage."

"I hope we get someone nice in there who likes to garden. It would be such a shame to see all of Nancy's work go to waste."

"I agree." We halted in front of my door. "This is your stop. Have a good day and try not to worry." He gave me a quick hug.

Cheryl, my assistant, greeted me. "The phones have been busy this morning. Clients want to know what Drew is going to do. We're telling them what you instructed, but I think a few of them need some reassurance. I've left their names and numbers on your desk."

"Thanks, Cheryl. I'll handle it. Did Rob call?"

"No. Were you expecting a call? Do you want me to interrupt if he does?"

"That's okay. I was just wondering."

I walked into my office and carefully shut the door, feeling Cheryl's curious eyes on my back. After hanging up my coat and stowing my purse, I glanced at my phone to see if any texts had arrived. Seeing none, I sighed and sat in my chair. I was going to have to make the first move with Rob. It was clear he wasn't going to call me.

CHAPTER 3

Patty texted me at four: "Sprung for a couple of hours. Patrick took Jenny, Cindy, and the kids to the movies. Want to meet at the Pickled Herring at five for a drink?"

"Works. See you there."

I smiled. Patty didn't get many chances to go out on her own, so I knew she'd be in a good mood. *Maybe this is just what I need to take my mind off things.* Making some last phone calls, I straightened my desk and headed over to the bar.

The town looked so festive with Christmas wreaths adorning the light poles. Most of the shopkeepers had already decorated their store windows, and the town tree was being decked out in the square. My mood lifting, I hummed as I turned the corner to the Pickled Herring. Patty was already sitting at the bar. She had a glass of red wine in front of her and faced one of the booths in the back.

I came up beside her. "What are you looking at?"

She jumped about a foot. "You scared me."

I laughed. "Most people look toward the door when they're waiting for someone. That way they don't get startled. Plus, then they can actually welcome the person they invited to join them." I pushed her shoulder. "What's so interesting?"

Patty nodded toward where she had been so focused. My mouth made an involuntary oval. Rob sat in one of the booths, and he was not alone. Amanda Thomas was with him, and she was practically sitting in his lap. Rob must have said something amusing because her laugh tinkled across the room as she leaned toward him and stroked his shoulder. Her long brown hair gleamed in the bar's soft light and cascaded down her thin frame.

I climbed up on the stool next to Patty and motioned for the bartender. "Ann, I'd like a glass of the house Pinot."

"Coming right up, Merry." Ann looked nervously over at Rob and Amanda. "Everything's okay, isn't it?"

"Just peachy."

"What are you going to do?" Patty asked.

"Nothing. I don't have a ring on my finger. He's able to see whomever he wants, even if she's supposed to be seeing someone else. And if he wants to sulk about an ex-husband I have nothing to do with, I can't change that either."

Patty turned me to face her. "Who are you and what have you done with my friend Merry?" I didn't reply. "Do you want to leave?"

"No. I have as much right to be here as he does. If I spend my life avoiding both Rob and Drew in this town, pretty soon I won't be able to go anywhere." My drink arrived, and I toasted Patty. "To us."

She smiled. "Through thick and thin." Twirling the wine, I put the glass to my lips and took a big gulp. She laughed. "I don't think you have to aerate the house wine." Whispering she said, "It's not that good."

I took another gulp. "Doesn't matter. It tastes good enough." I sighed. "The chamber meeting was this morning."

"And?"

"Amanda was very direct in telling me that it was my job to make sure Drew leaves town."

"Your job! Why does she think it's your job? Doesn't she know you're divorced?"

"I shared that fact with her."

The back of the bar was decorated with an antique mirror. I realized I could look straight ahead and see what Rob and Amanda were doing behind me. I frowned. Amanda was still sitting way too close to Rob for my liking. And she touched his arm.

Patty poked me. "I was talking to you."

"I'm sorry." I gestured at the mirror.

"Ah, that's easier and less intrusive than turning around."

"Sure is."

"Do you think she could get much closer to him?"

"Only if he became her second skin. But it doesn't look like he's uncomfortable with it."

"Maybe he's just talking to her about a story."

I caught Patty's eye in the mirror. "Uh-huh."

She had the good grace to blush. "Well, that might be all there is to it."

"I'd feel better about it if she wasn't such an attractive, single lady."

"Uh-oh." Patty gestured toward the mirror. I looked again. Philip Piper approached Rob and Amanda's table.

"This should be interesting." It took all my willpower not to turn around and to settle instead for the mirror view. Philip reached the table, and luckily his voice was loud enough that it carried.

"Amanda, you were supposed to meet me at six. I've been waiting for you." Philip towered over their table.

Amanda didn't seem to be in any rush to get up. I couldn't hear her reply, but Rob shifted in his seat. He scooted from behind the table, and I could just make out him saying, "It was time for me to leave anyway. Thanks for the information." Rob shook Amanda's hand. I might have been mistaken, but her brown eyes looked disappointed.

As Rob was putting on his coat, his eyes met mine in the mirror. He left it unzipped as he came up to the bar. "Merry, Patty, what a nice surprise. When did you come in?"

Patty was still focused on the drama behind us, so I replied, "About a half hour ago. You must have had your mind on other things."

He glanced back at the table where Philip and Amanda argued. "Oh. I met Amanda to talk about the fashion show she's putting on to promote the new spring lineup at her store, Shades of Gray."

I looked at Patty. "Aren't spring lineups supposed to be colorful?"

Patty snorted. "Don't do that when I'm drinking."

I laughed. Rob scolded, "You shouldn't make fun of the show. It's for a good cause. Some of the proceeds are going to fund breast cancer research."

"I know. I think it's a great cause. That's why Jenny and Cindy have agreed to be volunteer models for the show." Patty caught my eye, and I looked again in the mirror. Philip and Amanda were arm in arm as they left the bar. I shrugged. *Must have made up.*

Rob put his arm around me. "I've missed you. I'm sorry I haven't been in touch, but I've been busy catching up on some things. Dinner tomorrow? You and Jenny?"

"That would be great."

He kissed me. "I'll pick you up at your house at six." He waved as he left the bar.

Patty threw her cocktail napkin at me. "You really play hard to get."

"I'm getting too old for games."

My phone dinged with an incoming text from Andy Perkins: "Talked to Melissa. Drew's renting Nancy's house."

I grabbed my wine glass and drained it. Putting my head down on the bar, I stiff-armed the phone to Patty.

"Oh no."

CHAPTER 4

The next day arrived far too early for me. Patty came back with me after we left the bar, and we finished an entire bottle of wine as I bent her ear about Drew. *At least I only need to get one person up and out the door. Patty has four.* Stretching and downing two aspirin, I hopped in the shower. Turning the pressure up, I increased the heat and let the water play on my back. Feeling slightly better, I toweled off and padded down the hall to Jenny's room. I knocked once and poked my head in. "You up?"

One eye opened. "Yes, but I'm surprised you are."

"Smarty-pants. Don't forget, we're going to dinner with Rob tonight."

She wiggled her eyebrows. "Are you sure you don't want to be alone?"

"No. He invited you specifically."

"Oh, so he doesn't want to be alone with you."

"Whatever. Get up."

I started the coffee maker and fed the cats. *Something seems off. What is it? There is something I need to do.* I poured my coffee and took a sip, trying to clear my brain. Then I remembered. Crap. Drew's moving in next door.

Climbing back upstairs, I sat on the edge of Jenny's bed to wait for her to come out of the shower.

A moment or two later, she came back into her room toweling her hair and jumped. “I thought you left.”

“I needed to tell you something before you heard it elsewhere.”

Looking worried, she sat on the bed next to me. “What?”

“Your dad is going to rent Nancy’s house.”

“What? Why would he do that?” She frowned at the bedspread and traced the pattern with her finger. “I’m not sure how I feel about that. What will people say? Will they think we wanted him here?”

I hugged her. “Let’s figure out how you feel first and then worry about everyone else.”

She shrugged. “I guess it will be handy to have him next door so I can get to know him better.” A snowblower started up outside. “On the other hand, what if we don’t end up liking each other? He’ll be too close for comfort.” She put her arm around me. “How do you feel? Won’t Mr. Jenson feel weird?”

“First, your dad loves you. He’s going to be happy to see you anytime. Second, it might be a little weird having him so close at first, but I’m sure we’ll get used to it. I just want to make sure you are okay. You can take getting to know your dad again as fast or as slow as you want.”

She stood. “I need to get going. I don’t want to be late for school. Is it okay if we talk about this later?”

“You bet.” I hugged her. “See you tonight.”

As I left, Melissa came out of Nancy’s house, cleaning supplies in hand. “Melissa, wait a minute.” She paused, and I joined her on the porch. “I heard you’re renting the house to Drew.”

Shifting from one foot to another, she nodded. “No one wants to buy, and he had cash upfront to rent, so I took it. I’m sorry if it’s going to cause problems for you, Merry, but I need to pay the mortgage.” She talked even faster, seeming to sense that I was less than happy. “Plus, he’s taking it furnished, so I don’t need to make any quick decisions about what to keep and where to store everything.” Taking a deep breath, she held my arm. "I'm sorry, Merry, but what was I supposed to do?"

"It's not your fault, Melissa. Needless to say, I would have preferred that he found a place far away, but that didn't happen."

"Word is spreading that he's staying and that I'm renting the place to him. I received several angry phone calls already last night."

I hugged her. "Hopefully it will all die down once people get used to having him back. When is he moving in?"

She shot me a nervous look. "Later today."

Eyes widening, I took a step back. "Today?"

"He didn't have anywhere else to go, and I needed the money."

I groaned. "It will be fine. We will make it fine. I need to go now. Have a good day, Melissa."

"You too."

I trudged to work. Today. That means that he'll be in the house when I get home tonight. And he'll be here when Rob comes to pick us up. Ugh.

Somehow I made it to the office. Cheryl greeted me with coffee. "I heard about Drew moving in next to you." She handed me the mug. "Or do you need something stronger?"

I groaned and sat at my desk. "How am I going to make it through this?"

She sat in the chair opposite me. "You are the strongest person I know, and you have the town behind you."

"I hope you're right on both counts. And, now, I guess I should at least pretend to work."

She gave me a worried glance and then went through the list of items that needed my attention.

My mind wandered. What is Rob going to think? I better text him before he finds out from someone else. Who am I kidding? He already knows.

Cheryl stood, and my attention snapped back. “You haven’t heard a word I said.”

“Yes, I did.”

“No, you didn’t, but I expected that, so I printed off a list.” She handed it to me.

“What would I do without you?” She smiled and shut the door behind her.

I texted Rob, “Drew renting house next door.”

“I heard. Talk tonight.”

I next texted Jenny, “Will pick you up after school.”

“Why?”

“Just will. No biggie. Talk then.”

Feeling slightly better, I turned my attention to Cheryl’s list and worked steadily on the more urgent items. When it was time to leave to pick Jenny up, Cheryl knocked on the door. “You need to leave now if you want to be on time.”

“I’m going. I just want to take a few things home.” She helped me gather everything together and then gave me a quick hug. “It’ll be okay; you’ll see.”

The hike over to the high school seemed way too short, even though it was cold out. Jenny bounded out the door surrounded by her friends. I had to wait till she said goodbye to each and every one of them.

She finally joined me. “Brr, it’s cold out here.”

“Even colder when someone takes forever to say goodbye to people they will be texting all night and will see tomorrow.”

Putting her arm through mine, she smiled. “You raised me to be polite. Let’s go.” She stamped her feet. “I need to warm up. Why did you come by? I could have come home by myself.”

“If we start moving, you may warm up a bit.” She gave me an eye roll but started forward. “Your dad is moving in today.”

She shrieked, “Today? I’m not sure I’m ready.”

"Sometimes we're never ready for the things that happen in life." I squeezed her hand. "I'm sure everything will be okay."

"If you can stand it, I ought to be able to as well." As we got closer, my speed slowed with each step. "Mom, I can't keep on pulling you. At this rate, we won't be home till eleven."

"You're right." I sped up. *It's cold out. We probably won't even see him.* We turned the corner to our street and hurried along to the door.

"Howdy, neighbors." Drew must have been watching for us out his window.

"Hi, Dad."

"That's all. No hug, no kiss? We haven't seen each other in four years!"

I threw Drew a warning look. "Look, Drew..."

Jenny ran over to his porch and gave him a quick hug and peck on the cheek. "It's okay, Mom. I'll be back over in time to change." She disappeared into the house.

I stood there stunned by the sudden silence. Traipsing into the house, I sat on the window seat overlooking Drew's house. *I hope she's okay. Maybe I should go over and make sure. That's stupid. She's almost an adult, and he's her dad.* Shaking my head, I stood and put a load of laundry in.

An hour later, the back door burst open, and Jenny came in rubbing her arms. "Let's move somewhere warmer. It's too cold here."

"Not a bad idea. How did your visit go?"

"It was fine, Mom."

"What did you talk about?"

She gave me a look as she hung up her coat. "Not much. He just wanted to catch up on my life. He said his mother studied ballet when she was young too. It's kind of weird not knowing him but knowing him. Some things seemed so familiar about him, but it's been a long time. I think it kind of freaks him out that I've grown up."

"He's been living in a time warp."

"I know. I had to show him how to use his new smartphone."

"How could he afford a new smartphone? And how did he afford the rent? He had hardly any money left after I paid everyone back from his accounts."

"I don't know. Why don't you ask him? I need to get changed for dinner." She ran up the stairs.

I sat at the counter staring out the window. *How is he affording this?*

After a few minutes, Jenny hurried back down the stairs. "Mom, hate to tell you this, but you could do with a makeup refresh. And you may want to run a brush through your hair. It was pretty windy on our way back from school."

Starting out of my reverie, I headed for our combo half bath/laundry room. As I refreshed my makeup, Jenny jumped up to sit on the washing machine. "Mom, don't you think you should bake something and take it over to welcome Dad to the neighborhood?"

I almost took my eye out with the mascara. "I don't think that's a good idea."

She studied me in the mirror. "If it was anyone else who moved in, you would."

"You're right. But it wouldn't be appropriate for me to do that. It might give him the wrong idea." I tapped her shoulder. "I know, why don't you bake something for your dad after school tomorrow? I'm sure it will be that much more special if you bake it and take it over to him." I smiled at my reflection in the mirror.

The doorbell rang, and Jenny launched herself off the washer. "I'll get it."

I made a quick swipe with my lip gel and scrunched my auburn curls.

Sighing, I greeted Rob. He dangled a string, playing with Courvoisier, while Jenny did the same for Drambuie.

He stood when I came around the corner and hurried to give me a hug. "You okay?"

"Yes." I kissed him. "Mmm, it's good to have you here again."

"Mom, are you sure you want me to come with you?"

Rob gave her a crooked smile. "Up to you, Jenny. We're going to Fiorella's, though, if that's of any interest to you."

Jenny looked over at me. "Sorry, Mom. You're stuck with me."

I grabbed her coat and tossed it to her as Rob helped me with mine. "Let's go. I hope your car's still warm."

"It should be. Plus, you could use the seat warmers; they turn on pretty quickly."

Jenny and Rob strolled out the door. I followed, setting the alarm and locking the door behind me. As I got in the car, a curtain swung shut at Drew's house. *Well, at least he didn't come out.*

* * *

The next afternoon, I put the final touches on a presentation concerning the differences between various insurance deductibles. Looking at my watch, I was surprised to see that the day was almost over. I left and was shocked at the change in the weather. It almost felt warm. *Three cheers for the changing jet stream.* Smiling, I made my way home, exchanging pleasantries with others who were also out and about on this gift of a nice day.

I cringed as I turned down my street, concerned that Drew would be out. I didn't see him, so I gave a sigh of relief as I danced in the back door. My happiness was short-lived, as he was sitting at my kitchen table playing Monopoly with Jenny.

"Hi, Merry," Drew said. "I hope you don't mind, but Jenny suggested we come over here."

I raised my eyebrows at Jenny. She said, “Dad’s getting all kinds of phone calls. Some are threatening, some are heavy breathers, and others are dead silence.”

“Have you reported them to the police?” I asked Drew.

“No. I really don’t want to involve them.”

“I think you should. I have a friend in the department. I could call him.”

He shrugged. “If you think it’s best.”

I picked up the phone and called Detective Jay Ziebold. Jay, Rob, and I worked to solve a murder together, and although the beginning of the relationship could have only been termed as frosty, we ended up in a good place. “Jay, it’s Merry. We have a bit of a situation here, and I was wondering if you could come by when you get a chance. Fifteen minutes?” I eyed Drew. He nodded. “Yes, that will work. Thanks.”

“Why should the police help me, Merry? They put me away, remember.”

“I do remember that. Quite clearly. I also remember that you deserved what you got.”

Jenny frowned. “Come on, Mom. Lighten up.”

“Whatever.” I sat at the counter.

“Why don’t you play with us while we’re waiting? It’s a lot more fun with three people,” she asked.

There was a quick knock at the back door, and Rob came in carrying take-out chicken. “Hello, ladies. I thought you might want some chicken tonight.” He stopped dead in his tracks as he noticed Drew. His hand tightened on the bag. “Or maybe you’re busy.”

I jumped up and gave him a quick hug and kiss. “Don’t be silly. Thanks for stopping by.”

Jenny smiled at Rob. “Want to play Monopoly, Mr. Jenson?”

“I don’t think so, Jenny. Let me just have a quick word with your mom.”

I put the food in the oven to keep warm and then joined Rob in the living room. Keeping his voice low, he asked, "What is going on?"

"Drew's been getting threatening calls, and Jenny didn't want to be in his house with the phone ringing, so she brought him here."

Rob rolled his eyes. "Phones can be unplugged."

"I know. I'll be suggesting he do that after he talks to Jay."

"Jay's coming over?"

"Yep. Should be here any minute now."

There was a rap at the back door, and Jay called out, "Anyone home?"

Rob and I came back from the living room. Drew tried to shake Jay's hand, but Jay ignored it and strode over to Rob and me. "What's up? And why is he here?"

I poured Jay a cup of coffee. "Let's sit."

Like territorial lions, Rob and Drew vied for the seat near me. I gave Drew a dirty look, and he gave Rob the seat. I asked, "Drew, why don't you bring Jay up to date?"

He did.

Jay asked, "What do you want us to do?"

"Can't you trace the calls?"

"What I suggest is that you get caller ID so you can identify who is making the calls. Once you've done that, I'll take a trip over to whoever it is and ask them to refrain from making the calls. The other alternative is to turn your phone off. If the threats escalate, let us know. It might be better for everyone, including Merry here, if you moved on."

Drew stood. "It's a free country, and I can live where I want."

"True. I'm just saying that you hurt quite a few people around here. Seeing you reminds them of the dreams they had that weren't fulfilled." Jay rose. "If that's all, I'll be going. Thanks for the coffee, Merry."

"Thanks for stopping by. I'll go with you to your car." Once we were outside, I asked, "How bad do you think this could get?"

"I don't know. I hope people have enough sense to leave it alone, but I'm worried. Let me know if you have any problems."

Drew's house loomed over me. I shivered. When I hurried back inside, a tense silence greeted me.

Drew frowned. "I think I should go now." No one stopped him.

Jenny quickly set the table, and we all sat down to dinner. She fidgeted with her napkin. "Should I be scared for Dad?"

"He can take care of himself, honey. I'm sure everything will be okay." I shot Rob a quick glance. *I hope that's true.*

CHAPTER 5

While lying in bed on Saturday, I made a mental list of things to accomplish. The cats batted at my hand to make sure they were first on that list. Petting them, I rolled over and got out of bed. Shuffling down the stairs was treacherous, as they did their cat dance, weaving in and out of my legs. I ended up in front of their empty bowls. They looked up at me with wordless appeal. Opening the bag of cat food, the mews of anticipation started. Bowls full, they began to chow down.

Proud to have checked one thing off my list, I turned on the coffee machine and paced the floor till it finished. Smiling, I poured myself a mug. My eyes closed as I savored that first jolt of caffeine.

Feeling sufficiently fortified, I opened the front door and bent down for the paper. Emblazoned on the front page was the headline "Swindler Returns to Scene of Crime." Darn. I knew Rob would cover Drew's return. I didn't know that it would be the lead story or so sensationally written.

Reading it, I kicked the door shut and returned to the kitchen. Jenny came in two minutes later, rubbing her eyes. "Any chance of some hot chocolate and pancakes?"

I turned the paper over. "I think I could accommodate that request." I gave her a quick kiss on the head and started heating the milk.

There was a rap on the back door, and Rob came in. He gave me a peck on the cheek. "Good morning."

His gaze darted around the kitchen. When it lit on the paper, he frowned and gave me a quick glance. Jenny's focus was on her phone, so I shook my head and put my finger to my lips.

Jenny looked up, frowning. "What?"

"What, what?" I echoed.

"Why are you two being so silent? What's going on?"

I looked at Rob and sighed. "You may as well show her." Looking sheepish, Rob picked up the paper and handed it to her.

She looked at the headline. "That's so mean!"

Rob said, "That wasn't my intention. It's factual. Your dad did move back to town, and he was a swindler. It's news."

"If you really liked us, you wouldn't have printed it."

"Jenny, I'm sorry if it hurts, but my job is to report what's happening in town. It would look silly if I didn't report it."

"It doesn't hurt me; it hurts my dad!" She raced up the stairs.

Rob grimaced. "Was I too rough in the article?"

"She didn't read it. She stopped at the headline. It was snappy, attention getting, and I guess it'll sell some papers. It was also pretty incendiary in view of the town's mood."

"Are you mad at me too?"

I hugged him and gave him a kiss. "It's your job. A little warning would have been nice, but, no, I'm not mad at you. This is just going to be a difficult time."

"That's fair." He hugged me back.

I turned away. "I think I should go upstairs and see how Jenny's doing."

"Should I stay?"

"No. It's probably better if you go. I'll call you later."

I knocked on Jenny's door, and she asked, "Is he still here?"

"No, he left."

"Then you can come in."

She was lying on her bed, her pillow clutched tightly to her stomach. She punched it. "It's not fair!"

I sat next to her. "Which part?"

"Mr. Jenson's using Dad to sell newspapers." She turned on her side so her back was to me.

"Rob's reporting on the news. Unfortunately, your father is news."

She buried her head in her pillow. "Whatever. I just wish this would all go away. My phone is blowing up with kids asking me if I saw the article."

I rubbed her back. "Just turn your phone off."

She looked at me as if I'd asked her to cut off her right arm. "Mom, I can't. What if I miss something?"

I rolled my eyes. "I think you could take it for an hour or so."

She made sure her phone was out of my reach. "I'm okay now."

I sighed. "Do you still want pancakes and hot chocolate?"

She smiled. "Absolutely!"

A half hour later, we were enjoying our breakfast. I asked, "What are your plans for today?"

"Dad wants me to take him over to the library to get a card and to take a look at their computers."

"Nancy used to have Wi-Fi at her house. Didn't he pick it up?"

"Yes. I helped connect his laptop the other day."

"Then why does he want to look at the library's computers?"

Jenny gave me a dirty look. "What's with all the questions? Why do you care? He can do whatever he wants. Maybe he just wants to be around other people. And if he wants my help, I'm going to give it to him." She stomped off.

Note to self: tread lighter around Jenny when it comes to Drew. I texted Rob, "Want to get together later?"

"Yes. Where?"

"Late lunch at the Iron Skillet? One thirty-ish?"

"Okay. See you there."

I was in the process of cleaning the kitchen when Jenny sailed by. "Going to Dad's. See you."

From the bay window, I watched as she tripped lightly up the path and knocked at his back door. He gave her a big hug, and she disappeared inside.

I joined Rob for lunch just a few minutes late. After we ordered, I asked him, "Why would someone who has Wi-Fi at home use the library's computers?"

He looked thoughtful. "Maybe he or she has a data cap."

"Nancy had unlimited."

"Ah, so we're talking about Drew." He picked up my hand and caressed it.

"Jenny said she set up his laptop and phone so he could access the Wi-Fi, but he wanted her to go with him to the library so that he could use their computers."

He studied the table, straightening his silverware. "He might want to be around more people."

I rolled my eyes. "In this town?"

Rob looked straight at me. "Or he doesn't want anyone to be able to track where he's been on the Internet."

"Maybe we should stop by the library on the way home."

"Good idea." We finished lunch and sprinted over.

I blew on my hands. "I really wish this winter would be over."

Rob gently took my hand and tucked it with his into his coat pocket. He smiled at me. "At least one will be warm. You may want to think about gloves."

"I forgot to pick them up as I was leaving. But this feels pretty good." I squeezed his hand and leaned closer to him.

I was happy to see my friend, Evelyn Roberts, behind the desk at the library. She waved at us. "Merry, Rob, good to see you."

We exchanged pleasantries, and I said, "Evelyn, we stopped by because we know you have all the answers."

She laughed. "I think you're exaggerating, but ask away, and I'll try to help."

"Where are the public computers, and how does someone get access to them?"

"Let me show you." She came around the counter and motioned for us to follow her. "They're actually in a few different places. Since the library is pretty old, we had to locate them where we had available electricity. The first five are through here." She showed us a smaller room behind the stacks. There was only one older man in the room.

"Why is there a window into the room? Is that so you can see what's going on in there?"

She laughed. "No. It's so there's more light. If we didn't have the window, it would be like a cave in there, even with the overheads on." She continued the tour. "Then we have another two workstations around this corner." She pointed them out. "And there's also one that most people don't know about that's upstairs behind the mystery section. Do you need to see it as well?"

Rob smiled. "No, we'll take your word for it."

I asked, "How do you arrange for a workstation?"

"It's easy. You just come in and ask for one. If it's a busy time, then we have a sign-up sheet, and we impose a time limit so we can accommodate everyone. That doesn't happen often, though."

"So you don't track who is using what workstation or what they are doing on the workstation?"

She frowned, and even though she spoke in a low tone, I could hear the stridency in her voice. "Of course not. Libraries don't function as thought police. We have some safeguards for children, but that's about it."

I grimaced. "Sorry. I just thought that nowadays everyone tracks everything."

"We don't. If you don't have any other questions, I need to get back to the desk."

Rob shook her hand. "We appreciate the time and the tour."

She smiled at him. "For you, anytime."

As we left, I looked up at him. "I think she has a crush on you."

"Evelyn? She's seventy if she's a day."

"She's not dead yet, and you are pretty good looking." I smiled and tucked my hand back into his.

"Flattery will get you everywhere. What do you want to do next?"

"It's cold out here, and I don't really feel like going home. Drew living next door is like a black cloud over the whole block."

"My hot-chocolate making isn't quite up to your standards, but I'm willing to struggle through. I also have some popcorn and Netflix. How does a movie sound?"

I gave him a hug. "Sounds like just what the doctor ordered."

An hour later, we cuddled together on Rob's sofa, popcorn in hand, watching *Casablanca*. Ilsa and Rick were in Paris. They looked so in love. I kissed Rob. "This movie is so romantic. Thanks for suggesting it."

He kissed me back, and soon there was more action on the couch than there was in the film. I came up for air. "Stop the movie. Let's go in the bedroom."

"Don't need to tell me twice." He pressed pause, picked me up, and pushed the bedroom door open with his foot. Kissing me, he pulled the covers down with one hand and softly laid me on the bed. He joined me. "You're so beautiful. I'm glad you're in my life." He kissed me softly. "Are you sure?"

I stared into his seafoam-green eyes. "Yes, absolutely yes." I pulled him down to me.

Lying in his arms later, I stretched like a cat. I felt so safe and warm. It was comforting to hear his soft snore. *Why did I wait so long? He is such a good man.* Quietly leaving the bed for the bathroom, I stared at myself in the mirror. My hair was askew and my cheeks rubbed red from Rob's stubble. Smiling softly, I returned to the bedroom. *How did those pillows get all the way on the other side of the room?*

He was awake, and a slow smile spread across his face. "Hey, you."

"Right back at you." I crawled back into bed.

We finally finished the movie over a dinner of scrambled eggs and sausage. "Why does he always end up with the guy?" I asked.

"Because it was a beautiful friendship. Plus, the war effort would have suffered if Ilsa left Victor."

"She should have gone with love." I kissed Rob. "Much as I hate to say it, I need to get back." I stood.

Rob got to his feet and pulled me to him. "Are you sure you can't stay just for a little while longer?" He kissed me again and ran his fingers lightly up my spine.

"Tempting as that is, I have a few things I need to accomplish yet today. And I'm afraid if I stay, it won't just be for a little while."

He put on his shoes. "Let me drive you back."

"That's not necessary." I opened the door and shivered. "Yes, it is. It's too cold out there. I would really appreciate a ride."

He smiled and got his coat. "I aim to please."

"Yes, you do."

CHAPTER 6

I rolled over in bed the next morning and smiled. *What a day yesterday.* I started my exercises, and my phone dinged. I grinned. It was Rob. "Church? Ten thirty?"

"See you there." I added a blowing-kiss emoji.

He sent me two hearts intertwined. Smiling, I hopped into the shower.

As I dried my hair, I looked out my bathroom window. Amanda Thomas snuck out Drew's back door, a kerchief covering her head. *Like that's a disguise.* In case I had any doubt what she was doing, Drew caught her by the hand and laid a big kiss on her lips. She waved goodbye and slunk toward her car, which I noticed was parked pretty far down the alleyway. *Well, isn't that interesting. I wonder how long that's been going on.*

I made coffee, fed the cats, and threw a load of wash into the machine. Feeling accomplished, I opened Facebook and searched for Amanda's page. Single, interested in men, and not much else. Her photos were relatively mundane, though there were some cute ones of her playing with her dachshund. Looking further back into her history, I was surprised to see a photo of her with Drew standing behind her. It was obvious they were at a party, and the date was significant. It was from before he went to jail, while he was still married to me. He wasn't touching her or even looking at her, but there was something in the way he was standing, along with her smug smile. Plus, why would you post a random photo like that if something wasn't going on? She did have some other photos from the same party. Maybe nothing was going on. I rolled my eyes. *Next thing I know I'll be buying a bridge from someone.*

It hurt. It shouldn't, but it did. I found out four years ago that Drew was a con man, but cheating on me? That was a whole other kettle of fish.

I texted Patty, "Need to talk tonight. Eight thirty okay?"

"Have wine waiting."

Jenny turned the corner into the kitchen, still in her pajamas. The clock chimed.

"If you are going to the ten thirty with me, you should probably get a move on."

She yawned. "I'll go to the one at noon. Do we have any Cocoa Krispies left?"

I frowned. "How would I know? When was the last time you saw me eat that type of cereal?"

She slumped next to me and brushed her hair back from her face. "You might have noticed when you were making out the grocery list."

I sighed, getting up and striding the five steps to the cupboard. The box was front and center. "Jenny, if you just looked, it would have bit you."

She smiled. "Now that you're up, would you please pour me a bowl? OJ would be appreciated as well."

"If it will get you going, I would be pleased to oblige." I took the bowl and glass down. "How was your day with your dad?"

"It was fun. I took him over to the library and got him set up. Then he took me to the Iron Skillet for lunch. We ordered pizza for dinner, and I showed him one of the games I've been playing lately. He was surprised at how good the graphics were."

"It's probably been a while since he's played an online game." I poured her juice and handed it to her along with the bowl of cereal. "I need to get a move on. I'm meeting Rob. I'll text you and let you know if we're going out after."

"If you go for breakfast, would you pick me up a sticky bun?"

"Will do."

Rob met me on the steps of the church and gave me a big hug before we walked inside. *I wonder if anyone will be able to tell I slept with him.* Determined to keep my face neutral, I couldn't help but smile at him as we looked for a pew. Seeing Patrick and Patty with two of their boys, we squeezed in beside them. She gave me a cursory glance. My face heated up like a red beacon. Her eyes widened. *Busted.*

After the Mass, there was a logjam in the vestibule because people were chatting and no one was in a hurry to get back out into the cold.

Patty sidled up next to me and whispered in my ear, "I want full details tonight." She gave me a knowing smile and shepherded her crew through one of the side doors.

Rob and I saw Father Tom but together made a silent decision to merely wave from afar and not press our luck.

After we exited, Rob pulled me to him. "Why do I feel like such a wicked child?"

I laughed. "Maybe because you are."

"Have I sullied your reputation?"

"I think we both sullied."

"Let's sully some more."

I smiled. "Later. Let's get out of here first without attracting any more attention than we already are."

He wiggled his eyebrows. "Breakfast at my place?"

"I'd like that." We strode arm in arm down the street at a quickened pace.

Making it through the door, we dropped our coats first and then other parts of our clothing like breadcrumbs leading to his massive king-size bed.

Rob lifted me onto the bed. “Let me warm you up.” And he did.

I cuddled up to him afterward. “I’m really warm now.”

He kissed the top of my head. “I’m glad. Are you hungry?”

“Ravenous.”

“Omelets? I have some cheddar, and there’s some sausage left over from yesterday.”

“Sounds great. Do you need help?”

“I can handle it.” He stood and bent over for an impressive kiss. As I clung to him, he gently disengaged me. “Food first.”

I gave him a dirty look. “Do you have a bathrobe I can borrow?”

He laughed as he looked from his broad six-foot-tall frame to my diminutive five foot two with heels. “You’d disappear into it.” He rummaged in his closet and threw me an old sweatshirt.

It came down nearly to my knees. I laughed. “I see what you mean.”

He put his robe on and turned to go to the kitchen. “I hope I can keep my hands off you long enough to cook.”

I looked in one of his dresser drawers and found a pair of socks. They were way too big on me, but it was better than cold feet. I padded into the kitchen behind him and hugged him from the back.

“Nope.” He lifted me onto one of the stools at the kitchen counter. “You wait here and try not to distract me.”

I crossed my legs and swung my foot back and forth. “Guess who I saw this morning?”

He glanced back at me. “Who?”

“Amanda Thomas. And she was doing the walk of shame from Drew’s house at seven thirty.”

Frowning, he faced me. “And how do you feel about that?”

“Not so bad, even considering that she was probably sleeping with him before he went to jail.”

"But you were still married then."

"I know." I pointed behind him. "And your eggs are starting to burn."

"Crap." He moved the pan off the burner. "A little crispy but not too bad." He cut the large omelet in half and slid it onto plates just as the toast popped up.

I jumped up. "I'll get that."

Sitting down with our coffee, eggs, and toast, I heaved a deep sigh of satisfaction. "This tastes great. I didn't know I was so hungry." I put another bite in my mouth.

"Let's get back to what you were saying before I almost burnt the eggs. Why do you think that Amanda was seeing Drew before he went to jail?"

I took out my phone, opened Facebook, and showed him the picture. He studied it. "So they're at a party together. From the other photos, it looks like quite a few people are there. It could have been totally innocent."

I gave him a long look.

"You're not buying it?"

"Nope. A wife, or ex-wife, can tell. Look at their body language."

He looked at the picture even more closely. "Nope. Not seeing it."

I hopped down from my seat and started taking the dishes to the sink. "Doesn't matter anyway. All water under the bridge now."

He came up behind me and kissed my neck. "I'll do the dishes."

I kissed him. "You cooked." Then I slowly pulled his robe open, an invitation in my eyes. Before long, we were back on the bed, the dishes forgotten.

As we snuggled afterward, I said, "I promised Jenny a sticky bun. Do you think I might still be able to get one?"

He looked at his watch. "If we could manage to get ourselves out of the bedroom, we might be able to find one." He kissed my nose. "That is if there are any left now."

I groaned and jumped into the shower. A minute later, Rob joined me. I gave him a look, and he said, "It's faster this way."

Surprisingly, it was. We hotfooted it to the Iron Skillet and got the last sticky bun they had.

As we opened the back door, Jenny frowned. "Shut the door. You're letting all the cold air in. Some people are trying to study."

I held up the bag with the sticky bun and shook it slightly.

She perked up. "Sorry. Just a bit grumpy. Thanks for the sustenance!" She got herself a fork and dove in, her eyes closed. "This would taste even more amazing with some hot chocolate." She batted her eyes at me.

Without missing a beat, I grabbed a pan and poured milk into it. I gave Rob a look, and he nodded enthusiastically. "I guess it will be hot chocolate for three while we watch the football games."

At five, Rob said, "I hate to leave you, but the drama club is having their dress rehearsal tonight, and they want me to take pictures to drum up some business for the show next week."

I hugged him. "That's fine. I have a few things I should be doing too. Do you want me to give you a lift home?"

"No, I'm warm-blooded. I can take it." He adopted a Superman pose.

I hit him on the shoulder. "You're too funny." I stood on my tiptoes and kissed him.

"I could get used to this. Maybe I don't need to leave after all."

I smiled. "Call me tomorrow?"

"You bet." We kissed again, and he squeezed out the door, quickly shutting it behind him.

Jenny said, "See. That's the way you should come in. There's far less of a cold breeze making it into the house."

I threw a pillow at her and moved the wash to the dryer.

At eight thirty on the dot, the back door opened, and Patty ambled in. I poured some wine into glasses and handed her one.

She looked around. "Where's Jenny?"

"She finished her homework and said something about an online game tournament."

"Good. That means we can talk freely."

We went into the living room, and she sank into the chair. I sat opposite on the sofa. Drambuie jumped onto her lap, and Courvoisier nosed her way onto mine.

Petting Drambuie, Patty looked into my eyes. "You and Rob looked pretty happy this morning. And," she paused for effect, "dare I say it, satisfied?"

"Yep, pretty satisfied." I smiled broadly. "The stars, the sun, and the moon finally aligned. I think one of us was waiting for an interruption; luckily it never came."

"That's great. You are taking precautions, aren't you?"

I rolled my eyes. "Of course. I'm not a teenager. But what I really wanted to talk to you about is Drew and Amanda Thomas. They're seeing each other."

"Wasn't she the one who told you that it was your job to get him to leave town?"

"Yep. I think it was just a ruse. Plus, I think she was seeing him before he went to jail."

Patty shifted on the chair and put one of her feet underneath her. "What would make you say that?"

I pulled up the Facebook photo and tossed the phone to her. She caught it and used her fingers to zoom in. "Oh, yes, definitely."

"Rob said he couldn't see it."

"Men. How do you feel about it?"

"Knowing that he was cheating on me hurts. I don't know why it does, but it does. I'm divorced and in a relationship with a good man. This shouldn't bother me."

"You're not dead, and you just found out that Drew was even more of a rat than we thought he was. I'd be surprised if you weren't hurt."

The grandfather clocked chimed. “Wow. Is that the time? I need to get going. Keep the faith.”

CHAPTER 7

While having coffee the next morning, I was surprised by a knock at the back door. Drew stood there shuffling from one foot to the other. "I'm sorry to bother you, but I was wondering if you would do me a favor?"

"Depends on what it is."

"Can I come in?"

Since it felt like the polar vortex was whirling right into the house, I acquiesced. "Would you like some coffee?"

"I'd love some." I poured him a cup and then almost on autopilot put a teaspoon of sugar and enough cream in to turn it a rich taupe. He looked pleased. "You remember how I take my coffee."

Exasperated, I handed it to him roughly. "Drew, we were married for fourteen years. It's hard to forget things I did every day for that long. You said you needed a favor."

"I have the list of phone numbers of people who called either threatening me or hanging up and the number of times they called over the past few days. I was wondering if you would be nice enough to give it to Detective Ziebold."

"Why can't you give it to him yourself?"

He sighed. "I don't know if you noticed, but he's not my biggest fan. I think if you give it to him, he'll take it more seriously."

I rolled my eyes. “I’ll give it to him, but this is the last time I play go-between.”

Drew got up to leave. “Thanks. I do appreciate it.” He bent over to kiss me on the cheek just as Rob popped his head in the back door.

Rob scowled. “Am I interrupting something?”

I groaned. “No. Drew was just leaving. Give me the list, Drew.” I held out my hand, and he gave it to me. He sidled past Rob out the door.

Rob glared after him. “What list?”

“The list of people who have been calling and threatening Drew. He wants me to pass it along to Jay.”

“Why can’t he just give it to Jay?”

I hugged him. “I told him I’d do it just this once. I don’t want Jenny over there if there’s a chance one of these nuts will try something.” I rattled the paper. “I’ll drop it by the police station on my way to work.” I looked Rob up and down. “Why are you here so early?”

He nibbled on my ear. “Do I need a special invitation? And do you have any more of that luscious smelling coffee?”

I kissed him and poured a cup. “Why are you really here?”

“There’s been a report of kids using an unsafe crossing route by the railroad tracks to get to the high school. I was hoping to go to school with Jenny so she could give me her perspective.”

Jenny rounded the corner into the kitchen. “Go with Jenny where?”

Rob told her, and she said, “I don’t take that route, but I know some kids who do. Will they get into trouble if I show you?”

“I won’t use any names. The point is to let parents know about the problem.”

Jenny shrugged. “Fine by me, but we need to get going.”

Rob put his coat on and held out Jenny’s. He glanced at me. “See you later?”

“For sure.” I smiled at him and gave Jenny a kiss. “Be safe. Love you.”

She wriggled away. Rob stole a quick kiss from me before he left.

I rinsed the mugs and put them in the dishwasher. Taking one last look around the house, I left. A stiff breeze assaulted me, and I pulled my scarf tighter. Shivering, I opted for the car. I smiled as I zipped into a prime parking spot near the police station; striding in, I asked for Detective Ziebold. One of the clerks escorted me back to his office.

"Merry. Good to see you. What's up?"

"Thanks for seeing me, Jay. Drew stopped by this morning and gave me a list of the phone numbers of the people who have been calling to harass him." I showed him the spreadsheet. It contained the phone numbers, whether it was a hang up or a threatening call and the number of times.

"Why did he give the list to you?"

I avoided his searching look. "He thought that you might not be his biggest fan. Plus, he knows that I'm concerned about Jenny. I don't want her involved in any of this."

"I'll look into it. I promise."

Waving, I pulled on my coat again and wound my scarf around my face. Bracing myself, I opened the outer door and then scurried to my office. Yanking that door open, I wiped my feet and luxuriated in the warmth. I took off my scarf and coat and moved through the office, pausing to touch base with some of my associates.

While I hung my coat up in the closet, Cheryl stuck her head in. "Rob called. He wants to know if you can meet him at the Pickled Herring at noon for lunch."

I checked my phone. "Unless you know something I don't, that should be good."

"I'll let him know."

I massaged my fingers to try and get some blood flowing and then read the call list. Amanda Thomas was on it to talk about commercial insurance for her small business. I thought for a moment and then picked up the phone. "Good morning, Amanda. The reason why I'm calling is to see if you'd like to learn more about the products we offer for small businesses."

"It's funny that you would call today. I was just looking at my bill and wanted to know if the coverage I have is right for me. Is it possible for you to stop by at four? We're usually not that busy then."

I checked my calendar. "I can make that happen. Look forward to seeing you." I hung up. *This should be interesting.*

At noon, I bundled up and hurried down to the Pickled Herring. Rob waited inside the door. He laughed. "Are you in there, Merry? It's kind of hard to tell with the amount of clothing you have on. On second thought, I think you could have added another scarf or two."

My eyes were the only things peeking out from between my hood and scarf. I gave him a dirty look as I unwound it. "At least I'm warm." Kissing his cheek, I sat in the booth. "How was the walk to school this morning?"

He moved his silverware around. "It was fine, but Jenny couldn't stop talking about Drew. She's so excited he's living here now. I know it's not really any of my business, but I'm worried he's up to no good and he's going to disappoint you both again."

I took his hand. "Thanks for caring about us. I appreciate it. Drew worries me as well, but there's not a lot I can do about it." Our food arrived, and we ate for a while in silence. "I'm seeing Amanda Thomas this afternoon on business. It will be interesting to see if she lets anything slip about Drew."

"Doubtful, since she's been sneaking around."

"We'll see."

Just before four, I bundled up again. Cheryl said, "I don't envy you having to go out in this weather."

I glared at her for effect and then smiled. "Text me if you need anything."

I scurried the two blocks and practically leapt into Amanda's store, closing the door swiftly behind me. I glanced at Amanda. "So glad to be back in the heat again." I shed my coat and scarf, putting them on the old-fashioned hatstand by the door.

"Let me just finish up with Barbara, and then I'll be right with you."

A hand waved from the top of one of the white louvered dressing room doors. "Is that Merry?"

"Yes, it's me, Barbara. How are you?" Barbara was Jay Ziebold's wife. They had five boys, and somehow she juggled the havoc they caused very gracefully.

She emerged from the dressing room wearing a muted gray-and-white angora sweater over a pair of gray slacks. "How lovely," I said.

She turned to see herself in the mirror. "Are you sure it doesn't make my rump look too big?"

"No. If anything, I think the cut makes you look quite slender."

"Did you hear someone bought the Morning Pastry? I lost five pounds when that place closed." She smiled. "Still, I'm hopeful that the new owners can cook even half as well." Barbara looked at Amanda. "I'm going to take these and the scarf I gave you earlier."

"That's great. I'll start ringing you up."

Barbara changed quickly. "I'd like to stay and chat, but the boys have been home for an hour now, and who knows what damage they've caused." She grabbed her packages, waved goodbye to both of us, and left the store.

Amanda gestured to two café-style chairs with a small table between. "Why don't we sit over here?"

I pulled out my iPad and joined her. "Let me pull up the coverage you have currently, and then we'll talk about some things you may want to think about adding. You might also be able to save some money by bundling your coverage together." I talked her through some options.

"Thanks for explaining this to me, Merry. I'm going to have to think about it. I want to make sure I have the appropriate coverage, but I need to weigh the costs. I'll get back to you next week."

I put away my iPad. “Jenny’s excited about the fashion show next week.”

“She’s a natural. She’s so pretty and tall. My clothes look great on her. I’m sure she’ll do a super job, and we’ll make some good money for breast cancer research.”

“I’m glad you’re doing this. It’s such a great cause.”

She smiled. “It is. Well, if there’s nothing else?”

Here we go. I stood. “One thing—the last time I saw you, you were very concerned about Drew being back in town. I just wanted to tell you that I had no idea he was going to rent Nancy’s house.”

She stood and glanced down at the table, her finger tracing the lace under the glass top. “I think our worries were overblown. As you said, he paid his debt to society; he can live where he chooses.” She finally looked at me. “I’m sorry if I was a little rough on you.”

“No problem. I’m glad you feel that way.” I paused, caressing the material of one of the display sweaters. “This feels so soft.” Then, taking a deep breath, I plunged in. “I’ve been curious about something. I don’t remember, but did you know Drew well before he went away?”

Her eyes narrowed. “I knew him, certainly, like most people in town. What are you implying?”

“I’m not implying anything. I was just curious.” I put on my coat and scarf. “Let me know what you decide to do on the insurance. I look forward to the fashion show next week.”

My neck hairs bristled as I felt her gaze following me all the way down the block. She was definitely sleeping with him before he went to jail. *But for how long?*

Cursing myself for having left my car near the police station, I hurried past my storefront, head down, trying to conserve whatever heat I could. Not paying attention, I barreled straight into Drew and bounced off him into one of the snowbanks lining the sidewalk. “I hate winter.”

Laughing, he pulled me up. “Maybe you should pay more attention to where you’re going.”

I smiled. “Sorry for running into you.”

“Hardly felt it, pipsqueak.”

It all felt so familiar and comfortable. *You rat. You cheated on me.* I yanked my hand from his and frowned. “I have to go.”

“Don’t be like that. We need to try and get along for Jenny’s sake.”

I pushed my forefinger into his chest. “Maybe you should have thought about that before you slept with Amanda.”

He smirked. “Like you said, we’re divorced. I can sleep with whomever I want.”

I leaned closer to him. “I meant back when we were still married, you creep!”

He backed up, his mouth a perfect circle. “I didn’t.”

I put my hand down. “Whatever. I just don’t want Jenny hurt again.”

He flinched. “I would never hurt her on purpose.”

I glared at him. “I’m not happy that you qualified that statement. You should have left it that you would never hurt her.”

I stalked off to my car. As I unlocked it, I saw Drew ducking into the alleyway behind Shades of Gray.

I drove slowly past the store, but the lights were out, and I couldn’t see anyone. Changing course back to my house, I sped up. Remembering Jenny’s harangue about coming in the back door, I made my way carefully up the front steps and let myself in.

She was lying on the couch playing with her phone. “Shut the door! You’re making it all cold in here.”

Exasperated, I gave her a dirty look and trudged over to the closet to put my coat away. “I thought you would be doing your homework in the kitchen. That’s why I came in the front.”

“Can I help it if I finished early today? Do you know how hard my life is? Dad’s way more sympathetic than you are.”

I sat next to her on the sofa. "What's wrong?"

"Nothing's wrong. Did I say anything was wrong?" Her voice reached screeching proportions. Then she continued with a calmer voice. "Dad asked me to go away with him for Christmas. He wants to go to Jamaica. It would be warm there, and I'd get to swim every day. But I can't go. I can't leave you alone at Christmas." She broke off with a sob.

I took a deep gulp of air. "He wants you to go to Jamaica?"

"Yes, he asked me yesterday. He said that it would be a chance for us to get to know each other better. And he pointed out that you've had four Christmases alone with me."

"That's because he was in jail!" I stood and paced, trying to calm myself. *What a jerk.* I stopped in front of her. "Do you really want to go?"

She looked miserable. "Not really. I love traditions, and you make Christmas so special. I love the tree and all the decorations, Midnight Mass, and waking up to French toast that's been soaked all night and baked fresh in the morning." She smiled at the memory and then frowned again. "But am I being fair? Dad's been alone in prison for the past few years. He talks about how special it was when we had Christmas together. Maybe I need to adopt new traditions." She looked sad and far younger than her seventeen years as she pulled a throw pillow to her stomach.

I sat next to her and put my arm around her. "We don't need to make a decision right now. Let me talk to your father about it. Sometimes things change. And maybe that's okay too."

She hugged me. "I hate change."

I smiled. "I've heard that before."

CHAPTER 8

The rest of the week was a blur. Jenny had fittings for the fashion show seemingly every night. The VFW agreed to donate the use of their hall for the show; the Iron Skillet provided the hors d'oeuvres and staff to pass them. As I strolled in, my mouth dropped, for I was stunned by the transformation of the normally utilitarian hall. The volunteer high schoolers did a terrific job. White folding chairs lined either side of the long runway, and the stage was festooned with flowers and pink ribbons. Bars were set up in the corners of the hall, and crowds formed at each of them.

Rob eyed the lines. "The one over there seems shortest. Would you like a drink?"

I gave him my tickets. "I'd love a glass of Pinot." I turned slowly in place, admiring everything.

Patty swooped in. "They did a great job, didn't they?"

"Yes. I can't wait to see what the kids are wearing." One of the waiters came by carrying a tray of scallops wrapped in bacon. Patty and I each took one. I bit into it and smiled. "This is so good."

"It is. Too bad we didn't persuade him to stay."

I smiled. "Probably better for our waistlines. Where's Patrick?"

She pointed at one of the queues. "He's over there. It looks like he is edging closer."

I looked at the one Rob was in. "Rob's almost at the bar." Another waiter with tiny eggrolls appeared. Sampling, we both moaned with delight.

Rob arrived a second too late and missed the tray. "Hey, that's not fair." He handed me my glass. "How was the eggroll?"

I smiled. "Not half as good as the bacon-wrapped scallops."

Patrick gave Patty her wine. "Scallops?"

"Yes. You missed the scallops and the eggrolls," Patty said.

Rob shook his head. "Next time you get the drinks."

I laughed. "Patty and I will put our coats on the chairs to save us seats. Hopefully some good food will come by for you while we're gone."

We scampered over to the seating area and saw that other people had the same idea. Luckily we spied four together that were still left in the front row. We hurried over and claimed them.

"Good thing you had this idea," Patty said.

"I can't claim all the credit. Some other people thought about it before me." I nodded at the number of seats already taken.

"You thought of it in time." We wound through the crowd back to where the guys stood. "How's your Christmas planning going?"

I stopped. "Don't ask. Drew's thinking of taking Jenny to Jamaica."

She sighed. "I wish he would take me." I elbowed her. "Oops. Sorry, that wasn't funny."

"It's not. This would be the first Christmas Jenny would be away from me." I pointed toward Drew, who had just come in. "And there's the rat who's going to do it." I sighed. "Let's focus on tonight. It's going to be fun."

We rejoined Patrick and Rob. Patty asked, "Did we miss any good food?"

Patrick smirked. "Just crab puffs and tiny filet mignons with blue cheese crumbles."

Disappointed, I sighed. But then Rob showed me the hand he had hidden behind his back. "I did manage to grab one of the crab puffs for you."

Smiling, I took it from him and popped it in my mouth. "You're the best."

He laughed. "Yes, I am." The lights dimmed and went back up. "I think that's our cue to sit."

As we ambled to our seats, Patrick's eyes widened. Drew removed a reserved sign from a chair to the right of the stage. "How does he rate? And, wow, that's a nice bouquet of flowers."

Crap. I should have gotten flowers. "He's secretly sleeping with the woman running the show. And isn't it nice that he brought Jenny flowers?" Patty stared at me. "What? It is nice of him."

She shook her head in disbelief. "I don't know who you are."

A few minutes later, Philip Piper arrived. He removed the reserved sign from a seat to the left of the stage. I gestured with my eyes at Patty. Her eyes widened. I nodded at her. *Oh my. This should be interesting.*

The show started. I had no idea that there were so many different shades of gray. It was a relief that Amanda inserted some pops of color in the forms of scarves, belts, and shoes. Jenny looked spectacular in a charcoal-gray dress with fuchsia shoes. Drew beamed with pride as she strutted down the runway. Cindy had on lovely steel-gray capri pants and a matching top that included a vibrant turquoise sash. She looked like a natural, and both Patrick and Patty lit up as she sashayed past.

The show was soon over. Everyone was on their feet whooping and hollering, applauding the models. Just when I thought it couldn't get much louder, Amanda came out and joined the models for a bow. The crowd was with her. Then Drew leapt up on the stage, giving Amanda a kiss and handing her the bouquet. The sudden silence in the room was deafening. I stole a quick glance at Philip. His cheeks sported angry red circles. An uneasy murmur began as people reacted.

"You tramp!" Susan Clime threw her drink at Amanda.

It was like a switch had been thrown. The air was full of flying cups and elbows.

Rob pointed east. "Make your way to the side entrance. I'll get Jenny."

Clutching each other, Patty and I wove our way carefully through the angry mob. We huddled by the entrance. Before long, Rob and Patrick joined us with Jenny and Cindy. Rob had a long scratch on his face, and Patrick's nose was bleeding. Luckily the girls looked like they had escaped relatively unscathed, with the exception of some rips in their clothes. The police came in force through the front door.

Rob said, "We should leave."

Jenny crossed her arms. "We can't go. We have to get Dad."

I shook my head. "Jenny, the police are here. They'll help your father. We're leaving." I grabbed her hand, but she refused to budge.

"I'm not going without Dad."

I looked at Rob. He moved over and held Jenny's arms, making her focus on his face. "I'll only try to help your dad if you agree to leave with your mother."

"You promise?"

He nodded. "Yes. Now go."

I gave Rob a quick kiss and pulled on Jenny's hand. This time she came with me. I turned to look at Patrick, but he had followed Rob back into the VFW. Patty shrugged and gestured to her car. Running to it, we climbed in.

Cindy said, "Should we wait in the car?"

Patty shook her head. "Buckle up. We'll wait for them at the house." She drove slowly home.

Once there, we piled out and hurried into the kitchen. With the better light, I was able to see that Jenny had a bruise developing under her right eye. "What happened to your eye?"

She touched the spot lightly. "Someone was punching Dad, and as I came up behind him, his elbow hit me. Mr. Jenson picked me up and pulled me over to where you were standing."

After examining Cindy and finding her unhurt, Patty grabbed a bag of peas from her freezer and handed them to Jenny. "Here, honey. Put this under your eye. It will make it feel better."

Cindy asked, "Can we wait upstairs in my room?"

Jenny looked like she wasn't going to leave, so Patty nodded. "Go ahead. We promise we'll get you when everyone comes back." They ran upstairs. "Wine?"

"Yes, please."

She uncorked the bottle and poured two glasses. "What an evening. And it started out so well."

"It did. What the heck happened?" I took a sip of the wine.

"Your ex decided to out his relationship with Amanda in front of her current boyfriend and the rest of the town."

I rubbed my arms. "Drew's elevator never did reach the top floor."

Laughing, Patty choked on her wine and was soon coughing. I retrieved a glass of water, which she drank. "Don't do that to me. How did Philip take it? I didn't want to look."

"He was mad." I looked at my phone. "I'm starting to get worried. How much longer do you think it's going to be?"

Patty glanced at the clock. "Hard to tell. Let's go to the living room so we can be more comfortable. If they don't get here in half an hour, we'll go looking for them."

The back door opened. Patrick came in first, looking a bit worse for wear. Rob soon followed and had the beginnings of a great shiner.

Patty went to her freezer and pulled out a bag of mixed vegetables. "At this rate, I'll have no frozen veggies left."

Rob took the bag. "Har har."

I asked, "Where's Drew?"

Patrick said, "Rob and I pulled him out of the melee just as the police got there. The EMTs checked him out and sent him in the ambulance for X-rays. Luckily there were more grudges settled today than the one against Drew. If he'd been the only one they were piling on, it could have been much worse. Plus, it seems that no one in this town knows how to land a real punch. Drew looked a bit banged up, but he should be okay."

Jenny ran down the stairs. "How's Dad? Why isn't he with you?" I explained, and she said, "We need to go to the hospital. He's all alone."

I groaned. "Don't worry. I'll take you. Rob, would you mind driving us back to my house so I can get my car?"

He pulled his coat back on. "I'll take you over to the hospital."

I smiled. "Thanks. I appreciate that. Do you want me to drive so you can keep the mixed veggies on your eye?"

He handed me the keys as I hugged Patty. "I'll text you later."

We drove to the hospital in silence. As soon as we got there, Jenny hopped out of the car and ran into the emergency room. When we joined her, she was already talking to one of the admissions clerks.

Jenny stomped her foot. "But he's my dad. I need to see him!"

I moved next to her. "Is Drew March here?"

She looked up. "What is your relationship to Mr. March?"

"I'm Meredith March, his ex-wife."

"As I was explaining to your daughter, he's being treated. She'll have to wait until he comes out. He already has one person back there with him."

"Who?"

"I'm not at liberty to say. Now, if you'd care to stay, please move to the waiting room."

Jenny trudged over and opened the door. Rob and I followed. Seeing Jay Ziebold in the far corner of the room, we hurried to his side.

I asked, "What's going on?"

"You probably know more than me. Apparently, there was some melee at the fashion show at the VFW."

"Have you seen Drew?"

"No, I'm waiting to talk to him. They said that he should be through in about fifteen minutes." Jenny flounced to one of the chairs, threw herself on it, and pulled out her phone. Jay eyed her briefly. "Why don't we talk for a moment over here?"

Rob and I followed him farther away. I sat where I could see Jenny. Rob said, "You're right. It was some fight. Drew got up to give Amanda a kiss and some flowers. The place erupted."

Jay's eyes widened. "Amanda and Drew?" Rob nodded, and Jay frowned. "Never saw that one coming. I thought she was seeing Philip Piper."

"Surprised a lot of people, including Philip," Rob said.

I frowned. "Susan Clime threw the first cup. That's what got the crowd started."

Jay blinked. "Susan Clime who works for you?"

"Yep. Not sure about her continued employment, though."

The doors to the emergency room opened, and Drew and Amanda shuffled out. Drew was limping a little and leaning on her. Her dress was ripped at the shoulder, and you could hardly tell that her hair had been in a perfect chignon earlier in the evening.

Jenny jumped up and sped over to Drew. "Dad, are you okay? Wow, your face is pretty messed up."

He gently touched the bruise on her cheek and hugged her. "I'll be fine in a week. I'll look as good as new."

She gave him a searching look. "Really? No broken bones?"

He laughed and then grimaced. "Nope. Just a little bit of rearranging."

Jay motioned to Drew. "I have some questions."

Amanda glared at Jay. "He's hurt. Can't you talk to him tomorrow?"

Jay frowned. "I'd rather it be tonight."

Groaning, Drew sat. "Ask away."

I stood. "Amanda, are you going to take Drew home?"

"Yes," she sneered. "Unless I need your permission."

"No. Not at all. I just wanted to make sure he had a ride." I glanced at Jenny and Rob. "Let's go." Jenny looked like she was going to object. "Honey, your dad's tired, and this is probably going to take a while. You can see him tomorrow."

Wavering, Jenny looked at Drew. He nodded weakly. "Go home, smart stuff. I'll see you tomorrow." She leaned over to kiss him. He said, "Gently."

We left. As I got into the car, I said, "What a night."

"It sure was," they said in unison.

I finally went to sleep somewhere around three in the morning, after tossing and turning most of the night. The alarm rang. I cursed. *At least I don't feel as bad as some of the people in town will.* That brought a smile to my face, and I tore myself away from my pillow. *Why do they have these things on a weeknight?* Stumbling into the shower, I let the water stream over me and first pried one eye open and then the next. Somehow I got washed and dressed. Sleepwalking down the hall, I stopped at Jenny's door, remembering her bruise from the night before.

Sneaking in, I carefully tried to lift some of her hair so I could see her face. Two blue eyes stared at me. "Mom, I was asleep!"

"I'm sorry, honey. I wanted to see how your bruise was."

She moved her hair aside. I grimaced. She leapt out of bed and turned on the light by her mirror. "I look hideous."

"It's not that bad, honey. Does it hurt?"

She touched it gingerly. "Ouch."

"I'll run down and get you some ice." I grabbed an ice pack from the freezer, wrapped it in a towel, and took it back upstairs. Picking up Jenny's phone, I asked Siri to set the timer for twenty minutes. "When the buzzer sounds, take the ice off. Then you can get ready for school."

"Seriously? You think I can go to school looking like this?"

I hugged her. "If you use some concealer under your makeup, it shouldn't look that bad." I ignored the major eye roll I got for my troubles. "I'll leave you a muffin in the kitchen. Text me later to tell me how you are doing."

I left for work. Looking up at Drew's house, I saw him moving around in the kitchen. Should I check on him? Nope, if he's up, he's still alive. And he's someone else's problem now.

Later that morning, I jumped as police sirens echoed through the office. It seemed like they had just passed when they chirped and abruptly cut off. *That's strange. What's going on?* I peeked out the window and saw an ambulance zooming past. *That's not good.* Curious, I grabbed my coat and hurried out the front door. A small crowd gathered on the sidewalk two blocks up.

I came up behind Andy Perkins. "What's happening? Is it your shop?"

He shook his head. "It's Amanda's. But I don't think it's the shop. The police went upstairs to her apartment."

"Oh no. I hope she's okay."

We waited together for a few minutes, and then Rob ambled down from where the police had gathered. I asked him, "What's going on?"

He looked grim. "It's Amanda."

"Is she okay?"

He shook his head. "No. She's dead. They think she was murdered."

Clasping my hand over my mouth, I felt the street start to tip. Rob grabbed me. "Sit down."

I gave a strangled laugh as I looked around me. "Where? There's snow everywhere."

He brushed off a stoop and guided me over. He put his gloves down. "Sit on these and put your head between your knees."

I sat just as my feet gave out from under me. Rob crouched beside me. "Just try to breathe normally. That's it—in and out."

Andy bent down on the other side of me. "Is she okay?"

I turned to him. "I can hear you. I feel better now but foolish. It was just such a shock."

"Can you walk back to your office?" Rob asked.

Andy touched my arm. "My shop is right here. Why don't you both come in, and I'll fix us some tea."

Rob looked at him gratefully. "Thanks. That would be great."

He helped me up and steered me into Andy's shop. Andy carried a chair over, and I sat. "I feel so silly. I'm fine now." Rob rubbed my back.

Andy called out from the rear of the shop, "Is Darjeeling okay?"

"Yes, and put two teaspoons of sugar in Merry's."

"I don't need two teaspoons of sugar."

He kissed my forehead. "Yes, you do. You had a shock."

Andy brought out a tray with three cups and some scones. He poured the tea. "I thought it wouldn't hurt for you to have something to eat too."

Rob smiled at him. "Great idea."

I took a small bite of the scone and sipped some tea. I frowned at Rob. "How did you know what happened?"

"The police were upstairs in Amanda's apartment, and Samantha Smith was just sitting by herself in Shades of Gray. She looked pretty rattled, so I went in to ask her what happened. She told me that she opened the shop at nine this morning as usual. Amanda was supposed to meet her to go over the orders for the spring collection, based on the reactions to the fashion show last night. When Amanda still hadn't shown up by ten, Sam became worried. She went to Amanda's apartment and knocked. No one answered, so she pushed the door open. Apparently, Amanda was shot, and her body was lying just inside the door. Sam called 911, but it was too late. Amanda was dead."

"How scary for her. And poor Amanda. Who could have shot her?" We all stared at each other.

Andy said, "The police will figure it out."

Rob and I exchanged a glance. I said, "Thanks for the tea and scones. I feel much better now. I should get back to work; I'm sure everyone is wondering where I went."

Rob accompanied me to my office. "Are you sure you're okay?"

I smiled weakly. "Yes, I'm fine. I'll see you later." I gave him a quick kiss and ducked in the door.

CHAPTER 9

Rob popped his head inside my office door later on in the day. "How are you feeling?"

"Better." I hugged him. "Thanks for your help this morning. It was such a shock."

"Do you want to go out for dinner?"

"No. I don't feel like being around a lot of people tonight. Let's pick up something on the way to my house, and we can eat there." I shivered.

He held me close. "I have a better idea. Why don't I grab some chicken from that place we like and bring it back with me? That way you can go straight home."

"Are you sure? Truthfully, that sounds like a far better idea."

He grinned. "Anything for you. I'll see you there in about a half hour." He gave me a quick kiss and left.

Pulling together some things I needed to look at before the morning, I shrugged into my coat and scarf and headed home. The place felt empty.

Concerned, I texted Jenny, "Where are you?"

"At Dad's. Sad about Amanda. Can he eat with us tonight?"

I shuddered. "Yes. Rob's bringing chicken. Come in twenty."

"Will do. Thanks."

Grimacing, I texted Rob, "One more for dinner."

I set the table for four and then mixed a salad. Unable to resist any longer, I poured myself a large glass of wine and sat at the kitchen counter glaring at it.

Rob came in. "I'm glad I'm not that glass of wine."

I jumped. "Why?"

He kissed the top of my head. "Because you don't seem very happy with it."

I kissed him on the lips. "Good news—I'm very happy with you." I picked up the bag containing dinner and stuck it in the oven to keep warm.

Rob gestured at the table. "Who's our fourth?"

I groaned and put my head in my hands. "Drew."

"Drew?"

"Jenny was with him this afternoon, and apparently, he's pretty broken up about Amanda. She asked if he could have dinner with us."

Pouring himself a glass of wine, he took a sip and then stared straight at me. "Is this going to be a thing?"

"No, this is just a very particular circumstance."

Jenny burst through the back door with Drew limping behind her. She rubbed her hands. "It's cold out there."

I nodded and then gave Drew a sympathetic smile. "I was sorry to hear about Amanda."

He gulped. "Thanks. It was such a shock. Last night was a nightmare, and it definitely continued into today." Taking off his coat and gloves, he set them on one of the chairs at the counter. "Thanks for inviting me to dinner; it smells great." He tried to give me a kiss on the cheek, but I ducked at the last minute as I slid past him into the kitchen.

Rob glared at him, and I said, "Let's eat." I pulled the containers from the oven and set them on the table. Jenny retrieved serving utensils and we all sat. Drew stared at my wine glass. I shrugged. "Would you like some wine, Drew?"

"Don't mind if I do." He stood, retrieved a glass and poured himself a healthy amount. He returned to the table and we all focused on eating.

As we finished dinner, Drew said, "Boy, I really miss the cherry pies you used to make. They were the best. When I was in prison, I used to fantasize about those cherry pies."

I gave him a dry look. "Pity. I guess you'll just have to go on fantasizing, won't you?"

Jenny frowned. "Mom, you didn't have to say that. Dad was just being nice."

I rolled my eyes and took another sip of wine. "Whatever."

I stood to start gathering plates, but in a repeat of this morning, the whine of approaching sirens startled me. Next, the sound of screeching tires abruptly halting echoed through the house. "What in the world?"

As I ran to the front of the house, red-and-blue lights drunkenly swirled on the living room wall. I pulled the curtain aside just in time to watch the police racing up the walkway to Drew's lit porch. Banging on his door, they demanded entry.

Drew laughed. "Good thing I'm over here."

Glaring at him, I yanked the door open. "He's over here."

Like birds flocking, the police made a sharp right turn down the path to my front door. The lead policewoman, Becky Dryer, asked, "Is Drew March here, ma'am?"

I nodded and extended my arm as an invitation to enter the house. She marched in and found Drew sitting on the living room couch. Jenny stood in front of him. She blocked the policewoman's way. I snapped at Jenny, "Move."

Jenny spread out her arms protectively. "No. They can't take him again."

I gently took one of her arms. "Let's talk about this later. Let Officer Dryer talk to him."

She shook off my hand. “Okay.” Jenny stomped over to the armchair and plopped down.

Becky Dryer stood over Drew. “Drew March?”

“Yes.”

“You are under arrest for the murder of Amanda Thomas.” She read him his rights then cuffed him.

Jenny leapt up and grabbed for the cuffs as if to loosen them. “He didn’t do it. I know it.”

I pulled her hands down as Becky guided him out the door. Shutting it after her, I sat. “I can’t believe this is happening again.”

Jenny glared at me. “How could you let this happen? You have to help him.” Without waiting for an answer, she pounded up the stairs and slammed her door so hard the cats dove under the sofa.

Rob retrieved our wine from the kitchen and handed me my glass. “Well, that’s not something you see every day.”

I shook my head in disbelief. “No. But it does keep life interesting around here.”

“Do you think he did it?”

“It’s hard to believe. But then it was hard to believe that he was a con man. And it was hard to believe that he was cheating on me with Amanda. I guess I’m not the best judge of character.”

He sat and pulled me onto his lap. “You aren’t so bad. You chose me, didn’t you?”

I smiled. “Everyone has to get lucky every once in a while.”

“Would you like me to go down to the police station and see what I can find out?”

I kissed him. “That would be great. For Jenny’s sake, we’re going to need to help Drew.”

Rob moaned, “I can’t believe I’m going to help that man.”

“You and me both.” I tucked his scarf into his coat, zipped it up, and gave him a kiss. “Thanks. Keep warm.”

Rob left, and I cleaned up the kitchen. Feeling I delayed as long as I could, I retrieved an ice pack from the freezer, trudged up the steps, and knocked on Jenny's door.

She poked her head out. "You can only come in if you're going to help Dad."

I hugged her. "We're going to help him."

She smiled and opened the door wide. "What can we do?"

"First, put this ice pack on. Your face is looking better, and icing it will help." She rolled her eyes. "Second, I need to find out who his lawyer is. I know the one he used to use retired a few years ago."

She held the ice pack to her cheek. "I can help! When I programmed his phone, I put his lawyer's number in it."

"Do you remember the name and number?"

"No, but I know where he keeps his address book." Excited, she ran over to pick up her keys. She tossed the ice pack on the bed and the keys in the air. "I have Dad's key right here. Let's go."

I shifted uncomfortably. "I don't know if we should go into his house without him there."

"Mom, it's to help him. He won't mind. Let's go." Jenny ran down the stairs. I barely had time to put my coat on before she shot out the back door. "Hurry up, slowpoke." She grabbed my hand and practically dragged me to his back door. Unlocking it, she pushed the door open. Taking a deep breath, I followed.

The last time I had been in that kitchen was when I discovered my neighbor's body. I knew it was no longer there, but I shivered anyway and crossed myself as I passed the spot. Sprinting into the hallway leading to the office, I let out the breath I didn't know I was holding. Jenny tossed things from the desk. "I thought you knew where it was?"

"It was right under here. He must have moved it."

"You're making a mess." On autopilot, I started picking up the items Jenny threw onto the floor. Several pieces of paper looked like they were diagrams of some type of financial transaction. Setting them to the side, I moved closer to the desk and pointed to the windowsill. "Isn't that an address book?"

"Yes! What's it doing over there?"

I pointed to the portable phone lying next to it. "He must have been phoning from here and forgot to put it back." I looked out the window and realized it faced my living room. Had he watched us from here? I shook myself. *Focus!* "Can you find the name and number?"

She paged through the book. "Here it is."

I looked at the entry: Davis and Family, Attorneys at Law. In parentheses, Drew had written Kendall Davis along with her cell number. I picked up the portable phone and dialed. "This is Meredith March. I'm calling about my ex-husband, Drew March. I believe he is a client of yours." I explained our dilemma.

"Thanks for alerting me. I'll go to the police station right now. Hopefully he hasn't told them anything."

Jenny and I returned to the house. Shedding our coats, I asked, "Would you like some hot chocolate?"

"Would love some. What do we do now?"

"We wait, and you put another ice pack on. Hopefully his lawyer is a good one, and she'll be able to get him out on bail." I picked up the hot milk and stirred it into the mugs. I handed Jenny one. "I know this is hard, honey, but we'll get through it."

She hunched over her mug. "But I just started to get to know him again!" She put the mug on the counter. "Mom, you found the person who killed Mr. Ford and Ms. Piedmont. You can figure out who killed Ms. Thomas!"

I blew on the hot chocolate and then took a sip. "We'll see. I said I'd help, but I don't want to get your hopes up."

She smiled. "I know you can do it." She threw a few more marshmallows into her mug. "I need to work on a paper. Let me know when Mr. Jenson gets back." She kissed me, left the ice pack on the counter, and ran up the stairs to her room.

No pressure. What if Drew really did it? I gave up and put the ice pack back in the freezer. Moping around wasn't going to help, so I washed the dirty pot. I strode into the living room with a dust rag. Seeing no dust, I sank onto the sofa. I grabbed my book and curled up with a cat on my lap. Courvoisier took her position on the back of the sofa near my head. Reading a page that I had no recollection of, I reread it. *You have the attention span of a gnat!* Giving up, I checked my phone to see if Rob had texted me.

The back door opened with a bang and then just as quickly shut. The cats leapt up to explore, and I followed them.

Patty stared at the hot chocolate pot in the sink. "I can't decide. Do I want hot chocolate or wine? Tough choice." She poured a glass of wine. "What's all this about Drew?"

"You were talking to yourself."

"No, I wasn't. I knew you were there." She gave me a superior smile. "Anyway, we're off topic. I heard Drew was arrested for murdering Amanda. Is it true?"

I pushed past her and grabbed myself a glass. "Is what true? That he was arrested or that he killed Amanda?"

"The former and, I guess if you know the answer, the latter as well."

"He was arrested. Right here, as a matter of fact."

"What was he doing here?"

"Jenny told me he was sad about what happened to Amanda, so she suckered me into inviting him for dinner."

Patty gave me a sideways glance and then padded past me into the living room. I followed. She sat. "You're getting soft in your old age."

I joined her on the sofa. "You're right." The back door banged open again. "Can't anyone open a door quietly?"

Rob came into the living room. “Sorry about that—the wind is really picking up. I’ll be right back.” He returned a moment later with a full wine glass. He took a sip. “Investigating is thirsty work.”

I patted the sofa next to me. He sank onto it, putting his arm around me in one smooth motion. I asked, “What happened? What do they have on Drew?”

He looked over my head. “Hello, Patty. Good to see you again.”

I frowned. “Okay, politeness done. What did you find out?”

Rob pulled out his pocket notepad. “It looks like Drew was the last person to see Amanda alive. Jay was interrogating Drew when his lawyer showed up.” Rob glanced at his notes. “A Ms. Davis.”

I nodded. “Yes, I know. Jenny and I called her from Drew’s house.”

“You went to Drew’s house?”

“Keep on topic. What happened?”

“Jay saw me chatting with some of the police in the bullpen and waved me over. He said that Drew went back to Amanda’s apartment and they argued. She was mad because she thought he ruined the spring fashion show.”

I raised an eyebrow. “But she reserved a seat for him. She must have known that he was going to be there.”

“She did, but according to witnesses, she said she didn’t know there’d be a brawl that would overshadow all the good she was trying to do.”

“But that wasn’t his fault.”

Patty looked over. “No. But he must have known how people in the town felt. He was getting all those phone calls.”

I nodded slowly. “I don’t even know why I’m defending him.” I twirled the wine in my glass. “What else did Jay say?”

“Two of the neighbors heard an argument; one of them had just returned from the hospital. Apparently, the guy chipped a bone in his arm when someone threw a chair at the fashion show. Anyway, he described the argument in great detail. They haven't found anyone who heard the shot, though. Jay thinks that Drew had a silencer."

"He just got out of prison. Where on earth would he get a gun? He certainly can't buy one."

"It's been known to happen. Only a third of the states require background checks if someone buys a handgun at a gun show. And this state isn't one of them. Did Drew have any guns here when you were married?"

"Two, I think. A hunting rifle he got from his dad and a pistol he picked up somewhere. He knew how to use them, but I don't remember him ever going to a range. Plus, I'm pretty sure he didn't have a silencer. What would he need that for?"

"What happened to them?"

"They're in a lockbox in the basement."

We all stared at each other, mouths agape. As one, we stood and strode to the stairs. Rob led the way. He stepped aside after he opened the door to the basement. Turning on the light, I ran down the stairs in front of them. I stood on the step stool and pulled the key off the third rafter on the left and opened the gun cupboard. It was empty.

Rob frowned. "I think you better call Jay."

I relocked the cupboard and put the key back. Rob raised his eyebrow. "What?"

"It's empty. Why are you locking it?"

"Oh. Habit, I guess." I shrugged, and we all returned to the living room.

Jenny sat there petting Courvoisier. "What were you doing downstairs?"

"I'll call Jay." Rob left the room.

"Wimp." I shook my head. Patty and I sat on either side of her, and I told her what had happened.

Ashen, Jenny asked, "He took the guns?"

"Yes, I think so."

She cringed. "Did he take them when I let him come over?"

"He could have. But I think it would have been difficult. The shotgun would have been hard to hide from you. I never changed the locks or alarm code, so he could have come over anytime."

She looked a little relieved, and then she paled again. "But he couldn't have done it. I can't believe that my dad is a murderer."

"Let's not get ahead of ourselves, honey. He may just have wanted his guns back and knew that if he asked me, I would have told him no."

She brightened. "That's true. So you're still going to help him, right?"

"As much as I can. Why don't you go back upstairs now? It's getting late, and Detective Ziebold is coming over."

Looking uncertain, she hugged me and trudged slowly back up the stairs.

Patty took a sip of her wine. "You handled that as well as you could."

"Thanks. It was a tough one."

The back door banged open again. Rob welcomed Jay. Patty and I joined them in the kitchen. Rob made coffee as Jay took off his outercoat, scarf, and hat.

"Sorry about the door, Merry. That wind is really howling out there."

"I heard." Reaching into the freezer, I brought out some frozen cinnamon rolls I had made a few weeks ago. "Cinnamon rolls?"

Jay nodded his appreciation, as did Rob. Patty asked Jay, "You don't need me, do you?" He shook his head, so Patty rinsed out her wine glass and left it in the sink. She hugged me. "Patrick must think I left him. You okay?" I nodded, and she bundled up and left.

I put the rolls in the microwave to defrost, and Rob poured us coffee. Jay sat at the kitchen table. "Rob told me on the phone that Drew took guns out of the locked cupboard in the basement."

The microwave dinged, so I grabbed the plate. "Yes, but we don't know for sure that he did it." I shrugged, realizing how ridiculous that sounded. "Okay, he probably did it. Who else knew that I had guns and that they were locked in the basement? Plus, who knew where I kept the key?"

Rob and Jay turned to each other. "Drew."

"But I'm pretty sure he didn't have a silencer for the pistol. I would have remembered that."

Jay frowned. "Unless he didn't tell you. He could have kept the silencer somewhere else. Or he could have gotten that more recently. Do you know what caliber pistol he had?"

"I think it was a .22."

Jay popped the rest of his cinnamon roll in his mouth and washed it down with coffee. He stood. "Let's take a look in your basement."

Rob said, "I'll clean up. You show him."

I took Jay downstairs, again unlocking the cupboard and showing him that it was empty. "Do you remember the last time you saw the guns?"

"Not really. It would have been before Drew went to jail four years ago. I know I didn't open it the whole time he was away. I don't shoot, so there was no reason to."

"How did he get in the house?"

I looked at my shoes. "I never changed the locks or alarm code. He was in jail, so I didn't see any point, and I just didn't think about it once he was out. You can bet I'm going to change them now."

He nodded. "Let's go back upstairs." We did. "We got a search warrant for his house, which we will be executing tomorrow morning. I'll let you know what we find. And thanks for the coffee and the roll. It really hit the spot." Shrugging into his coat, hat, and scarf, he opened the door, holding onto it this time.

Rob helped push it shut. "I'm not looking forward to going back out in that."

I hugged him and gave him a kiss. “I wish you didn’t have to.”

He kissed me more deeply and held me closer. “I could stay.” He smiled down at me.

I pushed him away gently. “Jenny’s upstairs. You really do need to leave.”

He bundled up. “I want the record to show that you pushed me out into this cold, cruel weather.”

Winding his scarf around his neck, I pulled him to me. “We will find the time. Soon, I promise.” He kissed me again, and I felt it all the way to my toes. “Very soon.”

CHAPTER 10

As I watched from my bay window the next morning, the police entered Drew's house to search it. Melissa and his lawyer, Kendall Davis, were on hand. I assumed Melissa was there since she was the owner of the house. I found myself hoping they wouldn't do too much damage, as she would have to clean it up. One of the policemen carried out Drew's laptop. *It would be interesting to see what he has on that.*

Jenny ran down the stairs as I yanked the curtain shut. "What were you looking at? Is Dad back?" She hurried to the window and pulled back the curtain. "What are they doing? Hey, that's Dad's laptop."

I closed the curtain. "They're searching his house."

"Did they get a warrant? I learned they have to have a warrant. Did you see it?"

"Detective Ziebold told me they got one last night."

"But did you see it?"

"No, I didn't, but your dad's lawyer is there, and I know she wouldn't have let them in without it."

"Oh." She looked pensive and then shook it off. "Will you drive me to school? It's too cold out to walk."

"Can do, if you'll eat something on the way." I handed her a granola bar as she rolled her eyes. We bundled up and headed for the car, both staring holes in the house next door.

Jenny said, "It's not fair that the police can look through your house and you can't do anything about it."

"I'm sure since you learned about search warrants, you also know that they are only issued once a judge approves them." I pulled up at the school. "So, if you don't want them to search your house, you should keep your nose clean."

"Thanks for the gross visual, Mom. See you later." She bounded out the door and joined a group just entering the school.

I looked down at the cup holder and saw that Jenny had forgotten her granola bar. *Crap. Need to make sure she gets more nutritious breakfasts.* Shaking my head, I drove to work, looking at the icicles hanging from houses' eaves. *May get some ice dam claims.* As I passed the Morning Pastry, I noticed that the open sign was lit.

I entered the office and asked Cheryl to send an e-mail to my client distribution list with an attachment on how to prevent ice dams. Settling in to do some paperwork, I realized that my standing eight-thirty staff meeting was in a half hour. *There's sure to be questions about Drew. It'll go better if I feed them.*

I hurried down to the Morning Pastry. Bustling in the door, I was stunned by the assortment of baked goods. I stood in the short line and debated what to have. As I reached the front of the line, I ordered an apricot Danish ring and their large crumb cake. The new owner, Gary Johnson, was behind the cash register, so I introduced myself and welcomed him to town. The line was getting longer, so I didn't linger.

Hurrying back to the office, I handed off the bounty to Cheryl. She asked, "What was it like? Do they have the same things?"

"Similar offerings. It all looked yummy. We'll do the true taste test at the meeting."

We went to the conference room. The associates heard there would be food, so they gathered quickly. I sliced the pastries and Cheryl put out paper plates and plastic cutlery. For a moment, all we heard were sighs of satisfaction as people tucked into the food.

Cheryl grinned. "This might be better than the previous place."

"It is good. I think they are in the process of changing the name. Maybe they wanted to open before the sign was ready." Finishing the last bite of my Danish, I stood and addressed the group. "First, how were the pastries?" Everyone clapped. "Second, by now you've heard that Drew was arrested last night." Some people nodded, and others gasped. "I just want you all to remember that he hasn't been proven guilty. He obtained legal counsel, and that's about all I know. If clients have questions, please do not speculate. Is there anything further on that topic?"

Peter Boston said, "I didn't hear about it; my network must be slipping. What was he arrested for?"

"Murdering Amanda Thomas." There were more gasps. *Must have been a busy night if the town gossip mill overlooked this.* "Yes, it's serious, and I know we'll all miss her."

"I won't," a few people muttered under their breath.

Continuing as if I hadn't heard, I urged, "Again, let's not speculate. Now, if there isn't anything else, let's move on to business." I asked Jill Farber to come up and talk about the new CD rates that we're offering. I sat. *That wasn't so bad.*

Rob texted me in the afternoon: "Dinner tonight?"

"Yes, but I don't want to leave Jenny alone. I'll pick up something and meet you at the house at six."

"Okay."

At five, I left the office and stopped at the grocery store. As I perused the aisles, I noticed that conversation died down when I passed clumps of people huddled together. *I guess Drew's arrest is definitely out now.* I nodded blandly to the newly silent groups and picked up my pace.

The salmon looked good, so I put some in my cart, along with some fresh dill and lemons. Next, I retrieved bagged salad, tomatoes, and rosemary. I spied some iced brownies and tossed them in my cart. *Definitely deserve some medicinal chocolate.* Checking out, I felt the stares on my back. *At least they're not judging me for the brownie purchase.*

The potatoes were in the oven and I had just started encasing the salmon in aluminum foil when Rob arrived. He kissed me and took off his coat. "What smells so good?"

"Potatoes."

He sniffed the air. "With rosemary? That sounds tasty."

"I hope you're in the mood for salmon."

"I love salmon. Do you want me to set the table?"

At my nod, Rob gathered the plates and cutlery. "How was your day? I'm sure there was a lot of conversation about Drew."

"There was, but it died down whenever I came near enough to hear anything."

"Ah, you felt like a pariah?" He came behind the counter and gave me a big hug, lifting me off my feet. "Poor lady. Is this better?"

"Much." I smiled at him.

Rob uncorked a bottle of wine and pointed at it. "Bet you'd like a glass of this."

"Absolutely. It's been a very tense day."

He rubbed my shoulders. "You are tense. If we were at my house, I could show you a few ways to relieve some of that stress."

I kissed his hand. "I'm sure you could, and I'm looking forward to that. Right now, though, I need to concentrate on dinner and that kid upstairs." I pointed toward the ceiling.

He gently kissed my finger. "Pity." He took a sip of his wine and continued setting the table.

I texted Jenny, "Dinner in five."

"Heard."

I laughed. "Remember when your mom would have to yell up the stairs to tell you it was dinnertime?"

He smiled. "This seems so much more civilized yet a touch impersonal."

I handed him the tomatoes, bagged salad, and bowl. He made quick work of washing and slicing the tomatoes and tossing the salad. He grabbed a wedge of parmesan from the fridge and held it up. "Want some parmesan slivers?"

I nodded, and he used the potato peeler to add shards to the bowl. I took the salmon and potatoes out of the oven. "What did you hear today?" Jenny clomped down the steps. "Later."

She swung into her chair and took a long drink of milk. "Studying is thirsty stuff."

I smiled at her. "How goes it in the salt mines?"

"Not bad. What have we heard about Dad?"

I glanced at Rob. "Not much. I think you're as up to date as we are."

Jenny told Rob, "We saw them searching Dad's house this morning. I wonder if they found anything." She chewed her salmon. "They took his laptop. Why would they do that? She wasn't shot with a computer."

I touched her arm. "They're trying to find out if this was something he planned. He may have e-mailed someone, researched silencers, something like that."

"You think Dad's dumb enough to send an e-mail to someone saying that he was going to kill Ms. Thomas? Be real, Mom."

"It's unlikely, but it's the kind of thing they look for." I stood. "Does anyone want brownies for dessert?" Two hands went up. I looked at Rob. "Coffee?"

"Yes. I'll clean up while you get dessert ready." He started to load the dishwasher with items Jenny handed him.

I poured Jenny some more milk and then filled coffee mugs. Cutting the brownies, I used a spatula to transfer them to plates.

Sitting down again, Jenny bit into a brownie. “This is so good. It’s like chocolate overload with the frosting.” She studied me. “This isn’t like you, Mom. I love you showing your decadent side.”

I pushed her shoulder. “Be careful, or you’ll be having broccoli brownies next.”

“Ugh.” She carried her plate and glass to the sink. “Need to finish my homework. Thanks for dinner.” She kissed me and then disappeared up the stairs.

Rob sipped his coffee. “I would have come to your defense, but all of the chocolate made my lips stick together.”

“Better watch it. You could be eating broccoli brownies as well.”

He stood with his plate and kissed the top of my head. “Just kidding. Dinner was terrific, and I loved the brownie. Thanks for inviting me.” He held up his mug. “Want more coffee?”

“Yes. Let’s have it in the living room.” He topped off our mugs and handed me mine. We sat side by side on the sofa. “Now that we’re alone again, what did you hear today about Drew?”

“It wasn’t really about Drew. It was about Amanda. I don’t know if you knew this, but she wasn’t really well-liked in town. In fact, I didn’t hear a lot of good spoken about her today.”

“It’s strange you should say that. I mentioned something like ‘she’ll be missed’ in my staff meeting today, and I could have sworn I heard some people say that they wouldn’t miss her. I knew that she was abrasive to me a few times, but I thought that was just because we were so different.”

“You always think the best of people.”

“If that’s my only flaw, I’ll keep it.”

Rob ran his hand down the side of my face. “I don’t see any flaws.” He kissed me, and I lost myself in his warmth.

I broke free after a few minutes. “Thank you, kind sir. Did you find anything else out?”

“I met Caroline.”

"Caroline? Who's Caroline? Should I be jealous?"

He nuzzled my ear. "You have no reason to be jealous. Caroline is Amanda's sister."

I sat up. "I didn't know she had a sister."

"Well, she does. She said she was here for the reading of the will and to close up Amanda's shop and apartment. She stopped by to talk about the obituary."

I leaned back into his body. "Was she her only sibling?"

He put his arm around me again and pulled me tighter to his side. "Yes, and her parents are both deceased."

"Then Caroline will probably inherit whatever little there is."

"Let's not talk about her anymore." Rob's lips reached mine.

I heard Jenny's door open and leapt up from the sofa, fumbling to pull myself together. "We have got to stop doing this." The upstairs bathroom door shut. I sighed in relief and ran my fingers through my hair. "I need to figure out how to resist you."

Rob pulled me back to him and kissed me again.

"Stop that. You'll just get me all rumpled again."

He pulled on my collar. "What's wrong with that?"

"I just don't want to give Jenny the wrong idea."

He smiled. "Which one is that?"

I pushed him away. "You are way too cute for your own good. And now I am going to toss you back out into the cold."

He grimaced and put his shoes back on. "You're a mean person, Merry March."

I handed him his coat. "Yes, I am."

"It's a good thing that you are also irresistible." He gave me a long, lingering kiss. Breaking contact first he said, "Bye."

I went to the sink and splashed cold water on my face. *That man.*

* * *

As I stretched the next morning, my phone dinged with a text from Rob: "Thanks for dinner last night."

"My pleasure."

"Dinner out tonight?"

"Let me check with Jenny."

"Bring her if you want to."

The cats insisted on playing with my socks as I tried to put them on. To be honest, I may have dangled one to see what they would do. As I finished dressing, they ran in front of me and out my bedroom door.

I knocked on Jenny's door. "You up?"

"Yes."

"Be downstairs in fifteen."

She poked her ruffled head out the door. "Why fifteen? I have more time than that."

"Not if you want pancakes."

The door shut, and I heard a muffled voice say, "I'll be there."

After we ate, I managed to get a quick kiss and "love you" from Jenny. I put the dishes in the dishwasher and then stuck one hand out the back door. It didn't feel quite as arctic. Pulling on my coat and scarf, I decided to be virtuous and walk to work. As I got closer to the office, I quickened my pace. *It may not be arctic, but it's definitely cold.*

Midway through the day, Cheryl popped her head around the door. "Peter MacDougal's on the phone. He says he's representing Amanda Thomas."

"What does he want me for?"

"No idea. Should I put him through?"

"Please. Thanks." I picked up the phone. "Hi, Peter. How can I help you?"

"Merry, good to speak with you. You may not know this, but I was Amanda Thomas's attorney."

"I didn't know that."

"Yes, well, we've got kind of a situation here, and I was wondering if you could meet me in my office at three thirty. You'll need to bring Jenny with you. Oh, and Caroline Thomas will be here too."

"I'm sorry, Peter, but I don't know what this is all about."

"We'll be reading Amanda's will. I really would rather explain all this in person. Will you be able to come?"

"We'll be there." As I hung up the phone, a shiver rolled up my spine. *What is this all about?*

CHAPTER 11

I picked Jenny up from school, and she was full of questions. I sighed. "Jenny, I have no idea what Mr. MacDougal wants. We're just going to have to wait till we get to his office to find out."

We arrived a few minutes early. An attractive brunette with long straight hair and mocha-brown eyes waited in the lobby. Her resemblance to Amanda was remarkable.

I hesitated for a moment and then ambled over with my hand extended. "Are you Caroline? My name is Meredith March, and this is my daughter, Jenny. I am so sorry about your sister's passing."

She shook my hand. "Thank you. Do you know what's going on? I'm not sure why Peter wanted all of us here. Were you a special friend of my sister's?"

"I knew your sister, of course." I gestured at Jenny. "My daughter was one of the volunteer models in her fashion show."

She grimaced. "I heard it was a disaster."

Jenny looked stricken. I protested, "The show was wonderful; your sister was so talented. It was after the show that was a disaster."

Caroline looked thoughtful. "Did you say your last name is March?"

"Yes."

"That's the same name as one of the men my sister was dating. He's the one who has been accused of murdering her."

I shifted from side to side. "He's my ex-husband."

She glared at me. Peter MacDonald came out of the elevator. “Good. You’ve all met. Follow me.”

I grabbed Jenny’s hand and pulled her with me. Caroline followed. “Peter, I’m not sure why these people are here.”

He waved his hand. “I’ll explain in a few minutes.” He led us into a conference room. “Would anyone like coffee or some water?” We nodded for the water, so he poured several glasses and passed them around. Jenny and I sat next to each other on one side of the table, while Caroline sat on the other.

Peter sat at the head. “Thanks for coming. This is a bit unusual, so I hope you’ll bear with me. I’ll hand out Amanda’s will in a few moments, but I thought it would be better to discuss it first.”

He looked at Caroline. “Amanda wanted you to have her shop, the contents of her apartment, and the monies in her bank account, which before any debts from the estate comes to roughly $50,000.”

Caroline nodded; it looked like the amount was what she expected.

“This is the part where it gets a bit difficult. Amanda had another account. She left the proceeds in that account to Drew March.” Caroline gasped.

I frowned. “I still don’t know what that has to do with us. Drew and I have been divorced for four years.”

Peter said, “Let me explain in layman’s terms. As you know, Drew has been charged with Amanda’s death.” Caroline took a gulp of water as her eyes teared up. He continued, “If Drew is convicted, he cannot profit from her death. For all intents and purposes, it will be as if Drew preceded Amanda in death.”

Still confused, I said, “So that means the money in the account will go to Caroline if Drew is convicted?”

“No. The will is very clear on that point. If Drew were to die or be otherwise unable to inherit, the money in that account will go to Jenny.”

I crossed my arms. “How much money are we talking about?” Amanda wasn’t rich. It’s probably only a few dollars. Nothing to worry about.

Peter cleared his throat and took a sip of his water. He focused on the pages in front of him. “Somewhere north of a million dollars.”

I leapt up. “What? Where did she get that kind of money?”

Jenny and Caroline both sat there with their mouths wide open. Jenny said in wonder, “A million dollars...”

“Again, that’s only if Drew is convicted. If he’s proven not guilty, he would inherit the money.”

I sank back down on the chair and put my head in my hands. *Another nightmare.*

Caroline stood. “There’s no way Drew or his spawn,” she pointed at Jenny, “are getting that money. I’m getting another attorney, and I’m going to contest the will!” She stalked out of the room.

Peter sighed. “That didn’t go very well. It’s within her rights to contest, but she won’t be successful.”

Standing, I shook his hand. “Thanks for letting us know, Peter. I appreciate it. Please keep us posted.” I pulled on Jenny’s arm, as she seemed frozen to her seat.

She stood slowly. “A million dollars...”

“Come on, Jenny. We’ll talk in the car.” I guided her to the door and then waved goodbye to Peter.

Jenny sat in the car. “Mom, where did Ms. Thomas get a million dollars, and why would she leave it to Dad?”

I started the car and headed home. “That, my friend, is the million-dollar question. I don’t think you should mention anything about this to anyone. We don’t know where the money came from, and it could cause some hard feelings around town.”

She looked at me wide-eyed. “I wouldn’t even know what to say. No one’s going to hear about it from me.” Dazed, she shuffled through the back door and up the stairs.

I texted Rob, "We better eat here tonight. Have news for you. I'll cook."

I grabbed some chicken from the freezer, prepared chicken parmigiana, and put the dish in the refrigerator till it was time to bake.

Cleaning up, I took one last look around the kitchen as my mind continued to swirl. *Where did she get the money? She didn't have money like that. She wasn't hurting but a million dollars?* I poured myself a glass of wine and sat on the window seat, staring at Drew's house. *I sense your mind at work, Drew. What were you up to?*

Rob came through the back door, breaking up my wool-gathering. He kissed the top of my head. "A penny for your thoughts. You look like a thunderstorm about to happen."

"Let me heat up the oven, and then I'll fill you in." Turning it on, I took the chicken out of the fridge and put it to the side. I poured Rob a glass of wine.

"Thanks. A guy could get used to this."

I smiled and gave him a kiss on his cheek as I sat next to him at the counter. "I had a strange call from Peter MacDougal today."

"Peter the attorney?"

I nodded. "Yes. He's handling Amanda Thomas's estate."

"I can't imagine she has that much to distribute. She didn't really live high on the hog."

I choked on my wine and started coughing. Retrieving a glass of water, Rob handed it to me. I sipped it, and then, unable to stop myself, I started laughing.

He frowned. "What's so funny? Did she look rich to you?"

"She left Drew a million dollars."

He whistled. "That's a lot of cabbage."

"It sure is."

"But if he killed her, he can't benefit from her death, so the money would go to her sister, right? Where do you come in?"

I took a deep breath. “I don’t understand all of the technicalities, but apparently, the will was written in such a way that if Drew couldn’t inherit, it would go to Jenny.” The oven buzzed, signaling that the preheat cycle was done. I put the chicken in the oven and set a timer. “Noodles or potatoes?”

“How can you think about that right now?”

“We have to eat, so which will it be?”

He threw his hands in the air. “Noodles.”

I filled a pot with water, added salt, and turned the dial to high. Returning to my seat, I rubbed Rob’s arm.

“A million dollars...”

“Yes. Jenny’s been saying that a lot. We’re in shock. And we’re trying to figure out where Amanda got it from.”

Rob’s eyes narrowed. “It seems odd that they’ve only been dating for a short time, yet she left him so much money.”

“But have they been? I told you I’m pretty sure that she was dating him before he went to jail.”

“How long before?”

“The picture she had on Facebook was posted roughly five years ago. So she had to have been seeing him for at least a year before he went to jail.” I shuddered at the thought.

Rob put his arm around me and pulled me to him. “It’s okay. You’re not married to him anymore.”

“Then why am I still trying to clean up his messes? And this seems like a big one.” I put the pasta in the boiling water. “Would you mind setting the table?”

Placing the plates on the table, he stopped in mid-stride. “Were you able to account for all of the money that he embezzled?”

I nodded. “Yes, I told you that we paid everyone back, every penny.”

“What about gains on the money?”

I took a sip of wine. "He told the police and me that he suffered some losses and had very small gains. He said we were lucky the principal was still intact. I remember they did a search to find all of his accounts, and they matched what he told them. There weren't any other ones."

"Was he a good money manager?"

"I thought he was, but obviously I was mistaken."

"Maybe you weren't."

I raised my eyebrows. He continued to set the table. "What if he moved gains above a certain amount to another account and left the losses in the accounts you found? Of course, the account with the excess gains in it would have to be one that he didn't own." He finished with the table and faced me. "And maybe he'd only get that money in the case of death."

My eyes widened. "You'd have to really trust the person who owned the account."

"Yes, you would."

Jenny came hurtling down the stairs and around the corner into the kitchen. "When's dinner? I'm starving, and it smells so good." She switched on the oven light and peered in. "Chicken parm, my fav."

I tore my gaze from Rob. "Two minutes. Would you put the salad in a bowl?"

"Will do."

We were just about to sit when the phone rang. "Merry, it's Jay. Would you mind if I came by tonight? About an hour from now?"

"That's fine. See you then."

I hung up and sat at the table. "That was Jay. He wants to talk to me."

Jenny frowned. "Do you think he knows about the will?"

"I think he just found out."

We finished dinner. Jenny went upstairs to complete a report, and Rob and I cleaned up. There were some brownies left over, so I cut them into small pieces and put them on a plate. Turning the coffee on, I lined up three mugs.

Jay stuck his head in. "Anyone home?"

Rob said, "Come on in. The coffee's almost ready."

"Thank goodness. It's just about time for my caffeine fix." Jay took off his coat, hat, and gloves.

I gestured to the kitchen table. "We might as well sit there." I handed mugs around and put the brownies on the table. "What's up?"

"I just learned about the contents of Amanda's will."

I nodded.

"A million dollars is a heck of a motive."

"Not if you knew that killing that person meant you wouldn't get the money. It's not my place to defend Drew anymore, but Drew's smart. He wouldn't kill Amanda. How does that help him?"

Jay played with his napkin. "What if it was a crime of passion? They were arguing, he had a gun, and he shot her. He forgot about the money."

I rolled my eyes. "Drew never forgets about money. Never."

Rob looked up. "When was he supposed to have gotten the gun anyway?"

"What do you mean?" Jay asked.

"You questioned him at the hospital. He was there with Amanda. Didn't they go to Amanda's house from there?"

"Yes, that's what he said, and we have some witness statements that agree with that timeline."

Rob frowned. "Then how did he get the gun? There was the melee at the VFW, and I would have noticed a gun there. Then the ambulance took him to the hospital. I'm sure somebody there would have noticed a gun. Do you think he was keeping it at Amanda's?"

"We found a .22 and the shotgun when we searched Drew's house."

"So what you're saying is that Drew kept the gun at Amanda's, retrieved it, shot her in a fit of pique, and then took the gun back home with him and stored it with the other one he took from Merry?" Rob picked up a brownie, finished it in one bite, and sat back to chew on it, looking smug.

"When you lay it out like that, it does sound far-fetched. But stranger things have happened." Jay looked superior. "And there is the fact that she was shot with a .38 caliber pistol."

I sat up. "What? That means Drew didn't do it. He doesn't have a .38."

Jay gave me a hard stare. "That you know of."

I picked up a brownie and examined it. "If he had a .38 caliber pistol, why would he have taken the guns from me?" I popped half the brownie in my mouth.

"Because he could." Jay picked up a brownie and ate it as he stood. He started to put on his coat but bent over for a last sip of his coffee. "And don't forget, if he gets off on the murder charge, he will get the million dollars."

"That's a big if. Are you too focused on the easy suspect?"

"What do you mean?"

I stood to make my point. "Philip might have done it. He started dating Amanda last Valentine's Day. I remember watching them at the dance, thinking they made such a cute couple. Fast-forward to earlier this week. I saw his face when Drew kissed her up on that stage. He looked shocked at first and then angry. He probably felt humiliated, and it was worse because it happened in front of the whole town."

Jay glared at me. "Thanks for the vote of confidence, Merry. Let me lay it out for you. Which murderer do you think is more plausible? The town dentist, who in his spare time offers free dental work in Appalachia and who has never even gotten so much as a parking ticket, or a convicted felon who stands to inherit a million dollars. Thanks for the coffee and brownie." Jay tugged on his hat and slammed the door as he left.

I looked at Rob. "It could have happened. He's really focused on Drew."

Rob laughed. "Yes, he seemed pretty clear on that." Rob snagged another brownie. "You cut them so small."

I handed him a napkin. "More coffee?" He nodded, and I topped off his mug. "Since it's clear that the police aren't going to look at alternative suspects, I think we're going to have to."

Rob clinked his mug with mine. "I'll go along for the ride. As long as we're careful. Remember what happened last time."

* * *

After tossing and turning for most of the night, I gave up at six and figured I might as well bake. I checked one of my favorite recipes from the Internet, and the blueberry muffins were mixed and in the oven in short order. Satisfied at achieving something, I sat to focus on my coffee. *He was seeing Amanda for at least a year before he was arrested. He trusted her enough that he moved a million dollars into her account. Why didn't I notice anything?*

My phone buzzed with a text from Rob: "Are you up?"

"Yep. Making blueberry muffins."

"Coffee ready?"

"Yes."

"See you in ten."

I shuffled over to the cupboard and grabbed another mug. The oven bell chimed, signaling that the muffins were ready. I took them out and put them on a rack to cool. I had just taken a sip of my coffee when the back door opened and Rob scooted in. "Brr. It's cold out there." He filled his coffee mug.

"No kiss, no coffee."

"I can oblige." He leaned over and placed a sweet, soft kiss on my lips.

"Now, that's the way to start a morning."

He smiled. "Now can I have coffee?"

"Of course. You can even have a muffin once they cool enough."

He touched one of the wrappers. "Maybe another minute or so." He took his coat off and sat next to me. "I've been thinking."

"And?"

"If Drew didn't kill Amanda and if for the minute we exclude Philip, who did? Who else would have motive?"

"Didn't you tell me that she wasn't very popular?"

"I did. But people aren't usually killed just because other people don't like them."

The clock ticked. "There's something I keep on turning over in my head. It was just plain weird."

"What?"

"When Susan Clime threw her drink at the fashion show. She threw it at Amanda, not Drew. And she called her a tramp. Why would she be mad at Amanda?"

Rob hesitated. "Sometimes people blame the woman. You told me that there was a lot of animosity toward you after Drew's misdeeds were discovered."

"I'm not sure it's the same thing. I was married to him, and people thought I knew what he was up to."

"Who knows what goes through people's minds? Maybe she thought Amanda was betraying the town by dating him."

"It's still strange and something I think I want to understand better." I took a sip of my coffee. "On a separate note, how can we find out if Drew really did give Amanda the money to keep for him?"

"I'm not sure we will ever know. One thing that might help is to know when the account was opened. Jay might be able to get that information."

"True, but will he tell us? He seemed pretty mad at me last night."

Jenny stuck her disheveled head around the corner. "I heard voices. Why is Mr. Jenson here this early?" She grinned. "At least he's wearing different clothes."

"Jenny, that's an inappropriate comment," I scolded.

Rob cleared his throat. "Your mom texted me she was making blueberry muffins."

"In that case, I'm sorry for my joke." She sprinted in, grabbed a muffin, and dashed back up the stairs.

I shook my head. "That girl."

"At least you know where she stands. And she does have a sense of humor."

I smiled. "She does, no matter how inappropriate. I'm sorry if she made you feel uncomfortable."

He laughed. "Takes a lot more than that." Hugging me with one arm, he reached behind me and nabbed a muffin. "Cool enough now." He peeled off the wrapper, finishing it in three bites. "Tastes good." He took another sip of coffee. "I need to leave. I'll check on the money angle and see what I can find out."

"I'm thinking it may be time for a teeth cleaning. I'll see if I can get an appointment."

We smiled at each other, and he wrapped me in a hug. "Be careful. I wouldn't want my best girl to get hurt."

"I promise." He gave me a long, slow kiss and grabbed another muffin before leaving.

A few minutes later, Jenny came running by. "Love you, Mom. I'm late."

I barely had time to say, "Love you too," when the door closed behind her. Cleaning up quickly, I left the house and hopped in my car.

I parked a bit farther away than usual so I could get a few steps in. After I had cleared away some of the urgent items, I called Dr. Philip's office to schedule my cleaning. They had a cancellation, so I was able to get in the following morning. I strolled over to the Morning Pastry to pick up some lunch and realized that they had changed the name. It was now called Delightful Bites. *Nice name. Doesn't limit them to breakfast.*

I ordered an egg salad sandwich on rye and a large coffee to go. As I waited, Gary Johnson came around the counter. "Merry, I understand you sell property and casualty insurance."

"Yes, although we do carry other product lines."

"Would it be possible to set up some time to chat about our coverage here?"

"I'd love to do that. When would be most convenient for you?"

"Between two and three or after five when we shut down."

I checked my phone. "I could do next Monday at two."

"That would work. I'll see you then."

My name was called for my sandwich, so I waved goodbye to him. *Nice man. Hopefully I can help him with whatever he needs.*

Returning to the office, I told Cheryl, "New name for the Morning Pastry."

"Yes. Delightful Bites. I saw that yesterday. I think they are living up to their name."

I nodded and went into my office. Unwrapping my sandwich, I sighed with happiness. They had olives in the egg salad. The brininess tasted so good. I had a meeting with a client later that afternoon that I needed to prepare for, so I focused on not dropping any egg on the paperwork. Just as I finished eating, my phone dinged. Patty's text said, "GNO tonight?"

"GNO?"

"Girls' night out. Sheesh."

"Okay. Pickled Herring at six?"

"B there or B square." She signed off with a smiley face.

I texted Rob and told him I'd see him the following evening. Next, I texted Jenny that she would be on her own. She reminded me that she had basketball practice and that Patrick would be taking them to dinner before. Satisfied that plans had firmed up, I continued to prep for the afternoon meeting.

Patty waited for me in the same seats we had the night Rob and Amanda were getting cozy. Shuddering involuntarily, I gave her a hug.

Ann, the bartender, looked over. "Your usual, Merry?"

I nodded, hung my coat on the back of the barstool, and climbed up onto it. "I wish they made barstools shorter."

Patty snorted. "Then you wouldn't be able to reach the bar. Especially not with your T. rex arms."

I gave her a dirty look. "Whatever. How'd you get sprung tonight?"

She smiled. "Basketball practice. Luckily the boys get a kick out of watching their sister play. Patrick does too, so it works out well for me. The coach always lets them shoot a few during the break, so it gets them running around." She eyed me. "What's new with you?"

Ann handed me my wine, so I took a fortifying gulp. "You wouldn't believe me if I told you."

"I always believe you. And you tell some pretty far-fetched tales." Her gaze abruptly shifted to something over my left shoulder. "I don't believe we've been introduced. Was there something that you wanted?"

Startled, I swiveled in my seat to find Caroline's face inches from mine. She glared at me. I recoiled. "Patty, this is Caroline Thomas, Amanda's sister."

Caroline leaned even closer. "You bitch." Smelling the alcohol on her breath, I slipped off the stool and backed away. The bar went silent. She stepped in closer. "I talked to another lawyer. He said he can't break Amanda's will. That means either your ex-husband or daughter is going to get Amanda's million dollars. He killed her, and now he's going to benefit. And what do I get? A paltry $50,000 plus some odds and ends."

The whispers from people around the bar began. “A million dollars. Where did she get a million dollars?”

Ann came around the bar and grabbed Caroline’s arm. “I’m sorry, miss, but you’re going to have to leave. We don’t tolerate disturbances in the bar.”

Caroline started crying, making her mascara run. “She was my sister. I miss her so much, and now you’re getting her money.” Ann pulled her away, helping her on with her coat. Then she guided her to the door. Just before she stalked out, Caroline turned. “I’ll get you and your daughter!” Ann pushed her out the door and shut it firmly.

Ann returned to the bar. “Show’s over folks. Back to your own business.”

In shock, I climbed back onto the bar stool and took a big glug of wine. Patty asked, “Is there anything else you’d like to tell me?”

I bit back a laugh as I realized all eyes in the bar were on me.

John Little yelled over, “Is it true, Merry? Are you inheriting a million dollars?”

Patty rolled her eyes. “Just ignore him.”

I ground my teeth as I stared down into my glass.

Someone else asked, “Is it true?”

I slid off the stool and faced the people at the bar. “I’m not inheriting a million dollars. Amanda did leave money to Drew. It has nothing to do with me. We’re divorced. You know that.”

I sat and glared at my glass. Patty asked, “Do you want to leave?”

I nodded and threw some money on the bar. We bundled up and left. *I guess everyone knows now.*

Patty and I went back to my house, where I opened a bottle of wine. I sank onto my sofa. “Will you still love me if my daughter ends up inheriting?”

She giggled. “I’ll love you even more.”

CHAPTER 12

I groaned as I woke up the next morning. *Everyone knows about the money. Thank God it's Friday. Tomorrow I can just burrow in bed all day.* Courvoisier batted at my face. I picked her up to snuggle with her. Offended, she squirmed free and stalked off.

Drambuie leapt up on the bed to see what was keeping me. She head butted me and swatted at my hand. I swung my legs over the side of the bed. "I'm up; I'm up." She must have thought I was serious, as she padded out the bedroom door, her tail swishing behind her.

Remembering my dental appointment, I flossed carefully and spent extra time with my toothbrush. *I guess that means no breakfast or coffee. Great day this is shaping up to be.*

I knocked at Jenny's door as I went downstairs and heard a barely discernable, "I'm up."

Taking her at her word, I fed the cats and grabbed my phone. Rob had texted me: "I heard the million-dollar story is out. Didn't take long."

"Nope, sure didn't."

I put a muffin on a plate for Jenny and left. As I ambled to the dentist's office, I pondered how I could get Philip to talk to me about his relationship with Amanda. And, more importantly, where he was when she was killed.

The receptionist told me to have a seat. I sat by the enormous fish tank in the center of the waiting area. They must have fifty fish in the tank. I guess watching them swim around is supposed to calm your nerves. Give me a good Pinot any day.

The hygienist appeared at the door and called my name. "I think you were overdue for a cleaning, Merry. I'm glad you came in." She scraped my teeth. "Is it true? Did Amanda leave a million dollars to Drew?"

I nodded. She frowned. "That must make you mad—Drew getting all that money after you got divorced." She looked away. "What I wouldn't do for a million dollars."

She polished my teeth then stood. "I'm going to take some X-rays." She put the lead apron over me and completed her task. "Let me get Dr. Philip." I waved weakly at her departing back.

Philip came into the room. "Merry, it's been a while since we've seen you." He put on a mask and grabbed a probe. "Open wide." He gently tapped various teeth then dug into one area. "Any pain here?" I jumped, and he glanced at the hygienist. "Tooth number fourteen."

The hygienist asked, "Did you hear about Drew inheriting a million dollars from Amanda?"

Philip gasped and hit my sore tooth with the probe again. I jumped about five feet in the air.

He frowned. "Oh, sorry, Merry. I didn't mean for that to happen." He gripped the probe tightly as he continued poking my teeth. "Is it true?" I mumbled an answer. He removed the implement from my mouth. "What was that?"

I rubbed my jaw. "Yes, it's true."

He brandished the probe. "How can it be true? Why would she leave money to him? He killed her." He stopped mid-rant, his eyes narrowing. "And where did she get the money anyway? I tried to get her to go away with me to the Caribbean for Thanksgiving, and she said she didn't have enough money. I told her I would pay. She wouldn't let me." Shoulders slumping, he shook his head. "Just one more thing that she kept from me." He again swung the probe toward my mouth.

Cringing, I swiveled out of the chair and stood, bib still on. He blinked. "I'm not done yet. Don't you want to finish your appointment?"

"I just remembered an important meeting that I need to get to. I'll make an appointment to finish up later." I waved and grabbed my purse. Hurrying into the hallway, I hustled down the corridor and didn't stop until I scurried out the door. Ripping off the bib, I tossed it in a trash bin. I took a deep breath and returned to the office.

"Tough dental appointment?" Cheryl asked.

I nodded. "You have no idea."

The rest of the morning went quickly, and at lunchtime, Cheryl poked her head in the door. "Merry, Dr. Philip is here to see you."

He shoved past Cheryl. "Merry, I want to apologize for this morning. You took me by surprise. Please let me make it up to you. Do you have a few minutes for lunch?"

I said, "Thanks, Cheryl." She gave Philip the stink eye and returned to her desk. I nodded. "I can do lunch if it's a quick one."

"Let's go over to Delightful Bites. I've heard their food is good."

"I can attest to that." I put my coat on and joined him. We stood at the counter, debating the merits of the various sandwiches. I opted for roasted turkey with cranberry mayo on rye. Philip made his selection and paid. We sat to wait.

He cleared his throat. "Merry, again, I'm so sorry about this morning. I just can't believe she left Drew money. And so much money!" He hung his head. "It was such a shock at the fashion show when he leapt up on stage. After dating for eight months, I just assumed we were exclusive."

They called our names, and we retrieved our sandwiches and drinks. I took my time unwrapping my sandwich. I took a sip of coffee.

"You looked surprised. Was that the first you knew they were together?"

He stared at his sandwich and played with the paper. "To tell the truth, I had a feeling there was someone else. Amanda had gotten very secretive over the past few weeks. She broke a few of our dates too. I just thought it was nerves over the fashion show. I guess I was wrong." He pierced me with his eyes. "Did you know they were seeing each other?"

Taking a bite of my sandwich, I chewed slowly. *What should I say? Should I admit to having seen them?* "I try to think about Drew as little as possible."

"Yes, but he lived right next door. Did you ever see Amanda there?"

Darn, a direct question. "Just once, not that long before the show. It did surprise me."

He threw down his sandwich. "Why didn't you tell me?" People stared at us.

I put my hand on his shoulder. "Philip, I'm sorry things turned out the way they did, but it's not my fault that Drew was seeing Amanda." I wrapped up what was left of my sandwich. "And now I'm afraid I need to get back to the office."

"I just don't understand how I didn't know. It was so embarrassing to find out in public. I've worked hard to be respected in this town. My image is important to me. I want people to trust me as a dentist." He pushed away his lunch. "She made a laughingstock of me."

"People do respect you. And if anything, they feel sorry for you."

He stood, his eyes blazing. "I don't want people to feel sorry for me. I am not weak, no matter how that two-timing woman made me look." He grabbed his trash from the table. "You should get that tooth looked at. Decay is a serious matter." He stalked off.

Patty slid into the seat Philip vacated. "I don't think it's a good idea to piss off the town dentist. It might hurt."

I jumped. "Where did you come from?" I rubbed my jaw. "It already hurt."

She gave me a concerned look. "Oh, poor baby. You know, that's what happens when you put off the trip to the dentist."

"Thanks for your sympathy, I think. Why are you here?"

"The kids are in school, and I thought I'd treat myself to a lunch I didn't have to make. Do you have a few minutes to sit here with me, or do you have to get back?"

I checked my calendar. "I've got thirty minutes."

Patty started eating, so I unwrapped my sandwich and took a bite. She asked, "So are you going to tell me what got the good dentist all steamed?" I explained, and she grimaced. "You might want to steer clear of him for a while."

"I would, but he found a cavity. That means I'm either going to have to go back to him or find another dentist."

"You do make life complicated for yourself. Just be careful." Finished with our lunch, we both rose, putting our coats on as we left. "Plus, I don't know if you heard, but people are really buzzing about the Drew inheritance." She hugged me tightly. "Take care of yourself. I think things are about to get rockier."

Worst decision ever—marrying that man. My life will always be tainted by him. Only one good thing came out of my marriage: Jenny. I returned to the office and tried to forget about the world outside, at least for the rest of the day. I was somewhat successful, only having to field three phone calls from clients asking about Drew and his inheritance.

At five, Rob opened the door. "Dinner tonight?"

I pulled him inside and kissed him. "I really needed that."

He enveloped me in a warm hug. "Have a tough day?"

"Yes. But it's much better now."

He smiled at me. "Dinner out or in?"

"In. I'm starting to see the benefits of becoming a hermit."

He tapped my nose. "You could never be a hermit. You're too much of a people person."

"Okay, maybe just for a week or two."

"Pizza tonight? That way we don't have to cook."

"Sounds perfect—a pizza, a glass of wine, and thou." Rob helped me with my coat. We strolled out arm in arm.

The texts from Jenny started on the way home: "Where are you?"

"Almost home."

"Hurry. Everything's a mess."

We raced the rest of the way and pushed through the back door. Jenny paced in the kitchen, her eyes wide. I gave her a hug. "What's going on?"

She wailed and sank into one of the kitchen chairs. "We have to move!"

"Why?"

"Because everyone knows about the money."

I sighed and sat next to her. "You need to remind them that the money is not yours; it's your father's."

"It doesn't matter. They're saying that I won't have to worry about student loans, unlike them. They're saying it's like winning the lottery. It was bad enough that everyone gave me a hard time when Dad went to prison; now I'm getting it again." She rested her head on the table. "I wish he hadn't come back."

I rubbed her back. "Jenny, all this will die down. I know it was hard for you a few years ago, and it's going to be hard now. You have to remember that your true friends are going to stay true friends."

She wiped her face and looked up. "You're right. Losers will always be losers."

"I don't think that's exactly what I said, but if it helps, I'm glad."

Rob changed the subject. "What does everyone want on their pizza?"

Jenny sniffed. "Pepperoni and sausage, please."

Rob eyed me. "A bit heavy on the meat, but I'll go for it." He went to the living room to make the call.

I lifted Jenny's face. "We'll get through this together. We just need to buckle up for now." I kissed her cheek. "Would you mind setting the table?"

She nodded and got up to get the plates. Her phone dinged. She handed it to me. Cindy sent her a string of heart emojis.

I smiled. "It's good to have real friends."

The pizza came, and we polished it off with embarrassing speed. I looked at the empty box. "I guess we were hungry."

Jenny and Rob nodded. Jenny asked, "What's for dessert? Are there any of those brownies left?"

I retrieved the plate and put it in front of them. "There are just a few bits left. Have at it. I can't eat another bite."

They both picked up a piece. Jenny said, "This would be even better with milk."

I poured her a glass and set it in front of her. She mumbled her thanks. Filling two mugs with coffee, I sat.

Jenny grabbed another sliver of brownie, a napkin, and her milk. "Thanks. I'll be upstairs if you need me." She vanished around the corner, her ponytail swinging after her.

Rob said, "I heard there was some kind of commotion at Delightful Bites today."

"How did you hear about that?" Rob just stared at me. "Never mind. How does everyone in this town know about everything? Philip asked me to lunch to apologize for being combative when I was having my teeth cleaned."

"What on earth did you say to him?"

"I didn't say anything. My mouth was full of dental devices of torture. His hygienist told him about Drew inheriting money from Amanda. It was pretty evident from his reaction that it was the first he heard about it." I rubbed my jaw.

Rob scanned my face. "Did he hurt you?"

"No. Not really. He just poked pretty hard on a cavity."

"You should get that checked out."

I glared at him. "I did. That and a cleaning were the reasons for my appointment."

"I thought you were digging for information."

"That too." I paused. "At lunch he told me that Amanda had been acting strangely since Drew came home. He thought she was just overworked because of the fashion show. He said he was shocked when Drew hopped up on stage and kissed her."

"What caused all the commotion at Delightful Bites?"

"He asked me directly if I saw Amanda at Drew's house. I had to admit that I had. He was pretty miffed I hadn't told him."

"But you two aren't close."

"True, but he was annoyed nonetheless, which brings up another subject." I reached over and held Rob's hand. "Are we in an exclusive relationship?"

He leaned over and kissed me. "What do you think?"

I looked down at the table, playing with my napkin. "I think we are."

"What brought all this on?"

I started clearing the dishes. As I slid past Rob, he took my hand and pulled me onto his lap. "I thought we were having a discussion."

I stared deeply into his emerald eyes. "You seem to be avoiding answering my question. Are we in an exclusive relationship?" I held my breath.

"Of course we are! I don't think I've ever been this close with anyone." He kissed me deeply and held me on his lap. "Now, what brought all this on?"

"Philip said that he assumed his relationship with Amanda was exclusive. I just didn't want to assume anymore with ours."

He nodded. "Glad we got that straightened out." I got off his lap and continued clearing the table. He pulled out his phone.

"What are you doing?"

"Just texting my other girlfriends to tell them we're off."

I smacked him with a dishtowel. "Just in case you're serious."

He pulled me back onto his lap. "I'll show you just how serious I am." He followed up with a long, slow kiss, which was interrupted by his phone ringing. "Darn, I thought I turned it off." He looked at it. "I need to take this." I jumped off his lap, and he went into the living room.

Finishing cleaning up, I brought him his coffee. He gestured for me to have a seat. I curled up next to him. He hung up. "That was Jay. The account Amanda left Drew was opened two years before he went to jail." Eyes wide, I stared out the picture window. Rob waved his hand in front of my face. "Earth to Merry. Talk to me."

"He knew he was going to go to jail. He knew it before he was charged. That's how he was able to move the money."

"He might not have known. It might have only been plan B, if he were caught."

I shook my head. "Any way you cut it, he had to have been seeing Amanda at least three years before he went to jail." Standing up, I hugged myself. "Do you think he was going to leave me for her? Was that his going-away money?"

Rob stood and put his arms around me, drawing me close to his chest. "Much as I hate to defend Drew, I don't think that was his plan. The vast majority of the monies were in the accounts the Feds could find. Why would he settle for such a small piece of the pie?" I pushed away from Rob and gave him an offended look. "And it goes without saying that he would never leave the best woman in the world."

I sank back against him. "Quick save."

He tipped my face up to his. "It's all true."

I kissed him and then stepped away to pace the length of the living room. “Okay, so we know he must have planned out different scenarios. We also know that he was seeing Amanda. Since she left the money to him and hadn’t spent any of it on herself while he was in jail, we have to figure that she was going to give him access to it without him having to kill her off.” I stopped mid-step. “Wait. He must have already had access to it because he was able to pay for rent, his PC, phone, etc.”

“Maybe she threatened to cut him off after he outed her at the fashion show.”

I stopped pacing. “I keep getting stuck on the fact that she reserved a seat for him. I believe that she didn’t fully anticipate the crowd’s reaction, but she knew he was going to be there and must have known that people would be able to put two and two together.” I sighed. “Especially in this town.”

Rob sat and took a sip of coffee. He patted the seat next to him. “Sit down and let’s puzzle this out.”

I curled up against him, and he put his arm around me. Taking a drink of my coffee, I made a face. “This is cold.”

I tried to stand, but he pulled me back down. “We’ve had enough coffee. I’ll have trouble sleeping as it is.”

I put the mug on the table. “The police are only focusing on Drew. We should be starting with the premise that he’s innocent, and that means someone else must have done it. And I can tell you one thing: after today, Dr. Philip is definitely on my list.”

CHAPTER 13

Saturday dawned cold, and icicles glistened sharply out my window. *Brr. Time to burrow more deeply into the covers.* Putting them over my head, I contemplated my plans for the weekend. *Need to get the Christmas decorations down from the attic.*

Pulling my phone under the covers I texted Rob, "Feel like doing some decorating today? Or at least some heavy lifting?" I ended with a smiley-face emoji.

"If there is wassailing, I'm in."

"Don't forget, we're going to Andy and Ed's tonight for more frivolity."

"Okay, minor wassailing. Want me to pick up bagels on my way over this morning?"

"Yum. Bagels will be quite welcome. Might even be enough to get me out of bed."

I smiled and gingerly stuck one foot out from under the covers, moving it around to test the air temperature. *Too cold. Brr.* I pulled it back in. *Not going to get any warmer till I get up and adjust the thermostat.* Eyeing the distance between the bed and the controls, I jettisoned myself, ran to the hall, and moved the dial to sixty-eight. I dove back under the covers. *Might be a world's record.*

Hearing the heat crank on, I grinned. After patting myself on the back, I saw Courvoisier lying on the vent. *Not going to get any warmer in here that way.* I hurtled out of bed, picked her up and deposited her in the hallway, giving her an apologetic pet as I shut the door. Speeding back, I dove into the bed. Just as I was smugly pulling the covers back over me, I noticed Drambuie had taken Courvoisier's place and was sprawled out in such a way to ensure that every piece of heat hit her body. I sighed. *May as well get up. The world is conspiring against me today.*

After showering and dressing, I listened at Jenny's door. Hearing her soft snore, I tiptoed past and proceeded to the kitchen. I tossed the cats a few treats to make up for rousting them from the heating vents and then put the coffee on. I sat at the counter, pleading for it to be ready quickly.

Pulling over my iPad, I opened the Facebook app. Wow. Some people have way too much time on their hands. There was a lot of negativity toward Drew. I wish he had his own Facebook account so people would stop posting on mine. Sighing, I started to flip the case shut. I wonder what's been posted on Amanda's wall. I was surprised to see the name-calling there as well. Have these people no decency? She's dead! Coffee ready, I shut the iPad case and poured myself a cup.

The back door opened. Rob kissed me and handed me a bag. "Bagel delivery, ma'am."

I took them. "Yum."

"I also brought some cream cheese and lox, should you be in the mood."

"You are the best!" I poured him a cup of coffee. "This is far more pleasant than the Facebook posts I've been reading this morning. You should see what they're saying on Amanda's page."

"I did. I thought it might give us some ideas on other people who had it in for her."

"Good idea. I didn't look at it through that lens." I opened the bag of bagels and set some out on a plate. "Which type are you in the mood for?"

"Cinnamon raisin with cream cheese, please."

I cut the bagel in half and deposited it on a plate. I pushed it and the cream cheese across the counter to Rob. "Did anyone stand out to you as you reviewed her page?"

He spread the cream cheese. "Susan Clime. Her post was pretty negative. Here, I'll show you." He pulled my iPad toward him and retrieved Amanda's page. I put my arm around him. He pointed to a post halfway down: "Serves you right."

I shrugged. "Seems weird to me. Why would she be so upset about Drew and Amanda?"

"Didn't you tell me that she was pretty outspoken about Drew when he first got out?"

I nodded. "She seemed like she was still bitter about the money. Of course, we found out at the fashion show that a lot of people are." I cut a sesame bagel in half and spread it with cream cheese. Unwrapping the lox, I laid a piece on top and took a bite. "That's one bad thing about eating this. It's awkward. I always feel that I have to hold the lox in place with my fingers or it'll slide off. I hate it when I end up with the whole thing in my mouth on the first bite."

He smiled. "That's why I don't eat lox."

"You're the one who's missing out." I took another bite and closed my eyes, savoring the taste. I sat back down. "I'll have some questions for Ms. Clime at work on Monday."

Finishing his bagel, Rob wiped his hands on a napkin. "What's the plan for today?"

"I have my Christmas things stored up in the attic. I was hoping you'd help me bring them down. Then Jenny and I can decorate. How long can you stay?"

He smiled. "That depends."

"Uh-oh. On what?"

"There are some college games on TV today. If you're okay with me watching them here, I can stay till five. Then I'll need to go back to my place to change for the party tonight."

I kissed him. "You're on, as long as you don't mind us decorating around you."

Jenny poked her head around the corner. "Is it safe to come in?"

I smacked her shoulder. "Fresh. Mr. Jenson brought bagels."

"He's my fav." She gave him a one-armed hug and sliced a French toast bagel in half. She put it in the toaster. "Thanks for bringing these. I love a good sugar rush." She took out a plate. "Did I hear you say we are decorating today?"

"Yes. I thought it was time we started looking a little festive around here."

Jenny pulled the bagel from the toaster and buttered it. Taking a bite and looking blissful, her eyes lit on the lox. "Ugh. Mom, I'll never understand how you can eat that."

"You like salmon."

She rolled her eyes. "Not the same thing. Not the same thing at all."

I looked over at Rob for support. He shook his head. "Sorry, but I'm with Jenny on this one."

"I guess I'm the only one here with cultured taste buds." I wrapped the leftover lox and put it in the refrigerator. "No problem with that—just more for me to enjoy. Rob, are you done?"

Wiping his lips with his napkin, he slid out of his seat and put his dish in the sink. "Your muscle is all ready for work, ma'am."

I punched his shoulder lightly. "Very funny. Let's go up to the attic, and I'll show you where everything is."

Opening the door to the attic, I flipped on the light switch. Rob peered around my shoulder and whistled. "Merry, you are a closet hoarder."

"Don't even say that in jest. You saw Ben Ford's house when Melissa and I were trying to clean it out." I shuddered. "Now, he was a hoarder."

"Uh-huh." Rob scanned the piles around him. "Closet hoarder, definitely."

"Whatever. The boxes I want are over here." I led him to the left-hand corner of the attic where there were twenty large boxes and several smaller ones spread out, stacked from floor to ceiling.

His green eyes widened in shock. "How much Christmas stuff do you have?"

I stared at my shoes like a little kid who's been found out. "I like to make Christmas special." I looked into his beautiful eyes. "Maybe I got a little bit carried away over the last few years. I wanted Jenny to have fun memories, even if her dad wasn't around."

He hugged me fiercely. "That's what I love about you. You're always trying to make the world better for others." He grabbed two large boxes and, whistling, made his way down the stairs. I followed with a smaller box.

I pointed to a space by the front door. "Let's stack as many here as we can, and then we can spill into the dining room."

He groaned. "I suppose once you empty them I'm going to have to take them all back upstairs."

I smiled. "Yes sirree, Bob."

He leaned over and kissed me. "The name's Rob, not Bob, ma'am, and don't you forget it."

I kissed him back. "Got it, sir. Won't make that mistake again."

Jenny pranced in. "Gross. I thought we were decorating."

Rob and I jumped apart. I said, "We are. Want to help us bring the boxes down?"

"If I have to." She trudged up the stairs in front of me. "Why don't we just hire someone to do it for us?"

I swatted her butt as she ran up the stairs. “Not nearly as much fun.”

Twenty minutes later, all the boxes were downstairs covering the front door and stacked carefully around the edges of the dining room. I looked around in satisfaction. “Now comes the fun part.”

Rob laughed. “I’ll be in the living room watching the game if you need me.” He kicked off his shoes and stretched out on the sectional.

Jenny nodded toward Rob. “Can I watch the game with Mr. Jenson?”

“No. The sooner we get started, the sooner we’ll be done. Don’t you like how festive we make it?”

She smiled. “Yes, Mom, you know I love it. It’s just the process of getting there that’s a pain.”

I opened one of the boxes containing Santa Clauses and positioned several of the more delicate ones on the mantel, trying not to block too much of the television.

Rob chuckled. “It’s a good thing you’re so short. Your head barely reaches the bottom of the flat screen.”

I tossed a pillow at him. “Great things come in small packages!”

As I scooted past him, he pulled me onto his lap and nuzzled my neck. “I know, I know.”

Jenny said, “Mom, we’re never going to get this done if you keep stopping for smooch breaks.”

I stood. “You’re right. Let’s keep going.” Two hours later, we collapsed next to Rob. “That’s all we can do until we get the tree.”

He rose to stretch, and his eyes widened as he took in all of the decorations. “Are you sure you’re going to be able to fit one in here?”

“Yes, silly. It goes on the other side of the fireplace. We have to be careful that we don’t get one too full, or it’s a fire hazard.”

Rob smiled at me. “Everything looks wonderful, and it’s starting to get me in the mood. What do you want to do about lunch?” He looked at his watch. “No wonder I’m hungry.”

I tapped his arm. "Yes, I know. Lying on the couch and watching football is tough work. Since you're now on the second game, I'll make us sandwiches and bring them in here. Tuna okay?"

Receiving two distracted nods, I made my way into the kitchen and quickly whipped up some tuna salad. Putting it on rye bread, I grabbed a bag of chips and some drinks and deposited everything on a tray. I carried it into the living room. Rob jumped up to take it from me. I moved some of the Santas on the coffee table out of the way so he could put it down.

Jenny grabbed a sandwich and piled some chips on her plate. "Thanks, Mom." She turned her attention back to the game.

Rob said something similar and moved his legs from the couch so I could sit. A commercial came on, and he gave me a quick kiss on the cheek. "Thanks, Merry. Once the game is over, I'll take all the empty boxes back upstairs."

The action on the screen resumed. The score was close, so the ending was exciting.

Jenny picked up the empty plates and what was left of the potato chips. She carried the tray back to the kitchen as Rob started bringing the boxes back upstairs. I took a few of the smaller ones up, and Jenny brought a few as well.

Jenny said, "Thanks, Mr. Jenson. It was a lot easier with you here." She shut the door to her room.

Rob and I headed back to the kitchen. He said, "Now I really do need a shower. It's a good thing I skipped working out this morning. I'm pretty sure I got all of my stairs in."

I kissed him. "Thanks for the help. It was so much easier this year."

"I'll stop by at six, and we can go over to the party together."

I wandered back into the living room, turned on the fire, and sank onto the sofa, admiring how festive everything looked. Then I picked up my iPad and logged in to Facebook to take a better look at the posts on Amanda's wall. There was one from someone called Beatle Boy that read, "I'm glad you're gone, witch!" *I didn't think you were allowed to put fake names on Facebook. I wonder who that is.*

Putting the iPad down, I stood and wandered to the window. *People felt strongly about Amanda. Could one of the people on Facebook be the person who killed her?* Shuddering, I flipped the switch for the fire and went upstairs to shower and dress.

Rob came in just as I was putting green-and-red bows on the wine bottles we were bringing. I put them in a shopping bag, and he picked it up. Tucking my hand under his arm, we ambled along the path through my backyard to Andy and Ed's house. Luminaries lined their back deck, and twinkling colored lights adorned their evergreens. We bundled through their back door.

I said, "Everything looks so lovely outside."

Andy took my coat. "I hope you think it's lovely inside as well."

I grinned with delight at their Christmas town display, which took up a good deal of their living room. There had to be three hundred tiny people dotting the town, including ice skaters and children sledding down a hill. "How did you do the hill?"

Ed smiled and handed me a drink. "Papier-mâché. You didn't know I was so talented, did you?"

Pat and Patty came in the front door. Pat quickly joined Rob on the floor, and they played with the train.

Ed took Patty's coat, and Andy hugged her and gave her a drink. He looked down at Pat and Rob. "Do you think they want a drink?"

Patty laughed. "Maybe later, when they decide to be adults again."

There was a tray with breadsticks wrapped in prosciutto, along with several different types of cheeses, figs, and olives. I picked up a breadstick and savored the salty bite of prosciutto. "This is so good."

Andy said, "Thanks. Ed made the breadsticks."

I raised my eyebrows as I turned to Ed. "You made these?"

"Yep. It's not that hard. I'll show you one day."

The doorbell rang, and more neighbors piled in. Soon the living room and kitchen were quite crowded, especially with the Christmas village taking up so much floor space. It was hard to hear the playlist Ed crafted with the din from so many voices and conversations. I helped Andy load the buffet dinner onto the sideboards. Ed and he had outdone themselves with platters heaped with medium-rare roast beef, turkey, and a ziti dish brimming with sausage, peppers, and mushrooms. The salad was enormous and had radishes cut in the shape of roses.

Stunned, I asked, “How long did it take to do all this?”

Ed replied, “Squeezing it in with work and everything else, probably about a week.” He pulled a notebook off of the top of the refrigerator and opened it. He pointed to a spreadsheet, clipped inside. “I keep track of everything on this spreadsheet. That way I know what’s been done already and what needs to be done next.” There were rows upon rows of green check marks. He grinned. “I just love seeing all the green marks.”

Andy tapped his wineglass with a knife. “Food’s ready, folks. But before we eat, Ed and I want to thank everyone for coming.” He raised his glass. “To the best small town in America.” Everyone drank to that and formed into a sort of serpentine line.

I found Rob midway through and nodded to the people behind us. “Mind if I squeeze in?” They laughed and ushered me into the line. I looked up at Rob. “Great party! Wait till you see all the food.”

“It smells wonderful. I can’t wait to eat.”

As the line edged forward, I caught snippets of other conversations. John Little and his wife, Nancy, were two groups in front of us. His voice carried as he turned to her. “I can’t believe that Amanda wouldn’t let Ed open up a café using the shared alley behind their buildings. Look at this food. It was criminal for her to stop them.”

Rob gazed at me. “Wonder what that’s all about?”

"I don't know, but I intend to find out. How could Amanda have stopped them? She wasn't on the zoning board."

"She owned the building next to them. Maybe they needed a variance approved by the owners on either side."

Shuffling forward, we soon found ourselves in front of the buffet. After our plates were full, Rob nodded toward the stairs. "Let's join Patrick and Patty. I think if we maneuver carefully, there's just enough room." We wove through the crowd, and Patrick and Patty moved their feet so that we could climb to the steps just above them.

Patty said, "Wow, it's crowded in here."

I smiled. "It really is. Nice work sussing out a place to sit. I hate it when I'm balancing plates and glasses. I always spill stuff." I ate for a few moments. "Wow, this is so good."

She nodded. "It is tasty. I always love their parties. They have the best playlists and food."

"It's hard for me to hear the music over everyone talking. That reminds me. Did you or Patrick ever hear anything about Amanda blocking a café Ed was trying to open?"

Her mouth widened in shock. She quickly closed it. "Where have you been? There was a big uproar about it a month ago."

Rob and I exchanged glances and shrugged. I said, "Somehow we missed it. Fill us in."

She leaned closer. "Ed wanted to open up a tea shop as an extension of Andy's business. He'd researched antique shops that include food service and found that they drew more customers, which results in more sales."

I nodded, anxious for her to continue.

"So he and Andy went to the zoning board. They were told they would need to get a sign-off from the property owners on either side of them. Lauren Stamper loved the idea because she figured it would bring more traffic to her real estate business. Amanda, however, refused to sign. She told them that she was worried cooking smells would infiltrate her building and make her clothes smell."

"Wouldn't they have installed some kind of exhaust system?"

"Of course, and they met with her a month ago to go over the specs for it. It was top of the line and should have lessened any concerns she had. They also showed her the increase in foot traffic they expected, which would have helped her business. She still refused. I think she was just being ornery. Her death ended up breaking the stalemate. I heard that Caroline's already signed the variance."

"That was quick. I wonder how they got it in front of her that fast." I bit back a laugh. "What did they say? Sorry for your loss. Please sign this variance."

Patty gave me a dirty look. "You know Ed and Andy aren't that crass. Caroline was conducting an inventory of Amanda's clothes, and Andy brought her over some tea and some of Ed's famous scones. She signed that day."

Rob sighed. "I'd probably sign just about anything for Ed's scones. Now, if you'll excuse me, the line is dwindling, and I need to get just a bit more of the ziti. And maybe another piece of beef. Merry, would you like anything?"

"I shouldn't, but if they have any of those prosciutto-wrapped breadsticks left, I'd love one." I turned to Patrick. "I'm surprised you're not getting more."

"I heard that Ed made several of his cranberry-and-apple-topped cheesecakes. Patty and I are holding out for that."

I smiled. "I'm glad I just opted for another breadstick. I don't want to be too full for dessert."

Later on, the crowd dwindled. Helping Ed and Andy put the first load of dishes in the dishwasher, we vied for places to stow the leftovers in the refrigerator. Soon Rob and I were the only guests left.

Andy held up a bottle of champagne. "Celebrate with us?" We nodded, and he poured four glasses.

Sinking onto the sofa, I tapped my foot along to the Christmas carol that was playing. I held up my glass. "Are we celebrating something other than the terrific party you just hosted?"

Ed smiled. "Yes. We are celebrating getting our new venture, Tempting Treasures and Tasty Treats, off the ground."

Reaching behind the sofa, Andy brought out a rendering of the new sign. "Isn't it great?"

It used the elaborate script of the current sign with many of the same soft-blue hues. Dainty teapots had been added, along with lace-covered plates piled high with scrumptious-looking confections.

"It's lovely," I said. "I can't wait for it to open."

CHAPTER 14

My phone dinged far too early the next morning. *Whose bright idea was the champagne last night?* I grabbed it from the side table and pulled it under the covers. It was a text from Rob: "Good morning, sunshine. Nine o'clock Mass?"

"What's wrong with ten thirty?"

"Early bird gets the worm." He appended a smiley face.

I groaned. He didn't get much more sleep than me. How can he be so perky? "All right. Nine it is. But you owe me coffee."

Showered and dressed, I felt marginally better. By the second cup of coffee, I was almost human, and my brain had started to process. *How desperate were Ed and Andy to expand their shop? They didn't waste any time getting Caroline to sign the variance.*

I went upstairs to Jenny's room and poked my head in the door. "I'm leaving for church. Are you getting up?"

Indistinct mumbling came from under the covers that sounded like, "I'll go to the noon Mass."

Striding into the room, I picked up her phone and set the alarm for ten thirty. "I love you." I shut the door and made my way back downstairs.

In front of the church, Rob hopped from foot to foot while rubbing his hands. I smiled at him. "You could've waited inside."

"No chance. I love to see your beautiful face get closer and closer." He leaned down for a kiss. I brushed his lips briefly and backed up. His eyes widened. "Are you in a bad mood this morning?"

"No. Just tired. I'm also not a big fan of public displays of affection in front of the church with lots of people around."

He laughed because we were the only ones on the steps. "It's the nine o'clock Mass. Anyone going to this one is already inside."

I grinned. "You've got me on that one." I tucked my hand under his arm. Since there was hardly anyone there, we made our way closer to the front. I whispered to him, "Is it always this empty or just after one of Ed and Andy's parties?"

He chuckled quietly as the Mass started.

During the first hymn, there was someone toward the front singing who had a lovely soprano. My gaze fastened on a woman in the third pew. I elbowed Rob in the ribs and motioned with my eyes.

He mouthed, "Susan Clime?" I nodded and faced front. He pressed my hand and whispered into my ear, "Let's catch her after."

I nodded again and continued singing the hymn. After Mass, the few parishioners in attendance gathered in the vestibule, chatting with Father Tom. I waited till Susan finished speaking with him. "Susan, can I talk to you for a moment?"

"Sure. What's up?"

"Are you doing anything right now? Would you be able to have breakfast with Rob and me?"

She looked nervous. "I haven't done anything wrong, have I?"

I patted her hand. "No. Not at all. We just have a few questions, and it's hard to find time to have a conversation at work."

"In that case, I don't mind if I do."

Rob said, "Why don't we take my car, and I can drop you back here? We just want to say hi to Father Tom for a moment."

Rob and I approached Father Tom. I said, "Thanks for the homily, Father Tom. It was meaningful."

He smiled. “We usually have more of a crowd, but I heard that a number of people had a late night yesterday. Hopefully by the noon Mass, the laggards will get here.” He eyed us. “It’s been a while since we’ve talked. Perhaps we should set up some time.”

I avoided his gaze. “That sounds great. I’ll talk with Belinda to get something on the calendar.” After we both shook his hand, we joined Susan. “Ready to go?”

She nodded. “I don’t normally see you at this Mass, Merry.”

“That’s right. I usually attend the ten thirty. I like to hear the choir.”

She smiled. “I used to sing in the choir. It was fun, but it took a lot of time. They’re very serious about practice here.”

Rob said, “That must be why they sound so good. Would Delightful Bites be okay for breakfast?”

Susan smiled. “It would be great. I love their food. I think it’s almost better than the place that was there before.”

We bustled into the café and read the offerings off the blackboard above the cutout kitchen window. I decided on a spinach, mushroom, and artichoke quiche, Susan had the same, and Rob went for the overlarge apple fritter. Susan and I claimed a table and waited for Rob to join us.

I smiled at her. “It was fortunate we ran into you today.”

She laughed. “More fortunate for me since you’re buying breakfast.”

Rob carried over her cappuccino and my latte. After going back to retrieve his black coffee, he joined us. “They said the food would be out in just a few minutes. Thanks for joining us, Susan.” She smiled. “It’s been so busy I haven’t had a chance to ask you about what happened at the fashion show.”

Susan blanched.

Rob continued, “I was surprised that you felt that strongly about Amanda. After Drew kissed her you threw your drink at her.”

She flinched, and I kicked Rob's foot under the table and gave him a dirty look. *I thought we were going to start slowly.*

I cleared my throat. "What Rob means is that we've been surprised at the number of people who didn't seem to like Amanda."

She relaxed back against her chair. "She wasn't a good woman. Always taking what wasn't hers."

Rob asked, "Like what?"

"Nothing in particular. Just things I heard."

He smiled at her and waited. She stammered, "Like Philip. He was dating Lauren Stamper. They seemed happy, and then all of a sudden Amanda snake-charmed him into dating her." She sat back as she sipped her cappuccino.

"But that was eight months ago. Isn't that ancient history?"

She stared at him and then leaned forward, enunciating every word as if he were deaf. "Ancient history? You're still new to this town. Eight months is like it happened two seconds ago." She looked at me. "Tell him, Merry."

I stirred my latte. "She's right. This town has a long memory."

Rob frowned. "Okay, so Amanda took Philip away from Lauren. I still don't understand what that has to do with you, Susan."

Gary Johnson approached the table. "Who had the apple fritter?" Rob nodded, and Gary put the largest fritter I'd ever seen in front of him. It was chock-full of apples, and the glaze glistened under the fluorescents. "That must mean you ladies had the quiche. They just came out of the oven, so be careful." He set the plates down. "Enjoy."

I eyed Rob with envy. "You are going to give me a bite of that, aren't you?"

He laughed. "I think I could give everyone in town a bite and still have more than I could eat." He cut two small pieces off and put one on Susan's plate and the other on mine.

I savored it slowly. "That tastes like heaven!" Susan nodded.

I cut off a piece of my quiche and slid it onto Rob's plate. He took a bite. "Wow. The food is really good here. The quiche is so creamy."

We gave the food the attention it deserved. After a few minutes, Gary came back to the table. "How is everything?" Three satisfied faces nodded with appreciation. He smiled. "Good. I'll take that to mean you like the food."

I said, "I don't like the food. I love the food."

"Me too," Rob said. "Would you part with the recipe for the quiche? I'd like to run it in the newspaper, giving you full credit, of course."

Gary thought for a moment. "I'd be happy to. Business is good, but I don't think everyone knows that we're open yet."

Susan laughed. "If you keep putting out food this good, it won't take long."

Rob handed Gary a business card. "I'd appreciate it if you'd send me the recipe via e-mail."

Nodding, Gary put it in his top pocket. "What would you think about me sending you one per week? I don't mind doing it, and people might look forward to reading them."

"Let's put the first one in and then talk about how to position the rest."

I asked, "Aren't you afraid that if you give away the recipes, no one will come to the café?"

Gary laughed. "When was the last time you laminated dough?"

"Never."

"Then I'm not worried." He nodded at Rob. "I'll be in touch."

I raised my eyebrows. "I've heard of laminated countertops but dough?"

He shrugged. "Must be a baking thing. You're a good baker."

"Not at this level." I paused. "Maybe I could talk him into giving me lessons."

Rob smiled. "I think you could talk almost anyone into anything."

Susan cleared her throat. “Thanks for breakfast. I need to be going.” She stood.

Rob jumped up. “Let me drive you back to the church.”

“Thanks for the offer, but it’s not that cold, and I could use the exercise.” She walked out the door.

I said, “Rats. We never found out why she threw her drink at Amanda.”

Rob took my hand in his. “She was never going to tell us. We’re going to have to find out a different way.”

“Any idea on how?”

He smiled. “It’ll come to me. Want to get something to go to bring to Jenny?”

“You’re so thoughtful.” I hugged him. “Let’s get her one of the fritters.”

He drove back to my house, and we found Jenny in the kitchen. Rob presented the box with a flourish.

Taking it, she weighed it with her hands. “What’s in this? It’s huge and heavy.” She opened it, and her eyes widened with delight. “Wow. This looks delicious.” Ripping off a hunk, she grabbed a napkin and ran out the door with it. “Don’t want to be late to church.” A few minutes later I received a text from her: “The best ever! Give Mr. Jenson a hug for me. Can’t wait to eat the rest!” She followed up with two heart emojis. I chuckled and handed my phone to Rob.

He smiled. “I guess she liked it as much as I did. And I can’t believe how much of it I ate.”

I laughed. “You could’ve brought back what was left.”

“Nope. Before the end of the day, I would have eaten the entire thing. I don’t need that kind of temptation.” He eyed me and then drew me closer. “I have all the temptation I need right here.” He kissed me.

There was a sharp rap, and the back door opened. Rob and I jumped apart.

Andy popped his head in. He looked at us and laughed. "You look just like guilty teenagers." He held out a big bag. "Thought you might want some of the leftover goodies from last night."

Rob groaned. "We just came from Delightful Bites."

"That place is good. But Ed's will be better." He put the bag down on the counter. "Got to run! Be good." He disappeared out the door.

I opened it and yelled at his retreating back, "Last night was great. Thanks!"

He waved without turning around.

"More food. Just what we need." I opened the bag and rummaged through. "Ooh, he's put in some of the beef and a few of those breadsticks I liked. And," I pulled out a plastic-wrapped plate, "some of Ed's cheesecake."

Rob smiled. "Put it away. Maybe we'll want to eat it later."

"No maybe about it." I slid the bag into the refrigerator.

There was another knock at the back door, and this time the person actually waited for an answer. I opened the door. Melissa stood there, blowing on her gloved hands. I ushered her in. "Melissa, what a surprise. How are you? Take off your coat. Would you like some coffee?"

"That would be great. I'm chilled to the bone." She took off her coat, hat, and gloves, stowing them on one of the chairs at the counter.

"Have a seat." I started to make the coffee, and she sat at the kitchen table.

Rob joined her. "What brings you by today?"

She shifted in her seat. "I'm just going to jump right in. I know it's not right to ask you about this, but I'm not sure what to do about Nancy's house."

I raised my eyebrows. "What do you mean?"

"Drew paid his rent through the end of January. I don't have to do anything right away, but if I'm going to need to find another tenant, I have to get started. I know that doesn't really have anything to do with you, but I wondered if you knew anything. Do you think he'll be let out of jail? Maybe on parole?"

I brought two coffees over and then went back for mine. "You're right. It doesn't have anything to do with me, and I don't know any more than you do." Melissa looked miserable. "You could check with his lawyer, Kendall Davis. She may be able to help, and in any event, she can at least ask Drew if he has the money to pay the rent to hold the house longer." I stood and retrieved Kendall's card from where I had stuck it on the refrigerator. "Here. This has her contact info."

She smiled. "Thanks, Merry. I knew you'd be able to help. Do you need this back?" I shook my head, and she tucked the card into her purse.

"Melissa, since you stopped by, I have a question for you. Do you know any reason why Susan Clime disliked Amanda?"

She fidgeted with her mug of coffee and took a sip. "I wouldn't want to tell tales."

"Susan's been pretty open about the fact that she didn't like her, even going so far as to put a negative post on Amanda's Facebook page after she was dead."

Melissa's eyes widened. "Who would put a negative post on a dead person's wall?"

"See what I mean? She hasn't bothered to hide the fact that she didn't like her. We just can't figure out why."

Fidgeting again, Melissa looked me straight in the eye. "This is really awkward. I'm uncomfortable telling you this, but Susan was having an affair with Drew before he went to prison."

Mouth agape, I sat back in my seat. "An affair with Susan? But he was having an affair with Amanda."

She nodded with a grim expression on her face. "I know. He was a busy man."

I put my head in my hands. "Drew was having an affair with two women and hoodwinking the town. I missed all of it."

Rob rubbed my arm. "You were busy with your business and raising a great daughter. And to your point, he was good at lying to people. You might call it his special gift."

"I don't know if that makes me feel any better." I stared into my coffee mug, hoping that it would provide answers. "Was there anyone else? I mean, he was seeing two women and married to me. Was there a third or fourth?"

She barked a laugh and put her hand on my shoulder. "No, Merry, to my knowledge, he was only having an affair with two women behind your back."

Standing to get an antacid, I rubbed my forehead. Rob said, "Drew was seeing Susan and then broke it off to date Amanda. I can see why she would be angry."

Melissa took a sip of her coffee and then cleared her throat. "I'm not sure he ever broke it off."

In the midst of chewing the pill, I almost spit it out. "What?"

"I think the first Susan knew he was seeing Amanda was at the fashion show when he kissed Amanda in front of her."

Rob's eyes widened. "That would hurt. She waits four years for him to get out of prison, and he rubs her face in it."

I muttered, "I wonder how much money Susan was holding for him. And, more importantly, when she transferred it back to his control."

Rob smacked the table. "I really hate that man." He stood. "I better call Jay." He pulled out his phone and went to my office.

Melissa stood and pulled on her coat. "I'm sorry I was the one to tell you, Merry. But you did ask."

"I'd appreciate it if you wouldn't share what we talked about today."

"I won't." She rubbed my shoulder. "You're too good a friend. And besides, I don't want Susan to turn on me."

She scurried out the door. Shutting it behind her, I leaned up against it and tried to absorb all that I heard. *How blind can you be? Two women.*

Rob came back into the room and hugged me. “He’s the bad guy. Don’t put this on yourself. You’re a good person with sound morals. And remember, you divorced him.”

“I know. It’s just such a shock. I need some time to process.” Stepping out of the circle of his arms, I shivered. “I’m okay. What did Jay have to say?”

“He’s looking into it. He thought he’d have more info for us before the end of the day.”

CHAPTER 15

Dinner consisted of leftovers from Andy and Ed's party. Jay knocked on the back door and poked his head in. "Oh, sorry. I didn't realize you'd still be eating."

I stood. "We were just finishing. Would you like some coffee?"

"Always." Jay took his coat and hat off and put them on one of the chairs at the counter. He joined Rob and Jenny at the table.

I motioned for him to wait to talk to us until Jenny left.

Jenny rose. "No dessert for me tonight, not after finishing that fritter. Have a good evening, all." She disappeared around the corner.

I poured three cups of coffee. "Would anyone like some of Ed's cheesecake?" Rob and Jay nodded, so I cut three small pieces and brought them to the table.

Jay took one. "Thanks for letting me know about Susan. I checked the new account Drew opened after prison, and $200,000 was transferred into it from Susan's account the day before the fashion show."

I laughed. "I guess Drew didn't trust Susan as much as Amanda. She only got a fifth of what Amanda held onto for him."

Jay raised one eyebrow. "You're taking this better than I thought you would."

"It's either laugh or go mad. Plus, it reinforces how right I was to get divorced."

Rob rubbed my back. “Are you okay?”

I rubbed my face and then studied my nails. “As good as I’m going to be. That had to be some shock for Susan. She held money for Drew, waited for him to get out, and then as soon as she returns his money, he dumps her.” I paused. “And in front of everyone. She must have felt just the way Philip did.”

Rob shook his head. “There was one key difference: no one knew that she was dating Drew.”

“No one but Melissa and whomever told her. We don’t know how many people knew.”

Jay stirred his coffee. “In this town? You can bet quite a few people knew. So she may have been just as embarrassed as Philip.”

I stared at him. “Could she have been upset enough to kill Amanda?”

“Why would she kill Amanda? She didn’t use her.”

“At breakfast this morning she said Amanda always took things that weren’t hers. Maybe she blamed Amanda as a femme fatale?”

Jay stood. “Drew still looks good to me as the killer. Thanks for the coffee and the information. I’ll see you tomorrow.”

Rob and I cleaned up the kitchen and took our coffees into the living room. I flipped on the fire, and we sank onto the couch. Curling up against him, I sighed. *This feels so good.*

He put his arm around me. “I’m happy you decorated for Christmas. It’s been a long time since I’ve been in a place that looks so welcoming and homey. My last five Christmases were all in war-torn areas of the world.” He hugged me closer and kissed the top of my head. “Experiencing that kind of poverty makes you appreciate how much we have and how very lucky we are.”

I smiled. “We are lucky, and I’m glad you’re here with me.” He kissed me. I rubbed his chest. “Plus, after finding out everything that’s been going on, I need some warmth and good cheer around me.”

"We seem to be accumulating suspects. Amanda was not a popular person."

"No, and it looks like she may not have helped her cause. I wonder if she knew about Susan and Drew."

"I doubt it. Drew would have been worried about the money. After all, the bulk of it was with Amanda."

"You're right. He wouldn't have risked her finding out." I paused. "But didn't he do just that? He kissed Amanda in front of everyone, including Susan. Wouldn't he be afraid that Susan would tell Amanda?"

Rob sipped his coffee and stared into the fire. "Maybe that's why she's dead. If Drew killed her, he knew Susan wouldn't have enough time to tell Amanda about them. That way he gets the money from Susan early and from Amanda in her will."

I shuddered. "That's plausible. But it looked so real when Drew kissed Amanda on stage. It looked like he really liked her."

"The same way he liked you when he tried to get you into bed after he was released from jail?"

I took a drink of my coffee. "Don't remind me. I still have nightmares about that." I traced the faint herringbone design on the sofa. "I can't explain it. I just felt that Drew cared for her. I can't believe that he killed her."

"Okay, we'll go with your gut feeling. What if Amanda already knew about Susan? What if there was a master plan that they were both working?"

I pulled away from him. "You think that Amanda was okay with Drew seeing Susan? How would that work?"

He set his mug down and rested his arms on his knees. "She had to have known about his pyramid scheme. How else would he explain the money he was siphoning off to her account? She also knew that he was still living with you before he went to jail. That means she was already accepting of things that most people wouldn't have been."

I sighed as I leaned against him. “He may not have told her about where the money was coming from. What if he told her he was taking the money from our joint accounts and that he was preparing to divorce me?”

Rob put his arm around me again and squeezed. “Does that scenario make you feel better?”

I laughed. “No. It just seems more reasonable to me. Amanda might have been okay with pulling one over on the wife. He probably told her I didn’t understand him, yadda, yadda, yadda.”

“I get your point; however, she had to have found out what he was really doing when he was caught and stood trial.”

Frustrated, I strode to the fireplace. I straightened one of the Santas. “What difference does it make at this point in time? She’s dead, and we know what Drew was doing. Her motives don’t matter anymore. It’s the people around her that we need to focus on.”

Rob patted the seat next to him, and I sank back down. He put his arm around me. “You’re right. But you have to admit that this actually makes Drew look worse in Jay’s eyes.”

“Just because someone’s a swindler and a cheat does not make them a murderer.”

He tipped my face up toward his. “I admire the fact that you are still defending Drew in spite of everything he’s done.”

“I can’t help it. He’s the father of my daughter, and I can’t bear the thought that he might be a murderer.” I shuddered. “So I’m going to proceed as if he isn’t. I think we should have dinner with Andy and Ed to find out more about their feud with Amanda.”

“Do you want me to ask them?”

“No, I will. Look at your calendar later and send me a few dates that will work for you.” I stood. “I hate to kick you out, but it’s late and I have an early morning tomorrow.”

He picked up his coffee cup and followed me into the kitchen. I took it from him, putting both cups in the dishwasher. Rob pulled me to him and kissed me. "Get some sleep and try not to think about everything."

I hugged him. "That's going to be difficult, but I'll try." I handed him his coat and gloves. Kissing him good night, I gently pushed him toward the door.

Making sure the cats had food and water, I turned out the light and ran up the stairs. Stopping by Jenny's door, I rapped lightly and stuck my head in. She was sound asleep with the light on. Her books were scattered across the bed. I tiptoed in and moved some of the heavier ones away from her and shut the light off.

As I got ready for bed, I paced. Drew was seeing two women. *How could I have missed that? I really need to talk to Father Tom about that annulment.* I slipped under the covers. The cats joined me and settled into their usual places. Hearing them snore, I pretended that I was near the ocean. I focused on the waves crashing in and then moving out. Finally relaxing, I drifted off to sleep.

At six thirty, my phone alarm sounded. Unfortunately, when my arm shot out of the bed to turn it off, I hit the phone and sent it flying across the room. The cats glared at me as I scurried across the floor to turn it off. They huffed, stretched, and curled back up, determined to catch up on their beauty sleep. I considered returning to bed for a few minutes but decided that moving them again might put me in peril.

After showering and getting dressed, I headed for Jenny's room. "Time to wake up."

She scowled at me from the bed, papers around her. "I've been up since five, studying for this stupid test. I fell asleep too early last night!"

I kissed her forehead. "Sleep is good for you."

"Not when there's a tough test. Thank goodness I set my alarm or I'd really be hosed."

"I'll leave you to it. Scrambled eggs sound good? You need some brain food."

"I need more than that." She looked at her book.

"Answer, please."

"Yes, but give me twenty."

"You got it."

Rolling her eyes, she put her head down again. I headed for the kitchen and started the coffee maker. Putting some bacon in the oven, I grabbed a mug and poured myself a cup of coffee.

I sat at the counter and looked at my phone. There was a text from Patty: "What's going on? Haven't heard from you. Call or text."

Why didn't I see that last night? I sighed when I noticed the new moon symbol. *When did I set the do not disturb?* I turned it off and texted her back, "All okay. Drinks tonight?"

"Wine at nine? Your place?"

"Okay. See you then."

I scrambled some eggs and heated milk for hot chocolate. When Jenny pounded down the stairs, I placed the hot chocolate and orange juice on the counter. She sat with a huff and gulped down the juice. I quickly served up the eggs, bacon, and toast and grabbed the blackberry jam from the fridge.

She stared at the array in front of her. "No marshmallows?"

I grinned. "Your wish is my command." I plunked them in the hot chocolate.

Almost before I could blink, she finished her meal, grabbed her coat and backpack, and ran out the door. "Thanks, Mom!"

I texted her, "Good luck today!" and added a fingers-crossed emoji.

Cleaning up the kitchen, I stopped, mouth agape, and dropped the dishtowel. Drew unlocked his back door. *How did he get out?*

Pulling on my coat and scarf, I donned my gloves and sped out the door. Within seconds, I pounded on Drew's back door. He pulled it open and leaned against the jamb. "Merry, good to see you."

My mouth open, he pulled me in and sat me at the table. "But...how did you get out?"

"On bail." He poured himself a cup of coffee and took a long sip. "And if you don't mind, I'm tired and in desperate need of my own shower, shampoo, and soap. You can't believe what they make you wash with in prison."

"But it's a murder charge. And you're a convicted felon."

He gave me a lazy smile as he leaned on the counter. "What can I say? I have a great attorney. And now you have to leave." He eyed me. "Unless you'd like to join me in the shower." He wiggled his eyebrows. "We used to have some good times in the shower."

I leapt from the chair as if it were on fire. "Your girlfriend just died!"

"Yes, and I am in mourning." He moved closer, running his finger up my sleeve. "Now, how about that shower?"

I ducked past him toward the door. "You swindled half the town and cheated on me with two different women. I hate you!" Stalking out of the house, I slammed the door behind me and ran headlong into Rob. Wiping my arms as if to get Drew's slime off, I jumped back. "Oh, it's you."

"That's all I get?" I gave him a dirty look, brushing past him into my house. He followed. "I take it you discovered Drew's out on bail?"

I paced the hallway, waving my arms. "What's the good of having a police detective for a friend if he doesn't give you any warning? A quick call or text is all I ask." Pausing in mid-rant, I stopped pacing. "Would it be too much trouble to give me an, 'Oh, by the way, your potential murderer ex is about to be sprung?'"

The back door popped open, and Jay bundled through it, stopping in his tracks. "Oops. Guess she already knows."

Rob gave him a sympathetic look and nodded. "Yep. She was just coming back from his place when I ran into her."

I returned to the kitchen. "I can hear you." I glared at Jay. "No warning, no nothing. I was just cleaning up from breakfast when I looked out the window, and what did I spy? My lying, cheating, rotten ex unlocking the house next door!" I shook my finger at Jay. "A little warning would be good."

He put up his hands. "Why do you think I'm here? I just found out too."

Rob pulled me to him. "Calm down. We both just found out, and our first thought was to come here to tell you."

I twisted away and stomped my foot. "How on earth did he get out? Who did he pay?"

"He has a good attorney." Jay ate one of the leftover pieces of bacon.

Deflated, I sat with a sigh. "Yes, that's what he told me."

Rob sat next to me at the counter and grabbed the other piece of bacon Jay was eyeing. "What else did Drew say to you?"

"He invited me into his shower."

Rob put the piece of bacon down and stood, towering over me, fists clenched. "He didn't."

I pulled him back down. "I think he was just trying to get me riled up."

"From the way you looked when you left his place, I'd say it worked." Rob picked up the bacon again and took a bite. "Good bacon."

Jay nodded. "It is. Do you have any more?"

I rolled my eyes. "No, gentlemen. I did not expect company this morning. And, in fact, I have an early meeting that I am now likely to be late for. If you don't mind, please let yourselves out."

I texted my client to alert her that I would be a minute or two late. I hurried along, dodging the snow piles in my way.

Later that morning, I moseyed over to Tempting Treasures to see if Andy was free. I admired the new walnut armoire in the entryway.

Andy came around the corner. "Merry, what brings you by?"

"I love this piece. But it's so big. I have nowhere to put it."

He stroked the finish. “It is lovely, isn’t it? In a way, I’m hoping no one buys it, but that’s the way I feel about most of my stock.” He grinned. “Do you have time for some tea? Ed made scones.”

I checked my watch. “I do have a few minutes, and I love Ed’s scones.”

I sat at his tea table, shrugging out of my coat. “Rob and I wanted to check and see if you and Ed would be available for dinner sometime this week.”

He warmed the teapot with hot water, swirled it, and poured it out. Then he put in a scoop of tea and tipped in the rest of the hot water. “Give me a sec, and I’ll check our calendar.” He brought the teapot over, putting it on the heavy lace doily. “This needs to steep for a few minutes.” He studied his phone. “We could do Thursday night, as long as you’re okay with going at seven. We’re meeting with the architect for drinks right before that.”

“That would work. Let me text Rob so he doesn’t make plans. Fiorella’s or the Screaming Pigeon?”

“The Screaming Pigeon has great food, but I just can’t get past the name. Let’s do Fiorella’s.”

“I’ll make reservations. It’s our treat since you were so kind to host last weekend and give us your leftovers.”

Andy poured the tea. “That’s certainly not necessary, but if you really want to, we will graciously accept.” He jumped up. “Oh, I nearly forgot the scones.”

I laughed. “Like I would have let you.”

A few pounds heavier, I trudged back to the office. I made the reservations for Thursday and sent a calendar entry to everyone.

Andy texted back: “Ooh, so efficient!”

Just before five, there was a knock on the door. Cheryl stuck her head in. “Susan is wondering if you have a few minutes?”

“Absolutely. Show her in.”

Susan came in. I shook her hand and gestured toward a chair. "Have a seat, Susan. I enjoyed our breakfast this weekend."

She fidgeted as she sat. "I appreciated it." She glanced around. "I need to tell you something."

"The floor is yours."

"What?"

I smiled. "What did you want to tell me?"

"Oh. Well, the police came to see me."

"What about?" She started crying, and I pushed my box of tissues across the desk to her. "Take your time."

Wiping her face, she straightened her shoulders. "I was holding some money for your husband."

I attempted to look shocked. "Why would Drew give you money to hold?"

She looked at her shoes. "I met him at the Christmas party you threw for the staff at your house five years ago. We started talking and had a lot in common." She glanced up, her eyes welling with tears. "I really thought he was a good guy. I'm sorry to tell you this, but we ended up having an affair, and he told me he was leaving you. I feel awful about it, but I really thought we were destined for each other."

I took a deep breath, handing her a bottle of water from the small refrigerator under my desk. "Drink this." I gripped the desk to keep from vaulting over it and hitting her. "Did you correspond when he was in prison?"

She hung her head. "Yes, like clockwork. When we spoke on the phone, he always ended the call by telling me how much he loved me and how special I was. But I realized he had been stringing me along the night of the fashion show."

I stood and paced behind my desk. "Where did he tell you he got the money he gave you to hold?"

She dabbed the mascara from under her eyes with the tissue. She took a sip of water and cleared her throat. "He said he was leaving you but that you had all the money. He said you wouldn't miss it and we needed it to start our life together."

"Where were you after the fashion show?"

"I went home to shower. I was sticky from all the drinks that were thrown."

"Did you go out again?"

She stood. "Why are you asking me all these questions? The police asked them all before."

I stopped pacing and glared at her. "You slept with my husband when you were working for me. And you helped him when he said he wanted to take money from me and my child. I think you owe me the answers to any questions I have."

Quivering, she sat back down. "No. I didn't go back out that night. And before you ask, I don't own any guns."

"I guess you know what comes next."

Standing again and drying her face with a tissue, she nodded as if she were facing an execution squad. "I'm fired."

"Yes, you are. Please call Cheryl to arrange a time to come back and pick up your things when the office is closed." I held out my hand. "I'd like your key now."

She rooted through her purse, finally pulling out her key and laying it on my desk. I pressed the intercom for Cheryl and asked her to grab Susan's coat and gloves. She brought them in and left. Susan pulled them on, weeping silently. I escorted her from the office.

Gritting my teeth, I returned and asked Cheryl to come in. "I just fired Susan. Please see that her security clearance and password are revoked immediately. She will be calling you to arrange a time when the staff is not here to collect her personal items."

Cheryl nodded, ever the professional. "I'll see to it, boss. Are you okay?"

"Yes. Thanks for helping with this."

She opened the door and smiled. "I think there's someone you're going to want to see out here."

Rob came in and closed the door. I collapsed in his arms, hugging him. After a moment, I stepped away.

He stared at me. "Not that I object to a hit-and-run hug, but what happened?"

"It's not every day that your husband's mistress cries in your office because he misled her."

CHAPTER 16

I just finished briefing Rob when my phone dinged. Glancing down, I read the text from Jenny: "I can't believe you didn't tell me Dad was out. We're having dinner together tonight. Back by nine."

"You're not going OUT to dinner, are you?"

"No. Stop shouting. He called for food to be delivered. He wants to keep a low profile."

I groaned and put my phone on my desk. Rob asked, "What's wrong?"

"Jenny's having dinner delivered at her dad's."

Rob grinned. "Maybe we should have dinner delivered too."

"I just can't face having dinner at my house, knowing he's next door. It's like having Darth Vader close by doing that heavy breathing thing."

Rob laughed and then grew serious. "Is it safe for Jenny to be with him?"

I put my head in my hands. "I'm not sure of anything anymore." I lifted my head. "He wouldn't hurt Jenny. He loves her."

He gave me a speculative look. "So you'd be okay if we didn't have dinner at your place tonight?"

"That's what I'm trying to say. I'd be more than okay to have dinner somewhere else."

"Perfect." He stood, grabbed my coat, and pulled me up. "Let's go to my place. You haven't been there for a while, and I'd like your opinion on a piece of artwork I just acquired."

I smiled and batted my eyelashes. "You want to show me your etchings?"

He pulled me close and grinned. "Something like that."

We drove to his house and hurried in the door. He glanced at me. "Do you want the fire on?" I nodded, so he flicked it on. He helped me with my coat. "What kind of food are you in the mood for? I hate to admit it, but I have a folder of menus for places that deliver."

He handed me the folder. I sat at the counter, perusing the options. "Indian? I haven't had chicken tikka masala in ages. That and some naan and I'd be in heaven."

He picked up the phone to order dinner. "It's going to be about an hour—they just had a big rush of orders."

I yawned and stretched. "I'm not in any particular hurry. I did tell Patty I'd meet her back at my place at nine, though."

"I promise I'll have you back by then." Rob massaged my neck and shoulders. "You're so tense."

I rested my head on the counter as he worked on my neck. "That feels so good. I may just have to keep you around."

"You're tensing again. Try to relax."

I shifted in my chair. "Mmm. This is relaxing." I looked at Rob. "A glass of wine might make me relax even more."

Rob kissed my neck. "Happy to oblige, ma'am." He pulled a bottle from the wine fridge. "Merlot okay?" I nodded, and he poured two glasses. Handing me mine, he kissed me. "Do you want me to continue with your shoulder rub?"

"Yes, but let's go over and sit in front of the fire. I'm still a little chilly."

He pulled me out of the chair and hugged me, rubbing his hands up and down my back. "I could warm you up."

I chuckled and pushed him away. "I'm sure you could, but the fire will do well enough for now." I picked up my wine and ducked under his arm. Putting my free hand in his, I led him to the couch. I kicked off my shoes, curled my legs up under me, and leaned against him. I took a sip of the Merlot and sighed.

He put his arm around me. "Does this feel better?"

"Yes, I'm focusing on the beauty and warmth of the dancing flames instead of the pinball thoughts in my head."

Rob smiled. "Sounds like the right thing to do." He rubbed my shoulder and arm. "How did your conversation with Andy go?"

I took a sip of wine. "It went well. You got my text that we're going to dinner with him and Ed on Thursday, right?"

"Yep. It should be fun." I sat forward on the sofa, and Rob's hand moved to rub circles on my back. "They're meeting with the architect just before dinner to go over the plans for Ed's place."

His eyes widened. "They sure aren't wasting any time, are they?"

"I was lucky enough to have some of Ed's scones this morning. It's criminal that he was delayed in opening."

Rob looked around. "You didn't bring a doggy bag for me?"

I laughed. "Last I looked, you weren't a dog."

"I'm not, but if you were a true friend, you would have snuck one in your purse for me."

I kissed him, leaning back against the sofa. "Does that make up for it?"

He pulled me close. "It might. Depends what else you have in mind."

Thirty minutes later, the doorbell rang. Rob quickly dressed and tossed me an afghan to cover myself. I pulled it over me and sank down so that the sofa back hid me from view.

Rob paid the delivery woman and shut the door. "It's safe to come out now."

I poked my head up. "It smells good, and I'm hungry. I skipped lunch because I ate so many scones."

Rob put the bag on the counter, smiling. "Are we talking about scones again?"

I grinned. "Nope. I think that conversation's done for the evening." Draped in the afghan, I stood and gathered my clothes. I headed for the bathroom. "Can you put the food in the oven for a few minutes? I just want to get cleaned up."

I took a quick shower and dressed. By the time I rejoined him, Rob had set the table and was pulling the food from the oven.

He put the bags on the table and leaned over for a kiss. "I'm glad you're hungry. We've got a lot of food here."

I ripped off a hunk of naan. Spreading it with saag paneer and taking a bite, I groaned. "This is so good."

He followed suit. "You're right. It's amazing that they can get spinach to taste like this."

"I think it's the Indian cheese or maybe all the spices." I reached for the basmati rice and spooned a healthy amount on my plate. Next, I picked up the container of tikka masala and ladled some on top, making sure to be generous with the sauce. I dabbed some naan in it. "Yum."

Rob dug in, and we both savored the food. I mopped up the last of the saag paneer. "Thanks for dinner. As you can tell, I don't get to eat Indian food a lot. Jenny says it's too spicy for her."

"I'm glad you liked it. I'm a fan as well." Rob looked at his watch. "I hate to tell you this, but it's a quarter till nine. Didn't you say you were meeting Patty?"

I glanced at my watch, shocked that it was so late. "I'll help you clean up. I'll just text Patty that I'll be a few minutes late."

He smiled. "No need. I'll leave the dishes in the sink and throw out the trash."

My eyes widened at the empty containers littering the table. "Wow. No leftovers."

"Sadly enough, no."

I helped him clear the table and stack the dishes in the sink. He pulled on his shoes and coat and drove me home.

The car in park, I leaned over the console to give him a lingering kiss. "That was a fabulous way to end a really bad day." Smiling, I got out of the car and waved as he left.

Hurrying in, I froze when I saw Patty sitting on the window seat, looking out the window at the driveway. She smirked. "That was some goodbye kiss. I remember giving kisses like that way back in the dark ages before four kids." She took a sip of wine. "Hmm. Maybe that's why I have four kids."

I gave her a dirty look and poured myself a glass. "Very funny."

"Drew's lights are on. Did Melissa rent his place?"

"The grapevine must be working slowly today. Drew's out."

She sat up straight. "Out? How did that happen?"

I joined her on the window seat, tucking one leg underneath me. "That's what I would like to know."

Jenny came through the back door like a shot and then stopped short. "Oh, hi, Mrs. Twilliger. I didn't realize you were here."

Patty waved. "Just catching up with your mom."

I stood. "How was your test? Did you get enough food at your dad's? Do you want a snack?"

Jenny rolled her eyes. "Dad's perfectly capable of ordering takeout and so am I. I'm fine, and the test wasn't as bad as I thought it was going to be. I'm going upstairs now. Good night, Mrs. Twilliger." And with that, she disappeared.

"How do they do that?"

Patty laughed. "Boundless energy. Oh, for just one iota."

I pulled her up. "Let's go in the other room by the fire. It's cold by these windows."

"Yes, but it's so informative as well. You never know what you are going to see."

"I don't want to see anything else today. Let's go." She followed me into the living room. I turned on the fire. "Now, isn't this better?"

"It is. And it's so beautiful with all of your Christmas decorations." She rolled the Santa train back and forth. "When are you getting your tree?"

"I was thinking next weekend." We sat on the sofa.

"Do you need help? I know Patrick and the boys would be happy to do any heavy lifting." She smiled. "Oh, that's right. This year you have 'Mr. Big and Brawny' to do your bidding."

I laughed. "Maybe you're right."

"So what's new? Anything happening that you'd care to tell me?"

I took a fortifying gulp of my wine. "You're not going to believe the day I had." As I recounted what happened, Patty went from having her feet up on the table to pacing the floor.

"Drew is such a scum! I can't believe I used to like that man. And don't get me started on Susan. She has some nerve getting all teary-eyed with you about how he did her wrong." Patty plopped down next to me. "That has to be the worst day ever."

"It was pretty bad. But it's ending on a high note."

She smiled, raising her glass to me. "I'll drink to that."

My phone alarm rang while I was in the middle of an R-rated dream about a gorgeous Indian prince. *Gotta love that Indian food.* Stretching languidly, I felt Courvoisier bat my hand. I stroked her neck. Drambuie appeared and demanded some attention as well. I petted both and got out of bed. While brushing my teeth, I glanced out the window to see if it was snowing. Susan Clime scurried out Drew's back door. She waved to him, got into her car, and drove down the alleyway.

My breath fogged the window, and I wiped it clean. Returning to the sink, I shook my head as if to deny what I had just seen. Drew was with Jenny until nine. Susan was in my office crying past five last night, so she certainly hadn't been back with him then. *When did he have time to reconcile with Susan? What's wrong with that woman? Why would she go back with him?*

Shuddering, I passed Jenny's door and rapped on it. "Time to get up."

"Five more minutes."

I made my way downstairs. Turning on the coffee, I opened the front door and retrieved the paper. I brought it into the kitchen. I was mid-pour when I missed the cup and coffee went all over the counter. The headline screamed, "Convicted felon out on bail in fashionista murder case."

Anyone who wasn't aware that Drew was out certainly is now. Cursing under my breath, I wiped up the counter. I poured more coffee; this time into the mug. I took a sip and sat to read the article.

My phone dinged with a text from Patty: "Nice headline about Drew." She appended a smiley face. I texted a thumbs-up emoji and left it at that.

Eyeing my watch, I called Jenny on her cell phone. "You need to get up if you want to be on time for school."

"I said I wanted five more minutes."

"You had ten."

"What? Why didn't you tell me? I'm going to be late." She hung up.

I heard her banging around upstairs. Pouring her some juice and wrapping a defrosted slice of banana bread in some wax paper, I had everything ready for the hand-off.

Six minutes later, the sound of elephants tramping down the stairs preceded her dash into the kitchen. I handed her the juice, which she polished off in three gulps, and then pressed the banana bread into her hand. She nodded at me as she hurtled out the door.

I checked to see that the cats had food and water and left. I decided to swing by Tom Butler's house. He had some drywall that was ruined because of an ice dam in his attic. Turning left instead of right, I strode the two blocks to his house and knocked on his back door.

Tom's wife, Melanie, answered. "Hi, Merry. Are you checking on our claim?"

"Yes. I want to make sure that you feel everything was done to your satisfaction."

She smiled. "Would you like some coffee? I was just about to leave for work, but I have a few minutes."

"No. I had two cups at home while waiting for Jenny to get out the door, so I've reached my limit."

"It's always fun to try and get my son, John, up as well."

I laughed. "I guess they need the sleep, which they might get if we could only convince them to go to bed earlier. Where was the damage?"

"The upstairs closet. I think the repair crew did a great job. And they were so quick. Do you want to see it?"

"No. I don't want to delay you. I just wanted to make sure you were satisfied."

"I am. You know, I tell everyone I meet to do business with you. I really appreciate your personal touch. Especially in today's world where it seems like everything is done on the Web." Her gaze slid away from mine. "I read in the paper that Drew posted bail. Doesn't it make you nervous to have a murderer living next to you?"

I ground my teeth. "Melanie, you know he hasn't been convicted yet."

"Well, sure, not of *that* crime. But the police wouldn't have arrested him if he didn't do it."

"It's been known to happen." I glanced at my watch. "I don't want to make you late for work. Please say hello to Tom for me." I gave her a quick wave. *Oh, joy. It's going to be another good day.*

When I arrived at the office, Cheryl was waiting for me. "The phones have been active this morning. Clients are calling with questions about Drew. We've been giving our standard answer."

I nodded. "Thanks. I appreciate it."

She handed me a few call slips. "I think you better talk to these. The rest other people can handle."

I stopped by Chuck Pole's desk on the way to my office. "I just spoke with Melanie Butler. She's very satisfied with the work that was done on the ice dam claim. Thanks for keeping her up to date on what was happening. She appreciated our high-touch service." I smiled. "Happy clients bring more clients."

"I know. It makes me feel good to help people when they hit a bad patch. That's why I enjoy working here so much."

"I'm glad. Keep up the good work."

I continued on through the office, chatting with several associates as I passed. Finally arriving at my office, I put my head down and returned the calls that Cheryl had given me.

At eleven, Patty texted me, "Meet me at Delightful Bites at noon."

"Okay." *I guess I've been summoned.* I made a few last calls.

Patty was standing in line when I joined her. "What are you having?"

"I can't decide between the Reuben and the turkey club."

I laughed. "Tough decision: sauerkraut or bacon."

She pushed my shoulder. "Funny. What are you having?"

"I'm going to have a cup of their vegetable barley soup and a half of a grilled cheese sandwich."

"Great. That also sounds good. Now I have three things to decide between." She reached the counter. "May I have a cup of the soup of the day and a half a Reuben?"

Gary laughed. "Yes, you may. Merry, what sounds good to you?"

"Everything. But I'd like a cup of the soup and the half grilled cheese."

"Coming right up. Coffee for you?"

Patty and I answered at the same time, "Yes, please." He handed us two mugs, and we went over to the do-it-yourself coffee station.

"I really love this place. I'm going to get the mocha flavored." I held my cup under the urn and pressed the lever.

"Just plain java for me."

Coffee in hand, we sat at one of the booths.

Taking a sip, I smiled with pleasure. "Yum. Did you just want to get out of the house, or was there something you wanted to tell me?"

"You're not going to believe this, but I ran into Ann from the Pickled Herring as I dropped off the younger kids this morning."

"Is it unusual to see Ann?"

She gave me a dirty look. "No, silly, her son is in my son's class. What was unusual was what she had to tell me."

Our food arrived, and I ate a spoonful of the soup. "This is really good."

Patty took a bite of her sandwich. "The Reuben is great too."

"I'm so glad to hear. Are you going to continue with your story, or are you going to leave me hanging?"

She rolled her eyes and snuck in another spoonful of soup. "Ann told me that it was slow at the bar last night. Around eight, Susan Clime came in. She spilled her guts to Ann and pounded down a few martinis. Susan told her all about her affair with Drew and how unhappy she was with the way things turned out."

"That was yesterday's news. Thanks for making me relive it." I glared at her and then took a bite of my sandwich. Unable to control myself, I groaned a little in ecstasy.

"If you'd just wait for it, Ms. Smarty-pants."

I motioned impatiently for her to continue, and she did. "What's new is that Drew came in about nine fifteen. Susan went nuts. She yelled at him for using her as a bank and for cheating on her with Amanda."

My mouth dropped open. "He must have left his house just after Jenny came home. Why would he go to such a public place?"

"He was probably bored and figured that the bar would be empty that late on a Tuesday night. And Ann said it was pretty empty: just a few stragglers and Susan."

"Doesn't the bar close at ten early in the week?"

"That's right. Anyway, just as Ann thought she was going to have to come around the bar and intervene, Drew calmed Susan down enough to convince her to take a seat at one of the booths. Ann couldn't hear what they were saying once they moved away, but after about five minutes, they made up."

"If Ann couldn't hear them, how could she tell they made up?"

"They were canoodling."

"Yuck."

"Yes, yuck. Even worse, she sounded last call just before ten, and they left together with nary an inch between them."

"That explains why Susan was leaving his house this morning at oh-dark-thirty."

Patty chewed her sandwich thoughtfully. "I can't believe she believed whatever he told her."

"I'm just glad I fired her yesterday."

* * *

Rob picked me up after work. I sank into his car with a sigh. He looked at me with concern. "Is everything okay?"

"Yes, just a tough day. Where are we going?"

"I thought we'd try a new place that opened up called Fish + Game. It's about a ten-minute drive, so you may as well relax."

He put on some music, and I closed my eyes, enjoying the smooth ride of his car and the comfortable seat. It seemed like only a second had passed when I was awoken by Rob gently touching my shoulder. "I hate to wake you up, sleeping beauty, but we're here."

I smiled at him, and he kissed me. He came around the car and opened the door for me. I stood and stretched. My eyes widened when I took in the restaurant. It was an old Bavarian-style building with dark wood, sloped roofs, and gingerbread detailing around the windows. It even had stenciling on the window boxes. It looked like something out of a fairy tale. But hanging high above the door was a stark, ultra-modern sign that read, "Fish + Game."

"This doesn't seem to go together. Is the music inside polka or some new kind of techno?"

He laughed. "I guess we're going to find out. Either way, I've heard that the food is really good."

We entered, and the modern theme won out. All I saw were crisp lines and a preponderance of black and white.

I shook my head. "I don't know if I can wrap my mind around this." The host showed us to a comfortable booth near a roaring fire. I gestured toward the large fireplace. "Now, this is something I can truly appreciate."

Rob said, "Why don't you sit closest to the fire? You're always cold, and I run a bit hot."

I grinned. "You surely do." I studied the menu. "I think I'm going to have the quail with grapes to start and then the halibut for my main course."

"I think I'll try the grouse appetizer and then have the wild boar."

"You are far more adventurous than me, but I will have a taste just to say I've had it."

"How was your day?"

I launched into the Susan/Drew tale, and before long, Rob's mouth was hanging open. "What's wrong with that woman? Doesn't she realize she was played? And what's wrong with him? Why would he be gallivanting around town, knowing what happened at the fashion show?"

I nodded. "Patty thinks he was tired of being housebound. When we were married, he always wanted to be out and about with people. He's a true extrovert. It must be really difficult for him to be home without a lot of human interaction."

"He's not going to get sympathy from me."

I laughed. "Nor me."

Our appetizers arrived. Rob and I gave each other a taste. I took a piece of his grouse. "Wow. It's nice and tender." I wrinkled my nose. "There's a bit of a gamey under flavor, though." Rob nodded, and I asked, "What went on in your world today?"

"I had an interesting lunch."

"How so?"

"I went to the Golden Skillet, and since I was alone, I sat at the counter. Philip Piper ended up sitting next to me, so I introduced myself and told him that I was in the market for a dentist. One thing led to another, and he told me how stunned he was by Amanda's betrayal. He said it was worse than when he was seventeen and his first love dumped him for his best friend."

"Wow. Not the kind of friend I'd want."

Rob shook his head. "Me either. Then he told me that it had turned out 'okay.' He had gotten even with his friend. He didn't say how, but he was gesturing with his knife as he said it."

I pushed my appetizer plate away. "That's a pretty strong story to tell when talking to a new acquaintance."

"I thought so. But maybe he doesn't have that many friends."

I fixated on the fire for a moment, watching the flames tickle the wood. "Now that you mention it, I don't think he has a lot of close friends. I only remember seeing him with Amanda and then Lauren before her. Hmm. That's kind of sad."

"Maybe he's one of those guys who only have a few close friends, but the relationships are very deep."

"From the story you told me, it sounds like he lost one of those." Frowning, I put my hand on Rob's. He brought it to his lips and kissed it just as our entrees were served.

My halibut glistened on the plate, nestled in fingerling potatoes and crowned with a small number of delicately fried onions. "This looks yummy!"

Rob's boar was cut in medallions arrayed in a fan shape. Drizzled with red sauce and accompanied by creamy mashed potatoes, they looked wonderful. He cut a slice of the boar, making sure to include some of the sauce, and slid it onto my bread plate.

I took a bite. "I thought it would taste like pork, but it's kind of between pork and beef. Interesting."

Taking a bite and chewing slowly, he closed his eyes. "I don't care what you call it, it's tasty." He took my hand. "I didn't finish my story about Philip. During lunch, we also talked about hobbies. I told him that I like to go skeet shooting and asked if there were any good places around here to go."

"I didn't know you liked to shoot."

"It isn't one of my hobbies; that's for sure."

"Well then, why did you say it was?"

Rob sighed and ate another piece of the boar. "To see if he likes guns."

I laughed. "Sorry to be a bit slow on the uptake. I was enjoying this halibut so much that I stopped tracking with the story. I get your gambit now. Please continue."

"Philip lit up like a firecracker on the Fourth of July. His dad used to take him hunting, and he has quite a collection of guns. He asked me to go shooting with him on Saturday. I told him I'd love to."

I rubbed his shoulder. “I’m sure you know what you’re doing, but that man caused me pain in a dental appointment and now you’re going near him with a loaded gun?”

He caressed my hand. “We’ll be at a range. Everything should be fine.”

CHAPTER 17

Savoring my second cup of coffee, I pared down e-mail at the kitchen counter. Jenny pounded down the stairs. "Mom, there were a few decorations we didn't use this year. Would it be okay if I took them to Dad's? It looked kinda bleak when I was there earlier this week."

I tried to remember my Christian values. "Show me which ones you're talking about, and if I'm not saving them for some reason, sure."

She ran back up the stairs to grab the box and clomped back down. Balancing the box on the counter, she started unloading it.

"Whoa, let's bring this over to the table so that we don't drop anything."

Within a few moments, I had separated the items into things I'd be sorry to see leave and those I could face going out the door. I chuckled as I realized one of the items I was willing to part with was a particularly garish Santa Drew gave me when we were first dating. I tossed it in the box.

"Thanks, Mom." She bounded out the door, box firmly in hand.

I sighed as I looked at what was left on the table. Rummaging through the hall closet, I found a smaller empty box. I had just started loading the leftover decorations when Jenny came back carrying the original box.

I raised my eyebrows. “What happened? Wasn’t he home?”

“Yes, he was home. But he wasn’t alone. Ms. Clime was sitting at the kitchen table. And she was wearing his robe! And I don’t think she had anything on underneath it. Yuck.” She frowned. “Doesn’t she work for you?”

“Not anymore. Long story. Why didn’t you just leave the box there for later?”

“I would have, but she had already decorated the place. And not well.” She shuddered. “I can’t believe Dad hooked up with someone who worked for you. Awkward.” She left the box on the table and ran back up the stairs.

Groaning, I emptied the box from the closet and refilled the one Jenny returned. I dropped Drew’s Santa in the trash and put the used coffee grounds on top of it. Smiling, I put the full box at the bottom of the stairs in the vain hope that Jenny might put it back where it belonged. Resuming my seat at the counter and taking a sip of my coffee, I spat it out. Stone cold.

I went to the living room, clicked on the fire, and picked up my book. Two pages in, my phone dinged. It was Rob: “See you at three.”

“Be careful!” *Philip wouldn’t try anything at a gun range.* I tried to concentrate on my book.

A few minutes later, Jenny bounded down the stairs. “Going to Cindy’s.” Almost tripping at the bottom, she glared at me. “Why did you leave that box there? I nearly killed myself.”

“It’s the box you brought down. Would you please take it back up?”

“I don’t see why I have to do everything.” Pouting, she carried the box back upstairs, stomping as she went.

“All the way upstairs in the attic, please.”

The attic door opened, and the stomping continued. The door slammed, and Jenny ran back down the stairs. “Can I go now?”

I chuckled. “Yes, you may.”

She pulled on her coat and stalked out the door, slamming that one too.

Gotta love teenagers. Settling back into the sofa, a pillow on either side of me and an afghan around my legs, I tried to reimmerse myself into the book.

Patty texted me, “Susan at Drew’s table in robe?” She added a few pitchfork emojis for emphasis along with flames.

Tossing my book aside, I turned off the fire and threw a load of wash into the machine. Courvoisier leapt up on the sink counter next to me and batted at the door holding their treats. *Someone may as well be happy.* I tossed her two, and Drambuie came running, attempting to screech to a halt. Her momentum too fast, she slid past the open door on the slick hardwood floor. Slinking back, she stood in the doorway and mewed. I threw her two, and then put the packet away. Four eyes implored me. I said, “No more.” They waited for a moment. Sensing my resolve they padded away for another nap.

Pacing the floor at five, I finally received a text from Rob: “On my way. No holes in my body.” He added a laughing emoji.

“Very funny. Where have you been?”

“Be there soon. Putting phone down to start car.”

I pulled out a Cabernet from the wine fridge and poured myself a glass. While I savored the deep undertone of tart cherries, Rob came in the back door.

I frowned. “Where have you been? You said you’d be here by three.”

“I know, and I apologize, but when Philip and I finished up at the range, he invited me to see his weapon collection. There wasn’t really a chance to text you until I was alone again in the car.”

“He knows we’re dating. You could have just told him you needed to let me know you’d be late.”

Rob came around the counter to give me a hug. “I’m sorry. I didn’t mean to worry you. I just didn’t want to interrupt the flow of the conversation." He kissed me. "You taste good. What kind of wine are we having?" Picking up the bottle to inspect the label, he nodded his approval. "Nice vintage."

I retrieved a glass from the cupboard and poured the wine. "Let's move to the living room, and you can tell me what you found out." Turning on the fire and some muted Christmas music, I sat next to Rob. "Okay, spill."

He tasted the wine. "This is good."

I made a swirling clock motion. "Stop stalling. What did you find out?"

"Patience, Merry, patience." Rob laughed. "Okay, okay. Philip's a crack shot. If he missed the center of the target once, I'd be surprised."

I leaned back on the sofa and pulled one of the pillows to my stomach, my feet resting on the coffee table. "Interesting, but I'm not sure how much skill is required to shoot someone standing four feet in front of you."

"You'd be surprised. Plus, shooting someone is more about resolve."

I squirmed. "Thanks for the visual. Go on."

"His gun collection is amazing." Rob's eyes widened. "He has a separate hidden locked room with a steel door. Think real spy stuff. You enter through a bookcase in his study. And everything is neatly displayed on specially made shelves. You know how dentists' trays are so organized?"

I nodded.

"That's how structured it looked."

"Did you see a silencer?"

"There were several." Rob gazed into the fire. "I'm not sure that there was much he didn't have." He took another sip of his wine. "Let me put it this way: if the zombie apocalypse happens or if a small government needs to be overthrown, Phil's our man."

I ambled to the fire and warmed my hands. “So what you are saying is that he not only had motive, he has the weaponry that would have enabled him to kill Amanda.”

Rob kicked his shoes off and crossed his feet on the coffee table. “I can’t swear that he has the gun that killed Amanda.”

“Wouldn’t you think he’d get rid of it?”

Swirling the wine, his eyes fastened on mine. “I’m not so sure.”

“That he did it?”

“No, I could imagine that.” His eyes narrowed. “Philip was so enamored of his collection, I’m not sure I could see him being willing to part with any of it. Plus, it would leave an empty space in the room that would offend his sense of symmetry.” I shivered and sat next to him. He put his arm around me and squeezed. “Are you cold?”

I shook my head. “You really could imagine our dentist murdering someone?”

“Yep. He seems like a pretty determined guy. He told me where he attended high school. I’m going to see if I can find out anything more about his friend from school. Maybe we should look him up.” Rob pulled me tighter. “And by the way, Philip wanted me to remind you to schedule your follow-up appointment.”

I rolled my eyes. “Like that’s going to happen anytime soon.”

“I think I should call Jay and see if he has some time to swing by later tonight.” Rob got up to make the call. After a few minutes, he sank back down on the sofa. “Jay’s going to come around eight.”

“Good. That will give us enough time to eat. Speaking of eating, I should probably get the steaks out of the fridge to get the chill off.” I stood.

“Do you need any help?”

“Not just now, but I will later.” I kissed the top of his head and left for the kitchen.

Five minutes later, Jenny came through the back door. She eyed the steaks. "I'm glad I didn't take the Twilliger's up on their offer of dinner. They were having chicken."

"Patty's a good cook. I'm sure whatever she was making would have been terrific." I hugged her. "But I'm glad you decided to come home and eat with us."

"Are you going to grill outside?"

I laughed. "The grill's under about a foot of snow, and it's cold out. I'll be cooking inside."

She smiled. "Whatever. Steak is steak. It's going to be good. Do you need help?"

"Just set the table before it's time to eat."

"I'll knock that out now." She started to get the plates and cutlery out. "Dad texted me today."

"What did he want?"

"He wants me to go to Mass with him tomorrow."

"At our church?"

She laughed. "Of course at our church. It was his church too."

"Is Susan going to be there?"

Jenny frowned. "I hadn't thought of that. I don't want to go if she's going to be there." She texted him. "No, Susan's not going to be there. It will just be me and Dad." She looked up with a relieved smile. "What do you think?"

I tucked an errant plait of hair behind her ear. "I guess it will be okay. I don't think people would do anything, not at a church. And unlike at the fashion show, Father Tom won't be serving drinks." I paused. "Although there is wine at communion. Hmm."

Jenny giggled. "I've never seen anyone guzzle from the chalice." She finished setting the table. "I'll be upstairs if you need me. Text when dinner's ready." She walked out. "Hi, Mr. Jenson. I'm looking forward to dinner."

A few minutes later, Rob joined me in the kitchen. "Something smells great in here." Pouring himself some more wine and topping off my glass, he sat at the counter. "So Jenny's going to church with Drew tomorrow."

I gave him a part grin, part grimace. "Yep."

"Is that a good idea?"

"Nothing to do with Drew is a good idea. But of all the places he could be taking her, this one seems the safest. People are unlikely to get out of control at a church."

He nodded. "Want to go to the same Mass?"

I smiled. "Of course."

Rob raised his glass. "To great minds thinking alike." Taking a sip, he gave me a light kiss.

After dinner, Rob and I were enjoying coffee in the living room when the back door opened after a sharp rap. "Anyone home?"

I replied, "In the living room. Grab a cup of coffee and join us."

Jay came in and sat on the chair opposite, setting his coffee mug on the table. "It looks so festive in here." Getting up again, he strolled around the room, examining the Santas. "My favorite is the one on the train."

I laughed. "Thanks. I love decorating for Christmas."

He turned in a slow circle. "What is that smell?" He ambled to the dining room and picked up one of the oranges studded with cloves. "My mom used to do this." He held it close to his nose and sniffed. "It's such a spicy scent." He smiled. "It smells like home."

Setting the orange back down, he put on his cop face. "Now, what's so important that I needed to come out on a cold Saturday night?" He sat back down on the sofa and blew on his coffee before sipping it.

Rob told him about Philip's weapon collection.

"Last I looked, it wasn't illegal to have a weapon collection in this state."

I placed my mug on the table. "True, but Philip could have wanted revenge for his public humiliation. He's a crack shot and likely had or has the weapon that was used to kill Amanda."

"Sounds like a lot of supposition to me. You do know I have a prime candidate right next door."

I frowned. "How can you be so focused on one person when someone else might have committed the crime?"

Jay leaned forward. "Merry, unlike in TV dramas, the most likely person is usually the culprit. I can't waste time looking for alternative suspects when the person who did it has been charged and is now awaiting trial." Jay stood. "Unless you have something more concrete, I'll be on my way home."

Once Jay left, I sat on one of the kitchen counter stools and hung my head. "I can't believe he didn't listen to us."

Rob sat next to me, rubbing my back. "He did listen. He also said to come back to him once we have some proof."

"Did he just give us carte blanche to investigate?"

He smiled. "That's what I heard. But we need to be very careful. You know what happened the last time you investigated."

I nodded. "Don't worry. I never want to be faced with death like that again."

I shivered, and he stood, pulling me up into his arms. Cradling me to his chest, he spoke down into my hair, "You're important to me, and I couldn't face losing you."

I hugged him. "You need to be careful too. I've gotten kind of attached to you."

CHAPTER 18

The next morning, I woke up dreading church. Gritting my teeth, I got out of bed and into the shower.

After dressing, I padded by Jenny's door and knocked. "Time to get up for church." Hearing a groan in reply, I continued downstairs. Turning on the coffee machine and putting an English muffin in to toast, I asked the cats, "Is anyone hungry?" Excited meows seemed to answer that question, so I put food in their bowls.

Still not hearing any signs of life from upstairs, I called Jenny on her cell phone. "Are you up? Do you want an English muffin?"

"Yes and yes. I'll be down in ten."

I buttered my muffin and stood in front of the open refrigerator. Weakening, I grabbed the strawberry preserves and slathered the toast with it. I made Jenny's muffin and poured her a glass of orange juice. As I bit into my English muffin, melted butter oozed from the side of my mouth. I wiped my lips. *So good but maybe a tad heavy on the butter*. I took another bite and groaned. *Nope. Just right.*

Jenny bustled into the kitchen. She slathered the English muffin with the butter and jam. I smiled. *Like mother, like daughter.*

There was a sharp rap on the back door. Drew said, "Hey, smart stuff, are you ready to go?"

She took one last bite and guzzled her orange juice. She donned her coat. "Ready now." She waltzed out the door.

Drew nodded at me as he left. “Merry.”

I texted Rob, “They just left. Meet me at the church in ten.”

“Will do.”

I put the dishes in the sink and then got ready to brave the cold. Hurrying to the church, I smiled as I saw Rob waiting on the steps for me. I gave him a quick hug. “Did they see you?”

“No. I haven’t seen them. They must have gone in earlier.”

“Hopefully they sat up front.” We crept into the church, scanning the rows as we went. I whispered, “We’re in luck. Drew and Jenny are in the third pew back.”

Moving forward, we sat five rows behind them. Drew had his head bent toward Jenny as she talked to him, waiting for the Mass to begin. Susan Clime scurried past me to Drew and Jenny’s pew. Jenny scowled as Susan scooted past her to sit on the other side of Drew. Shoulders slumping, Jenny faced forward, ignoring Drew’s whispered pleas.

I gave Rob a sidelong glance. “That’s not going well.”

“No, it’s not.”

The Mass began. I missed most of it watching the show unfolding in front of me. Susan tried to put her arm around Drew’s waist. He batted it away. Settling for tucking her hand in his elbow, she smiled up at him. He disengaged it, glaring at her, and pushed her hand down to her side. She faced forward. Her shoulders trembled. After a few minutes, she stood, pushing her way out of the pew. Then she raced past us, her face wet with tears. Jenny swiveled to follow her progress, eyes wide.

Rob shook his head. “You don’t see that every day.”

Drew put his arm around Jenny and pulled her to him, his other hand holding the hymnal.

The Mass ended. As Rob and I gathered our things, Drew strode by with Jenny just behind him. She mouthed, “OMG,” to me as she hurried to keep up. Rob and I followed behind them. Drew stopped to shake Father Tom's hand. After a moment's hesitation, Father Tom took it and said something to Drew. Drew glared at him, grabbed Jenny's hand, and strode out the door.

Waiting in the line to greet Father Tom, Rob and I inched forward. Conversation buzzed around us. We finally reached him. After we congratulated him on his insightful homily, he laughed. "I don't think anyone was paying attention. Susan and Drew caused quite the scene."

I edged closer. "What did you say to him?"

"I told him that if he was going to continue to upstage me, I'd prefer that he pick the early Mass because then he'd do me a service by waking everyone up."

I giggled all the way home.

As we came in, Rob asked, "Not that I'm complaining, but are you going to laugh all day?"

"I'll stop. I swear." And then I giggled some more. "It was all that tension. And then to hear something so unexpected..." I laughed again. "You have to admit, it was funny."

He smiled. "It was."

"Do you think that's it for Drew and Susan?"

"She wouldn't be dumb enough to forgive him for another public humiliation."

"One would think. But she hasn't proven that she's the brightest bulb in the box."

Rob started the coffee machine. "What's the plan for today?"

I rubbed his arm. "Are you feeling strong?"

"Absolutely." He adopted a strongman pose. "I can't believe you even need to ask."

I laughed. "Let's get the Christmas tree today. I can't wait for the smell of pine throughout the house."

"Do you promise you'll water it? It's a little early for a cut tree. I don't want the house to burn down." He hugged me. "Especially with you in it."

I laughed as I held up the middle three fingers of my right hand. "I Girl Scout Pledge it."

"Then I would be happy to be your muscle for the day. When do you want to go?"

"Let me text Jenny." My phone dinged. "She said she'll be home by one."

"Do you mind if I work on a story while we wait?"

"No. That would be fine. I have some things I need to do anyway. You're welcome to use my office if you'd like." He nodded, disappearing with his MacBook.

Picking up a magazine that Andy wanted to read, I readied to brave the cold air. I flew through the alleyway and up Andy and Ed's steps.

Andy opened the door before I could knock. "Girl, you should go out for track the way you were moving."

I laughed and handed him the magazine. "I finished reading that magazine you wanted."

"Oh, good." He paged through. "I love getting new design ideas for the store." He set it on the kitchen counter. "Can you stay for a moment? I'll make tea."

I took off my coat. "Just for a few minutes. Rob, Jenny, and I are picking up our tree today."

"I'm so glad those days are behind us. We just wheel the tree out from the spare closet, flip it over, put the top on, and, voila, ready to decorate. No more chilled hands or scratching the top of the car." He poured the tea. "It just seems so much more civilized."

"I love the tradition. And the incredible odor of fir." I sniffed. "Speaking of which, if you don't have a live tree, why do I smell one?"

He gave me a smug smile, pointing to a candle burning at the end of the counter. "I repeat, so much more civilized."

I rolled my eyes. "Whatever." I sipped my tea. "Ooh, this is lovely. What is it?"

"A special blend called Ancient Happiness. Do you like it?"

"It's floral, but it doesn't overpower." I took another sip and closed my eyes. "Yes. This is lovely."

"I hate to interrupt you, but since you stopped by, would you like to look at the plans for the shop?"

"I'd love to."

Unrolling the blueprints, he anchored them to the counter using the teapot and some salt and pepper shakers. He pointed. "This is the existing shop. Customers will have to go through the shop to get to the tea room, which will be accessed through the French doors right here. Then the kitchen will be here, and both open to the patio right here."

"It all looks wonderful." The notes section of the blueprint included the date. My eyes widened. "You had these done three years ago."

"Yes. We've been working on them for some time. Amanda blocked us from creating our dream for three long years. Thank God the witch is dead."

My mouth opened in shock. "Andy, a woman died."

He shrugged. "She was evil. I don't want to pretend that we miss her. She made our life a living hell, and I, for one, am glad she's gone." He stood. "You can pretend that you miss her, but I remember that she wasn't your favorite person either."

"It's true that she was abrasive. But no one's life should be snuffed out early. That's evil too."

"You really are a Pollyanna." He kissed my forehead. "That's what I love best about you. You're a calm sea of innocence in a turbulent and messy world."

I smiled. "Thanks, I think." I caught sight of his clock. "Is that the time? I need to run."

Rob and Jenny were waiting in the kitchen as I propelled myself through the door. Jenny said, "Where have you been?"

"At Andy's. I'm sorry. I lost track of time. Are we ready to go?"

CHAPTER 19

Exhausted after putting up the tree, I crawled into bed for what ended up being a dreamless sleep. The next morning, I was enveloped in the lovely scent of fir. I scampered down the stairs and sat on the third one from the bottom. *That tree's not too big. It looks just right.* A feeling of peace washed over me as I leaned against the rail and admired our handiwork from the day before. *I love Christmas.* Courvoisier sat next to me and head butted my hand. I pulled her to me, stroking her fur.

A disheveled Jenny opened her door. "What are you looking at?"

I smiled dreamily. "The tree."

"It's too big."

"Nope. It's just right. Come see." I patted the stair.

She sat next to me and draped her arm across my shoulders. "It does look pretty good."

I studied her face. "Are you sad your father's not going to be able to take you to Jamaica?"

"Not really. It means I get to spend Christmas with you. And besides, he told me he'll take me there to celebrate once these stupid charges against him are dropped." She sighed. "I remember the last Christmas we had with him. We went to New York City to see *The Nutcracker*. It made me want to dance." She smiled and leaned against me. "It was so much fun."

The living room grew brighter as the rising sun refracted against the tree's clear glass icicles, setting them aglow.

"I'm really glad you're going to be here. It wouldn't be Christmas without you." I put my arm around her waist. "I love you, Jenny."

"I love you too, Mom."

I kissed her. "I don't want to move, but it's getting late."

She groaned and cozied up closer to me. "Why don't you call in sick for both of us? We'll sit by the fire drinking hot chocolate, eating bonbons, and admiring the tree."

I smiled. "That sounds like a great idea, but I remember someone telling me they had a drama club lunch today."

She jumped up. "That's right. We can't play hooky today. Maybe tomorrow?"

I laughed. "Let's do it on Saturday."

Later that evening, Rob and I cuddled by the fire after dinner. I asked, "Remember how I went over to Andy's house yesterday?"

He stroked my arm. "Yes."

"He showed me the plans for their business expansion."

"And?"

"They were dated three years ago. He was pretty bitter about how Amanda blocked their progress. In fact, Andy said that he was glad she was dead."

"That's pretty harsh."

"I thought so. I can't think of Andy, or Ed, committing murder. But they had a pretty good motive. And with Amanda's death, their plans are steamrolling along." I looked into Rob's eyes. "I hope it just looks bad versus being bad."

He kissed my forehead. "Me too." He frowned. "Ed wouldn't be able to make those scones of his in prison."

I smacked his chest. "Not funny."

He smiled and pulled me closer. "Enough murder talk."

I lifted my face for a kiss. He was kind enough to oblige. I said, "I wonder how Susan is doing after yesterday."

"Didn't we put a stop to the talk of murder for the evening?"

"You did; I didn't."

Rob laughed. "John Little told me he saw her in the grocery store. She was creeping around the edges like a skittish mouse who didn't want to be seen."

"I feel bad for her."

"It's not as if she's some innocent. She brought this on herself."

"True." I sat up. "I just don't like to see anyone hurt." The clock chimed eleven. "Wow, how did it get so late?"

"I guess that's my cue to leave." We stood. He pulled me to him for a lingering kiss. Groaning, he broke away. "It's getting harder to leave you."

I touched the tip of his nose and smiled. "That means you're that much happier when you see me again."

"Or something like that." He readied himself for the shock of the weather, giving me one last kiss.

I was in the midst of shutting the door when his arm came back in. He crooked his finger, so I stuck my head out the door. "What's wrong?"

He put his finger to his lips and pointed toward Drew's back door. Susan, bathed in the light from Drew's porch, was hunched against the door, knocking. After a few seconds, the door opened, and she was pulled inside.

My eyes widened.

"What is wrong with that woman? Has she no pride?"

"Apparently not." I shivered.

He pushed me gently back inside. "Warm up. We'll talk more tomorrow." Giving me a kiss on the forehead, he eased the door shut.

I texted Patty, "Susan's back for more."

"No sympathy. She deserves what she gets. Lunch tomorrow? Noon?"

"Okay. Sweet dreams."

As I spooned clam chowder into my mouth, my eyes nearly rolled back into my head. Patty laughed. "You make it look like you haven't been fed in years."

"Can I help it I enjoy my food? Especially when all I had to do was buy it? And when it tastes this good? I mean, just look at those pieces of bacon."

"I'm one to talk." She dove into her hot pastrami on marbled rye.

"Did you come for the food? Or was there something you wanted to talk to me about?"

Putting up her forefinger to tell me to wait a minute, she finished the bite of her sandwich. "Mmm. That is good." She dabbed her lips with the napkin. "I had lunch with Samantha Smith yesterday."

"The woman who worked in Amanda's shop? You do get around."

She smiled. "It's nice to have excuses to eat good food."

"And?"

"She and her husband are thinking about buying Amanda's shop from Caroline. She wanted to pick my brain on some design ideas, should they be able to complete the purchase." Prior to becoming a stay-at-home mom, Patty was an interior decorator. She still kept her hand in on jobs that struck her fancy.

"Did she hire you to design it?"

"It was just a preliminary conversation. On the positive side, I did get a free lunch."

"Somehow I don't think that's why you wanted to talk to me. What else happened?"

"She said that Andy had a meeting with Amanda the morning of the fashion show. He didn't know Samantha was there because she was working in the back of the shop on last-minute alterations."

"And?"

Patty leaned closer and put her hand on my arm. She glanced around. “He was making a last-ditch effort to get Amanda to sign on the dotted line for the Tasty Treats expansion. It didn’t go well. Samantha was busy, so she wasn’t paying much attention. Sudden shouting startled her. Amanda said she would die before she signed the variance. And that she was tired of them wasting her time with their smelly ideas. Andy yelled back that Amanda was a stupid cow with no design sense. Then he lowered his voice. Samantha said she really had to strain to hear him. Andy told Amanda that if she continued to block the tea room, her death could be arranged. The door slammed, so Samantha crept out of the back room to see if Amanda was okay. Red faced, Amanda screamed for her to get back to work.”

I sat back, my meal forgotten. “Wow. Did she tell the police about the argument?”

“No. She likes Andy and Ed and didn’t want to cause them problems. I told her that she could get in trouble for withholding information from the police and gave her Detective Ziebold’s number. She said she would call him this morning.”

“Do you think she followed through?”

“I know she did. Jay was leaving here just as I came in. He thanked me for telling her to come to him.” She eyed me. “You don’t seem very happy. I thought you were trying to clear Drew.”

“Andy and Ed are friends. I want Drew cleared but not at their expense.”

Patty frowned. “I know what you mean. Maybe I shouldn’t have told Samantha to call Jay.”

“No, you did the right thing. I’m sure they have an alibi for the time of death.” I drummed my fingers on the linoleum table. “I think I’ll go over to Ed and Andy’s tonight to see how they are doing.”

“Keep me posted.”

I wrapped up the half sandwich that came with my soup to have for lunch the next day. Giving Patty a kiss on the cheek, I returned to the office.

Andy couldn't have killed Amanda. I refused to believe it.

Rob texted that he'd meet me at my house at six. Eyeing the clock, I thought I had just enough time to drop by Andy and Ed's house. When I approached their front door, Jay was striding down their steps. I ducked behind one of the massive street oaks. After he drove off, I scampered up their steps and rang the doorbell.

Andy swung it open. "What else?" He jumped when he saw me standing on the porch. "Sorry, Merry. I thought you were someone else."

"You thought I was Jay?"

"How did you know Detective Ziebold was here?"

I pointed to my eyes. "Aren't you going to let me in?"

"Of course. It's just so strange to see you at the front door." Andy moved aside so I could enter.

"It's strange for me too. I'm seeing all of your art from a different perspective."

Andy smiled. "Is it better? Or worse?"

"It's always impeccable."

"Ed's in the kitchen getting dinner ready."

I followed Andy and claimed a chair at the island so I could watch Ed work.

Andy sat next to me and placed a glass of wine by my right hand. I grinned. "You know me so well." I took a sip. "Why was Jay here?"

Ed looked up from dicing an onion. "Andy had an argument with Amanda the day she died. Some interfering nosy parker reported it to the police."

"What was the argument about?"

"The same thing it's been about for the last three years. This is old news."

"What did you tell Jay?"

"Just what we told you."

"Did he ask where you were when she was killed?"

Andy raised his glass to Ed. "I think someone's been watching too much TV."

I took a sip of wine and swirled it. "Very amusing. So you just told him your story, and he didn't ask any other questions?"

Andy tapped my nose with his forefinger. "Don't be silly. Of course he wanted to know where we were."

"Well, where were you?"

Ed rolled his eyes at Andy. "Speaking of nosy parkers..."

Andy said, "Ed was in West Virginia. He got a hot lead on some eighteenth century teapots. He was supposed to come home that night, but a snowstorm dumped three feet in his path."

"And you?"

"After such a disappointing day, I worked on the books and then braved the weather to get a drink and dinner at the Pickled Herring. I sat at the bar. Ann's always a hoot. Plus, it was pretty empty with the whole town at the fashion show. There was no way I was going to show up there to give that witch the satisfaction of seeing me." Andy slammed down his wine glass, and it broke.

Ed grabbed a dishtowel, using it carefully to wipe up the wine and pieces of glass. Shaking the dirty towel out over the trash, he left it crumpled at the far end of the counter. "I'll deal with that later." He filled another glass with wine and handed it to Andy. "Temper, Andy, temper. I like these glasses."

Andy took it from him. "Sorry. I'll be more careful." Ed rubbed his back and then scraped the onions into the pot to soften.

I said, "The bar closes at ten early in the week. Where did you go when it closed?"

"If you must know, I hung out with Ann while she closed up shop. After she was done scrubbing down the bar, I accompanied her to her car. Then I came back here, got ready for bed, and went to sleep. I have no alibi for the time Amanda was murdered. It's a good thing the police already have their man, or I'd be in hot water. Is there anything else you wanted to know? The brand of underwear I choose?"

I stood. "This was awkward." I looked into Andy's blue eyes. "Thanks for humoring me. I'm glad we're friends." I hugged him.

Ed frowned. "What am I? Chopped liver? Don't I get a hug too, Ms. Busybody?"

I laughed. "Of course. Although you don't deserve one after that snide comment."

I hugged him, and he whispered into my hair, "If the shoe fits..."

I pushed him away. "Very funny." I put my coat on and left.

Making my way across the alley, I ran up my back stairs. Rob held the door open for me. "I saw you coming across from Andy and Ed's. What were you doing there?"

"Are you cooking bacon? I love that smell." Straining my neck to peer around him, I checked the stove. Bacon sizzled in a frying pan. "Yum. What are you making?"

"Spanish rice. It's my mother's recipe."

I examined the items lined up on the counter. "Looks kind of complicated."

"Not very. Plus, it's a one frying pan dish, so the bonus is easy cleanup."

"Love that. I can't wait to try it."

Rob handed me a glass of wine.

I smiled. "This is my lucky day. In the past hour, two hot men have given me an unbidden glass of wine." I sipped it. "Thanks."

"I'm assuming that the other hot man was either Ed or Andy? Does that mean I don't have to worry?"

"Yes, you're safe."

"Are you going to tell me why you were over there?"

I gave him the details. "So Andy doesn't have an alibi, and Jay doesn't care." I put my head on the counter. "What do we do next?"

Rob rubbed my back. "First, we check Andy's story with Ann. Maybe she knows something. Feel like an after-dinner drink tonight?"

"It's a school night."

"Merry, live on the edge."

I laughed. "Okay, then that's our next step. I guess a small glass of Bailey's wouldn't hurt."

"One last thing before Jenny comes down."

"What?"

"I talked to a reporter in the town where Philip went to high school. He searched the newspaper archives and found that a senior at the school died accidentally while cleaning his gun. It was just after their fall dance."

I frowned. "That's so sad."

"It gets worse. It was the year Philip was a senior. Here's a picture of him and the boy who died in the yearbook. They were both on the basketball team." Rob held out his phone and pointed to a posed picture of two smiling boys holding the same basketball.

"That's Philip."

"Yes, with the boy who died."

My mouth dropped. "You think it wasn't an accident."

He shook his head. "I don't know. It could be a coincidence. I told Jay about it, and he looked into it. The police said that there was no doubt it was just a tragic accident."

I shivered. "When you told me he got back at his friend, I was thinking that he gave him a wedgie. Not that he killed him."

Jenny ran down the stairs, swinging into the kitchen. "Something smells great. Let's eat!"

I gave Rob a warning look, and we set the table.

CHAPTER 20

After cleaning up the dinner dishes, Rob and I left for the Pickled Herring. Ann was working. Lucky for us, it wasn't that crowded. She served us drinks, and we chatted about some school events that were coming up.

I leaned forward. "I was talking to Andy earlier. He mentioned he was here with you during the fashion show."

"He was. I remember because it was so slow that night. If he hadn't come in, I would have been bored to tears. He stayed with me while I cleaned up and then took me to my car. Normally he's so funny, but, boy, he really bent my ear about Amanda. Do you know that she blocked their plans for three years?"

"I heard that."

"He made a last-ditch attempt to get her to sign that morning, and she laughed at him. By his count, she cost them thousands of dollars." Ann rubbed a spot on the bar with a cloth and then leaned against the back counter. "Anyway, I was worried he'd have a stroke. His face was beet red. He pounded on the bar. I couldn't believe he got so worked up. After he escorted me to my car, I saw him stalk away up toward Tempting Treasures. It's a good thing Amanda was at the fashion show, or I think he might have given her a solid piece of his mind." A customer came in. She jumped to attention. "Sorry, got to go."

"Did Andy mention any of that?" Rob asked.

I shook my head. "No. He definitely left that part out."

* * *

The next morning, I towel dried my hair while looking out the window. Susan hurried away from Drew's. I rolled my eyes. *That woman will never learn.* Finishing dressing, I knocked on Jenny's door to make sure she was up and then made my way to the kitchen. I fed the cats and left for the office.

Work was busy, so it was a good thing I still had my leftover sandwich from the day before. I finished it quickly at my desk and moved on to my next task. At five, I realized I barely left my chair. Waving goodbye to Cheryl, I hurried out the door to the chamber of commerce meeting at the library.

Evelyn was behind the desk. "Conference Room B."

I nodded my thanks as I headed in that direction.

It was a quick meeting, with the stickiest point of conversation being when everyone would decorate their shops for Valentine's Day. The consensus was three weeks prior. Some people left grumbling that four weeks would have been better.

As I walked out, Evelyn beckoned to me from her position behind the circulation desk. "Merry, stop for a moment."

I joined her. "How are the grandkids? Are they excited about Christmas?"

"They are jumping out of their skins. They're at that age when they still have no conception of time, so every day they ask if it's Christmas."

I laughed. "We'll have to catch up soon. What did you want?"

"Drew's been here a lot since he got out of jail. It's making some of the other patrons uneasy."

"So?"

"Just thought you'd want to know. Good to see you." She pivoted in place and began to load returns onto the book truck.

I raised my eyebrows at the quick dismissal. Shrugging, I turned to leave, hitting Drew, bouncing back against the desk, and ending up at his feet.

Drew pulled me up. "Merry, we keep on running into each other."

Hazarding a glance behind me, I saw that Evelyn's eyes were wide, and her mouth was shaped in a perfect circle. I pushed out of his grasp.

He said, "It's always such a nice surprise. Are you going home?" Without thinking, I nodded. "Great. We're going the same way. I'll join you."

He linked his arm through mine. I shoved it away. "We can go together, but no touching."

Drew laughed. "You're such a stick-in-the-mud. But, okay. No touching. Is there a mandated number of inches we need to be separated by?"

I rolled my eyes. Drew followed behind me. "What's going on with your case?"

"My lawyer says they're having difficulty matching the bullet to the guns I have. Plus, I don't have a silencer, and they know one was used."

"That must help."

"Not really. The police are still so sure I did it they aren't even looking at anyone else. I'm hoping that someone confesses because, otherwise, it looks like I'll be going to trial. And you know how long that takes."

I gave him a dark look. "Yes, I remember all too well."

"Oh, Merry. Don't get snippy and bent out of shape. You should have some sympathy for me. I'm going through tough times."

I stopped and glared at him. "All of this is your fault. Just like before. It's really hard to feel sorry for you when you leave death and destruction in your wake. Just think what this is doing to Jenny."

"I told her I'd take her to Jamaica when this is all over."

"That's it? A trip? You think that will make everything all right? I've got news for you: a trip to the Caribbean is a start, but you've got a lot of making up to do. And what's going on with Susan?"

He laughed as he tried to kiss me. "Why, I do believe you are jealous. Susan and I are just friends."

I jumped back. "No touching. We agreed no touching."

He put his hands up. "Okay, no touching."

We resumed our walk. I frowned. "Plus, if you want to take Jenny somewhere, I'd appreciate it if you'd talk to me first. I need to make sure that the dates line up with her school break, and it would be good if there are no surprises."

"Always the organized one."

"Someone has to be. And you sure aren't."

He stopped at my gate. "I believe this is where you get off."

Susan appeared like a Valkyrie, two inches from my face. "What are you doing with Drew? I know you're trying to get him back. It's not going to work. He's with me now."

Through gritted teeth, I said, "You two are welcome to each other. And, in fact, you deserve each other. Have a nice life." I opened the gate, slammed it behind me, and stalked up the path into the house.

Jenny jumped away from the window. "What happened out there? It looked like you were going to take a swing at Dad, and then I thought he was going to deck Susan. After you came in, he grabbed her arm and yanked her into his house."

Sinking down on the sofa, I gestured for her to join me. "One of the things you will learn is that relationships are hard and endings are even harder. But the good news is that you have two parents who love you."

"Thanks, Mom. A little less drama might be welcome, though."

"You're the only one who saw us."

My phone dinged with a text from Patty: "Heard threesome went south on the sidewalk. Maybe next time move away from the streetlight?"

I groaned and put my arm around Jenny. "I'll try to do better."

CHAPTER 21

In the middle of the night, my jaw started throbbing. *Oh great, my tooth*. I got up, took two aspirin, and rubbed the area with a dab of clove oil. After a few minutes, it felt slightly better, and I was able to get back to sleep. In the morning, the pain was worse. I called the dentist's office to leave a message that I needed to see someone that day.

The dentist's receptionist called me just past eight. "I can't get you in to see Dr. Philip this morning, but Dr. Malcolm just had a cancellation at ten. Would that work?"

I smiled at this twist of fate. "That would be great. Thanks." I took some more aspirin and put another dab of clove oil on the spot.

I tried to focus through the pain, and I actually accomplished a few things at work. Leaving earlier than necessary for my appointment, I traipsed the three doors down in the hope that Dr. Malcolm would be able to take me earlier.

The receptionist greeted me. "I was just about to call you. Dr. Malcolm's a bit backed up. It should only be a half hour or so. Do you want to come back, or would you like to wait?"

I groaned and sat. "I'll wait."

Holding the side of my face, I tried to relax by watching the neon tetras dart around the fish tank. A school of swordtails swam into my field of vision. I tried leaning back in the chair to get more comfortable. *This is not working. I'm as tense as when I came in.* Giving up on the fish, I took my phone from my purse and scrolled through my e-mails.

The hygienist appeared. "Merry, Dr. Malcolm can see you now." I rose, still holding the side of my mouth. She gave me a sympathetic look. "Poor thing. Does it hurt a lot?"

I nodded as she led me back to the room themed with stars. Somehow they glowed even though the room was well lit. Sidling up to the dental chair, I hesitated.

The hygienist put her hand on my arm. "Don't worry. We'll try to make this as painless as possible." She looked at her computer screen. "Tooth number fourteen. That's the one we talked about last week." Realizing that I still hadn't sat in the chair, she rubbed my arm. "Do you need help getting in the chair?"

"No. I can do it." I eased into the chair, stretching my legs out in front of me. Every muscle tensed as she pushed the lever to lift the chair to a comfortable height.

She hooked the bib around my neck and rubbed my arm again. "You're stiff as a board. Try to relax. It really isn't going to be that bad. Open your mouth."

I did as instructed. She poked around with the probe. When she hit my sore tooth, I shot up like a rocket.

"Ow!" I glared at her.

"Yep, that's the tooth. Sorry about that. I'll get Dr. Malcolm."

I rubbed my jaw. Dr. Malcolm came in. "Hi, Merry. I understand that you have a tooth that's giving you some pain?" I nodded, rubbing my jaw again. "Let's just take a look. Open your mouth." He took the probe, tapping a few of the teeth surrounding the one causing me problems. "Does this hurt? This? This?"

I shook my head. Then he poked my sore tooth. I jumped again. "Yep. That's the tooth."

I groaned. "I told you that was the tooth."

"I know, but sometimes it's really a different tooth. Now that we know for sure which one it is we'll take an X-ray to see what we're looking at."

The hygienist came back in and took the X-ray. After she brought it up on the computer, Dr. Malcolm bent over it. He nodded. "Yep. Look at that decay. It's a good thing you came in now, or we might be talking about a root canal." He patted my shoulder. "Let's get you numbed up and fix this tooth. Try to relax. I'll make this as painless as possible."

After what seemed like a hundred shots of lidocaine, he said, "We'll give this a few minutes. I'll be back."

Mercifully, after a few minutes, my tooth didn't hurt anymore. *Maybe this will work.* My body relaxed for the first time that morning. Letting my eyes wander to the stars above, I recognized the Big Dipper. I followed its outer stars, looking for the North Star. It wasn't there. *They should have the North Star. And where are the Seven Sisters?*

"Merry. I heard you were here. I told you that tooth was going to cause problems."

I jumped as Philip shot into my peripheral vision.

"I see Dr. Malcolm has the lidocaine working." He looked down at me, "You really should relax. You're so tense." He frowned. "You shouldn't feel any pain at this point. Does your tooth still hurt?"

I shook my head. "No, I can't feel it at all."

"Well, then there's nothing to be worried about."

"Are you going to work on me?" I winced, waiting for the answer.

"I'd like to, but I have patients stacked all day today. Dr. Malcolm will take great care of you. I just wanted to stop by to say hello." He patted my shoulder and left.

Letting go of the breath I hadn't realized I was holding, I felt every piece of my body go slack. *Thank goodness he was booked.*

Dr. Malcolm came back in. "Let's fix this tooth."

Two hours later, various parts of my mouth began to wake up. *Minor areas of soreness, but nothing like it was this morning.* I sighed in relief and returned phone calls.

Rob appeared in my doorway at quitting time. I rose to give him a big hug. "You are a sight for sore eyes. And mouth."

"I heard you had that tooth looked at." He tilted my face up. "Is it all better now?"

I laughed. "Yes, all better. And I'm starving. I wasn't able to eat lunch."

"We'll need to fix that. I could make you my signature scrambled eggs if you'd like something easier to eat."

I kissed his cheek. "That does sound tempting, but I think I could handle something more challenging."

"Tell you what. Why don't you go home, get into some comfy clothes, and I'll pick up something on the way. Shall I surprise you?"

"I trust you. You're so good to me." I kissed his cheek again. "A girl could get used to this."

He gave me a look that made my legs want to melt straight off my body. "I hope you do get used to it." Giving me a soft kiss on the lips, he groaned as he pushed himself away. "Meet you in a half hour."

"I'll have the wine waiting."

Blowing me a kiss, he left. I pulled some things together and followed soon after. When I got home, I changed into my favorite sweat pants and T-shirt. I added a hoodie for warmth. Running lightly back down the stairs, I turned the corner and ran straight into Jenny.

"Mom, make a little noise why don't you."

"Sorry. I didn't realize you were here."

"I just got here. What's for dinner?" She put her hands on her hips.

I laughed. "I have no idea."

She pouted. "But I'm hungry. We had basketball practice. You know that chews up a lot of calories."

I patted her arm. "Not to worry. Rob will be here soon with dinner." I opened the refrigerator and took out some carrot sticks. "Munch on these while you get changed. I promise he'll be here soon."

She took three, biting one as she pivoted and ran up the stairs. I poured two glasses of wine and a glass of milk for Jenny. Just as I finished setting the table, Rob came in with dinner, holding bags from our local gourmet grocer.

He held them up. "I figured rotisserie chicken, some green beans, and mashed potatoes with gravy would be best." He smiled. "Some comfort food for you."

"Yum. I especially love comfort food I don't have to work for." I helped him unload the bags. I held up a chocolate cream pie. "Is this part of making me feel better?"

"I'm willing to go along with that."

Jenny thundered down the stairs. "Something smells great!"

Everyone sat to enjoy the food. After dinner, I cut the pie and handed slices around.

Jenny stared at hers. "Would anyone mind if I took mine upstairs? I need to study."

Rob and I nodded our agreement, having already taken a bite of the pie. Jenny grabbed hers and headed upstairs.

Rob finished his mouthful. "She studies a lot. Do you ever worry she's missing out?"

I traced circles through the whipped cream with my fork. "No. She's getting good grades and participates in other activities. I worry more about what this whole thing with Drew is going to do to her."

"She'll be fine. You've given her a great grounding." He gestured toward me with his fork. "You're a good mom."

I smiled as I took another bite of pie.

"Guess who I ran into at the store?"

"Who?"

"Susan. She was picking up some food for her and Drew. While we were in line, she made sure to tell me they've been talking about moving in together."

I raised my eyebrows. "She's moving in? I guess moss doesn't grow on her." Shifting in my seat, I frowned. "Drew's not setting a good example for Jenny. And it makes me rethink whether he really cared for Amanda. Maybe he did kill her." I stared hard at Drew's house. "This is so confusing."

Rob rubbed my shoulder. "I don't want you to take this the wrong way, but Drew doesn't seem like someone who believes in commitment."

I twisted my napkin. "I think you may be right."

* * *

Rubbing the steam from my bathroom window, I read the outside thermometer: thirty-four degrees. And the trees weren't doing their normal wind-whipped shimmy. *Positively balmy*. Smiling, I finished dressing, rapped on Jenny's door, and danced down the stairs.

I opened the back door to feel the air. Drambuie bounded past me, sensing freedom in her grasp. She got about two feet from the house and realized there was still a lot of white stuff in the yard. Almost levitating, she shook all four paws at once. She used the open door as a springboard to propel herself back inside. Courvoisier yawned from her perch on the kitchen stool and gave Drambuie a baleful look that seemed to say she was an embarrassment to the species.

I laughed, retrieved my coat, and decided to take the long way to work. That brought me past Tempting Treasures. The construction noise was deafening, even out on the sidewalk. Looking through the window, I saw Andy talking to the general contractor. I poked my head in the door and waved.

He shouted, "I can't let you in without a hard hat, so I'll come outside." He joined me on the stoop and slammed the door. "That's much better. I can hear now."

"If you think this is better, you should be wearing earplugs inside."

He grimaced. "You may be right."

"I can't believe you're already building the new place out."

He rolled his eyes. "We've had the plans for three years. All of our tinkering ended long ago, so we're very clear on what needs to happen when. We were lucky that the contractor we wanted just finished a job." He rubbed his forehead. "Huh. Maybe we should thank Amanda for that." He paused. "Not."

"That's not very nice."

"No. I suppose it wasn't. What did you want?"

"Nothing really. I was just looking in and thought it would be rude if I didn't stop."

Andy pierced me with his baby blues. "How long have I known you? What did you want?"

"I was just wondering if you saw anyone else the night Amanda was killed?"

"Why do you want to pin this on me? I thought we were friends." He glowered at me. "As far as I'm concerned, they've charged the right person. And the last time I looked, you hated Drew. I'm warning you: leave it alone."

I backed away with my hands raised. "You are my friends, my very dear friends." I closed the gap between us and put my hand on his arm. "I just don't want my daughter's father to be a murderer. He may really have done it." I shook my head. "I don't know how she would survive that. It would just be too awful." Sinking down onto his front stoop, I put my arms around my legs and rested my head on my knees.

Sighing, he sat and put his arm around me. "You're strong. Jenny's strong. You will survive this, and so will she. I'm sorry I yelled at you, but it's unnerving to have the police asking questions, and now you're doing it. Ed and I had nothing to do with this. Amanda cost us money and time, but that's not something either one of us would kill over. You're going to have to trust me."

I leaned against him. "I know that. Drew really messed with my head. And my heart." I put my arm around him and squeezed. "I'm sorry I made you mad." I got up, brushing off my slacks.

He stood and kissed my forehead. "You're a good person, Merry, but you need to drop this."

That certainly could have gone better. Note to self: be more discreet with my questions. I continued to my office, my mood improving as I admired the Christmas displays in the shop windows. Stopping in front of a pop-up Santa shop, I drooled over one in chaps saddling his horse. *Need to start dropping hints with Jenny.* Turning in at my door, I was pleased to see that everyone looked quite industrious. I made my way back to Cheryl and gave her a cheery wave as I shut the door.

Cheryl knocked briskly as she opened the door. "Sorry to bother you, but you may want to return this call." She placed a message slip on my desk and scurried out.

I looked at it and sighed. It was from Susan Clime. *May as well get it over with.*

She answered on the first ring. "Hi, Merry. Thanks for returning my call. I'm sure Rob told you that Drew and I are thinking about moving in together." I pulled the phone away from my ear, staring at it. "Merry, are you there?"

"Yes, I'm here. But I'm still wondering why you called. Why would I care?"

"I wanted to talk to you so that we can set some ground rules with Jenny. I don't want her bopping in and out whenever she pleases. When I start living there, it'll be my house too. I want to have a set schedule that we stick to..."

Rolling my eyes, I put my head down on my desk, unable to believe what I was hearing. I sat up. "Susan, I'm not going to discuss my daughter's visitation schedule with you. I'm also not going to limit her access to her father. If he wants to call me to talk this over, I'll take that call. Are we clear?"

"I bet you think he doesn't want me to move in. Well, he does. He's in love with me, not you, and he was never in love with that witch Amanda. I'm glad she's gone. I wish you and your stupid daughter were gone too. Hmm. Things have been going my way lately; maybe I'll get lucky."

"Is that a threat? Listen here. You're welcome to Drew. But I don't want you within ten feet of my daughter. Do you understand?"

A click sounded. Mouth agape, I stared at my phone. *She hung up on me?* I threw it down, leaping up. Pacing, I stormed from one wall to the other. I kicked the wall.

Cheryl stuck her head in. "The wall's going to win every time."

I rubbed my foot. "You're right. That was a bad idea."

"Are you okay? I'm sure your conversation wasn't pleasant. Is Susan trying to get her job back?"

I choked out a laugh. "Nope. It's worse than that. Can you see if you can reach Detective Ziebold for me and ask him if he can swing by?" I tapped my cheek. "No, wait a minute. See if he's available for lunch. My treat at the Golden Skillet."

"Will do. Let me know if you need anything else." As she left, she tossed a worried glance over her shoulder. A few minutes later, she knocked again. "You're on for eleven thirty." I still stood in the same place, staring out the window. "Are you sure you're okay?"

"No. But I will be." I put my hand on her shoulder. "Thanks for your help. I really do appreciate it."

As she left, I sat at my desk. Trying to power through, I opened a spreadsheet. After several mistakes, I closed it. I grabbed my purse and coat and nodded to Cheryl on my way out.

Jay waited for me by the host station at the Golden Skillet. "I love a free lunch, but I have a funny feeling I'm going to be paying for it."

I nodded. "You may not be far off." We ordered lunch, and I told him about my conversation with Susan.

"I'll have a talk with her, but I question if it was a direct threat." Jay put more salt on his fries. "You should know that after the episode at the church, Susan met with me."

"Really? What did she want?"

"She said that she was willing to testify that the money Drew gave her to hold was from the scam he pulled in town."

My eyes widened. "That's not what she told me. She said she thought that the money she got was from my account." I frowned at the table. "If she's moving in with him, why would she want to turn him in? That doesn't make any sense." I looked up. "Why would she do that?"

He gestured with a French fry. "That's easy. She was mad at the time. Not surprisingly, she stopped by yesterday and tried to recant. It's too late for that. The Feds are involved now and it's not looking good for Drew. If he gets off on the murder charge, this will be hanging over his head."

I slumped in my chair. "If he finds out that she's working with the Feds, he's not going to be happy."

Jay nodded. "I know I can trust you to keep your mouth shut. I'll talk to Susan today. You have my promise. And now I have to get back on duty." He tipped his hat to me as he left the restaurant.

Stirring my tea, I took one last sip before leaving. One thing for sure, I need to talk to Drew and give him a piece of my mind.

CHAPTER 22

I called Drew from the office and asked him to meet me for dinner. The terms were I'd meet him there, we'd go Dutch, and there would be no touching. After some teasing, he agreed.

I texted Rob, "Meeting Drew for dinner at six at Fiorella's to talk about Jenny visitation. Can you come by my house at nine?"

He replied with a shocked face emoji. "Fine. See you then. Be safe."

I sent him a thumbs-up.

As I drove to the restaurant, my palms slid on the steering wheel, and I popped two antacids. *Be an adult. Divorced people have these conversations all the time.* Scanning for an empty spot in the parking lot, I spied one and swung into it. I took a deep breath and put my head down on the steering wheel. A sharp rap on the window sounded like a gong going off next to my head. I jumped. Laughing, Drew peered in.

I scowled as I opened the door. "You scared me."

He grinned. "I don't know why. You knew I was going to meet you here."

"Inside. I thought we were going to meet inside."

He rolled his eyes. "We got here at the same time. Why would I ignore you?"

"Whatever." I shoved past him. "Let's go in."

They had a booth ready, and we slid in on opposite sides. Drew tilted his head, giving me a wistful smile. "Remember the old days when we used to sit next to each other?"

I glared at him. "Thank goodness those days are long over."

"I just thought of a new rule we should have for tonight. No snarkiness."

Leaning back, I exhaled. "You're right. Let's talk like civilized people. The point of this dinner is to try and set some rules on visitation for Jenny."

His eyebrow rose. "Isn't everything okay the way it is now?" He frowned. "Has Jenny been complaining?"

"No. I just thought it would be easier down the line if we set up some ground rules now."

He picked up his napkin-wrapped silverware and shook the cutlery out. Placing the napkin on his lap he mumbled, "You and your rules."

I shook my finger at him. "No snarkiness."

He grabbed my finger and kissed it. "You're right. My bad."

I snatched my hand back. "And no touching."

He grinned. "Getting back to our conversation, what prompted your concern?"

"Since Susan's moving in with you, I assumed things would be changing."

His face slackened. "Why would you think Susan's moving in? She's just a friend, and, anyway, I just lost Amanda."

"Drew, I've seen Susan sneaking out of your house in the mornings. Jenny found her in your kitchen in your robe. We're not stupid."

He leaned forward. "Okay. So she's a friend with benefits. But I haven't asked her to move in. I'm fine with the way things are." He paused. "I probably shouldn't say this to you, but I really cared about Amanda." His voice cracking, he stared at the ceiling and took my hand. He stared down at it. "I miss her."

I yanked my hand back. "It's tough for me to believe you when you've lied about everything." I frowned. "At any rate, you really have to do something about Susan. She called me today and told me she was moving in. She also said that she didn't want Jenny around as much."

Drew's face turned an impressive shade of burgundy. He stood. "That bitch! I'm going to kill her." He stormed out of the restaurant.

The waitress sidled up to the table, concern etching her face. "Will you be dining alone tonight?"

My mouth still open, I shook my head. "I think I'll go home. Sorry for putting you out."

I texted Rob from the parking lot: "No dinner. Feel like making me your special scrambled eggs?"

"No problem. Meet at your place in fifteen?"

"Yep."

Rob arrived a few minutes after me. Giving me a kiss on the cheek, he held me at arm's length, concerned eyes running over me for any visible hurts. "Are you okay?"

I hugged him. "I'm fine. But I'm not sure about Susan."

He pushed me away again and looked down at me. "Susan? Was she there?"

I sat at the counter, shaking my head. "Drew was surprised to learn that she was moving in with him."

"What? They hadn't agreed on it? Then why did she tell me they had?"

"Who knows?" I poured myself a glass of wine. Raising the bottle toward him, he nodded, so I poured him one as well. I sat back down. "Susan called me today. She said she didn't want Jenny dropping by unannounced anymore."

His eyebrows rose. "What did you say?"

"I told her that it was a matter for Drew and me." I took a long sip of my wine and then gestured with the glass toward Rob. "Oh, and Drew was surprised about her weighing in on Jenny too."

"Wow. What did he say when you told him?"

"He stalked out and said he was going to kill her."

My phone dinged. A text from Patty read, "Heard crossing of swords at Fiorella's tonight. Drew's going to kill someone?"

"How did you hear that?"

"Patrick's nephew is a dishwasher there."

"Unbelievable. I'll call you tomorrow."

She sent me a hug emoji.

I handed my phone to Rob. He said, "Word does travel fast. And Fiorella's is two towns over."

I nodded. "That's why I picked it. I figured we wouldn't be as noticeable there."

Rob stood. "Now you know that the ears in this town are super powered." He pulled the eggs, butter, and cheese from the refrigerator. "Ready for some food?"

"Yes, please." He worked his magic and placed the plate in front of me.

Jenny trudged through the door but stopped when she saw what I was eating. A smile brightened her face. "Breakfast for dinner. My fav!" Dropping her coat and knapsack on the floor, she joined me at the counter, eyeing Rob expectantly.

He sighed. "Just call me a short-order cook." He reached for more eggs.

I elbowed her. "Weren't you supposed to be eating out tonight?"

"I was, but when I realized how much homework I had, I decided to come home and fend for myself." She smiled at Rob. "But this is so much better than anything I would have made."

He handed her a plate of eggs and buttered some toast. "Anything else?"

She smiled at him. “I hate to put you out, but can I have some jam for the toast?”

Laughing, he pulled it from the fridge and handed it to her.

She took a bite of the eggs and closed her eyes. “Did you put cheddar in this?”

“Yep.”

“Tastes great.” She gestured with her fork. “You can cook for me anytime.”

“It would be my honor.” He leaned against the sink and took a sip of his wine.

Jenny finished her plate. “What happened with you and Dad? I thought you were having dinner with him?”

“He needed to get back, and I was still hungry.”

She raised an eyebrow. “I heard you had a fight at Fiorella’s. I’m guessing you didn’t even eat.” She scanned the kitchen. “I guess that means you didn’t bring home any cannoli.”

“Sorry, kid. And I’m not even going to ask how you knew we had a fight.”

She looked smug. “I know all.” Her face darkened. “Was it the usual, or is it something I need to be worried about?”

“Nothing you need to worry about. Your dad and I still love you.” I kissed her cheek.

“Well if you didn’t bring me cannoli, what else do we have for dessert?”

“You could look.” She just stared at me. “Off the top of my head, we have ice cream in here and muffins and cinnamon rolls in the freezer outside.” I opened the pantry door. “And we have some store-bought cookies.”

“Tough choice.” She elbowed me out of the way and grabbed the chocolate chunk pecan cookies. “Maybe not so tough after all.” She poured a glass of milk.

Rob asked, "You're not planning to take that whole bag upstairs, are you?"

She smiled. "No, of course not." Taking two cookies out, she laid them on a napkin and then exited with the rest of the bag and her milk. Laughter echoed up the stairway.

Rob frowned. "Could she spare them?"

I laughed. "Eat those, and if you want more, I have another bag in the back."

He smiled and popped one of the cookies in his mouth. "You know, these aren't half bad." He ate the second one and looked at me expectantly.

I sighed and rummaged through the pantry. Successful, I held up the bag.

Rob ripped it open and downed another cookie. He stared out the window. Then he backed up and turned off the kitchen light.

"What are you doing?"

He pointed toward the alley running between my house and Andy's. I caught sight of Andy as he ducked into one of the shadows past Drew's back porch lights. He looked like he was dressed to blend into the darkness. "Where do you think he's going?"

CHAPTER 23

Swiping a dust rag around the living room the next morning, I took care to return all the Santas to their previous positions. Next, I began the mindless task of vacuuming, running it back and forth across the rug. It pinged as it picked up dead needles from the tree. Then a low moan rose over the roar of the vacuum, ending with a high-pitched squeal. *Great. Need to shop for a new vacuum. Just what I want to spend my money on.* I bent over the canister and tried to figure out where the noise was coming from. I jumped when Jenny clasped me on the shoulder.

She switched off the machine. "Mom, it's the police, not the vacuum. They're at Dad's again."

We rushed to the bay window just in time to see Drew being led out of the house in handcuffs. "What on earth?"

Jenny dove for the phone and pressed it into my hand. "You have to call his lawyer."

Looking over at the refrigerator for her card, I moaned. "Darn. I gave her card to Melissa."

Jenny pulled out her phone and googled the firm. She read the number to me, and I called Kendall. "Drew was arrested!"

"Not surprising. I heard about his threats last night. It's not exactly the low profile I advised him to take. I'll meet him at the station."

"Please let me know what happened."

"I'll call to give you an update later today." She hung up.

Jenny clung to me. "What's going on, Mom?"

I rubbed her shoulder. "I don't know, but I'll find out."

Rob rushed in the back door. "Did you hear?"

"Yes, they just took Drew away. I guess making a public threat is a violation of parole."

He panted. "Not about Drew. About Susan." Jenny and I gave him blank expressions. He grabbed my hand. "She's been killed. And it looks like it was the same person who killed Amanda."

Jenny paled, swaying like a willow in the wind. Rob raced over to catch her just as she started to sink to the ground. He put her in a chair.

I bent over her. "Put your head between your knees and breathe. You'll be okay in a minute. You've just had a terrible shock."

I rubbed her back. After a few minutes, she raised her head. "I'm feeling better now." Still looking pale, she tried to stand and then sank back down.

I turned to Rob. "Can you make her some hot chocolate? I have some instant in the cupboard, so you just have to nuke some water. Put an extra teaspoon of sugar in it."

He bustled around the kitchen and brought over a steaming mug piled high with whipped cream. Jenny lifted her head, taking a sip. Color returning to her face, she sat back.

I said, "Try to take a little more, honey."

She complied. "Maybe some marshmallows would help."

Relieved, I gave a short laugh. Rob retrieved them and handed her the bag. She dropped in a handful and took another sip. "Much better."

Rob sat. I mouthed, "Thank you."

She finished the hot chocolate and stood, both of us gripping her arms. Impatient, she shook us off. "I feel better now." She took a few trial steps. "Thanks. I'm going up to my room."

I frowned. "I'll go with you."

"I'm not ten. I can go up to my room by myself."

"I'll just see you up the stairs. You've had a shock, and I don't want you tumbling down."

She rolled her eyes. "If it will make you feel better."

I needed to jog to keep up with her as she raced up the stairs. Reaching her door, she looked back over her shoulder. "Told you." She shut the door, and her music filled the air, the dull thud of the downbeat echoing through the hall, causing the floor to vibrate.

I returned to Rob. He asked, "Is she okay?"

Nodding, I poured two cups of coffee and sat at the counter. "Tell me everything you know."

He leaned against the sink. "She was killed sometime last night. Similar to Amanda, one gunshot wound. She was found just inside her door, as if she answered it and whoever was there shot her."

I frowned. "That looks bad for Drew."

Rob came around the counter and rubbed my back. "It certainly does."

"How was she found so quickly?"

"She was supposed to be volunteering at the church for the rummage sale."

"And?"

"Drew's threats were the talk of the sale. When she didn't show up on time to help set up, the police were called. Her door was ajar, so the police entered and found her."

"Wow." The mug clanged as I misjudged the distance to the counter. Jerking up, I walked over to the window and stared out. Arms folded across my chest, I faced Rob. "Hear me out."

"Of course."

"Everyone in town knew about his threat last night. That means it would be a perfect chance for whoever killed Amanda to murder Susan. The killer would know Drew would be charged."

Rob stared at me in disbelief. "That's pretty convoluted. What possible motive would someone have to kill both of them?"

"To cement the fact that Drew was the killer." I threw my hands up in the air. "I don't know. It just looks bad for him." I stared at the counter. "And I know something that makes it look even worse."

Rob raised his eyebrow. "What could possibly make this worse?"

"After the church debacle between Drew and Susan, she went to Jay. She told him and the Feds that she'd be willing to testify against him."

Rob's eyes widened. "And now she won't be able to."

I nodded and put my head down on the counter.

He rubbed my back and tilted my face toward his. "You're going to have to prepare yourself. Jay could be right. Drew may be the killer."

* * *

Later that evening, Drew's lawyer called. "They're holding him without the possibility of bail. I'll be preparing for trial on both counts."

"What can I do to help?"

"Pray."

I hung up the phone and crept upstairs. As I pressed open the door to Jenny's room, the hall light glanced off her face. She was sound asleep. Tears flowed as I blew her a kiss and softly closed the door.

Unable to sleep, I pulled out an old photo album. Jenny must have been around five. Drew and I looked so young, so innocent. I laughed at the picture of Jenny with her face pressed against the goldfish bowl. Poor Goldie. Her life ended way too soon, a victim of overfeeding. As my finger caressed the picture, I remembered Drew conducting a funeral for Goldie as we buried her in the backyard, even picking out solemn music for Jenny's procession with the shoebox-encased body. *He was so kind then, and we were so in love. What happened?*

I put the album down and paced. Drew probably did it. No, Philip or Andy must have done it. I stopped in my tracks to make a vow. Tomorrow I'm going to dig further. I need to know who killed Amanda and Susan. The clock chimed two. Swallowing a sleeping pill, I lay back down, my eyes squeezed shut and teeth clenched. Must relax.

My phone dinged. Flinging out my arms, I tried to grab it but knocked my lamp off the end table. It teetered for a moment but then fell to the floor with an impressive crash. My door banged open, and the cats ran out.

Jenny stood there, eyes wide. "Mom, what happened?"

I yawned. "I knocked over my lamp."

She came around the side of the bed. "It's a goner."

Leaning over and viewing the carnage, I nodded.

Jenny hopped into bed. "Scooch over. It's cold out."

I complied, and she yanked the covers over herself, hogging them. "Hey."

She laughed. "You snooze, you lose." Relenting, she gave me some. "Why did you knock the lamp over?"

"I heard a text come in."

"From whom?"

"I don't know." I gestured for her to hand me my phone. She glanced at it. "It's from your boyfriend. He wants to know if you want to go to the ten-thirty Mass."

I groaned. "It's only seven." I texted back, "Fine." I burrowed more deeply under the covers. Shutting my eyes and hovering at the edge of sleep, I was yanked back to consciousness by the poke of a sharp fingernail. "Ow."

"Wake up, Mom. I want to talk."

I pried one eye open to find Jenny staring at me. Sighing, I put two pillows behind me and sat up. "What would you like to talk about?"

"Dad. What else?"

"What would you like to know?"

She winced. "You don't think he did it, do you?"

I touched her face. "I really hope he didn't. But things don't look good right now for him."

She nodded slowly. "When are they going to let him out on bail?"

"They're not. I spoke with his lawyer last night, and she said he'll be in until the trial."

Jenny put her head on my shoulder. My pajama top soon became sodden. I stroked her golden hair. "I can't promise you that everything is going to be okay, but he has a good lawyer. She's well respected. It's going to take time, though."

She broke away and sat up. "Dad will miss Christmas. He'll be in jail again. Just like the last four years."

"I know." I put my arm around her and pulled her to me. Her snuffling finally gave way to light snoring as the ceiling fan continued its slow revolution above the bed. Feeling pins and needles in my arm, I gently maneuvered it out, replacing it with a small pillow. Murmuring in her sleep, Jenny turned over. I got out of bed and padded downstairs.

Coffee maker on, I fed the cats and toasted myself a bagel. I made my way into the living room. Setting my food and mug down, I plugged in the tree and flicked on the fireplace. As I sat, I pulled the afghan around me and took a bite of the bagel. The clock chimed nine. *Need to think about a shower.*

Jenny shook my shoulder. "Weren't you going to meet Mr. Jenson for the ten-thirty?"

I stretched. "I must have dozed off. What time is it?"

"Ten. You left your phone in bed. He texted to find out if you wanted to have breakfast after church."

Screeching, I leapt off the couch. "Text him. Tell him I'll be late and will meet him inside."

Running upstairs, I took a quick sink bath and threw some mascara on. I dashed into my clothes and was back downstairs in twenty minutes.

Jenny smiled from her prone position on the couch. "A new world's record."

I threw a pillow at her. "You better be planning on going to the noon Mass." She nodded as I raced out the door.

The choir was on the first hymn as I eased myself into the seat next to Rob. He looked at me with a question in his eyes.

I whispered, "Don't ask."

Finally calming down halfway through the homily, my eye was caught by a couple sitting a few rows in front of us. I elbowed Rob and said out of the corner of my mouth, "Philip and Lauren Stamper." I nodded in their direction.

Rob's eyes widened. "They must be back together."

At the end of Mass, I saw them ahead of us in the vestibule talking to Father Tom. I nodded at Rob. "Let's try to catch up with them."

Rob ducked into the next pew and moved from the clogged center aisle to one of the side aisles. I followed. We emerged in the vestibule just as Philip and Lauren were saying goodbye to Father Tom.

Rob waved at Philip. "Wait up."

Philip and Lauren smiled, stopping by the door. Rob joined them. "Merry and I were just going for breakfast. We'd like to have you join us."

Lauren looked at Philip, and he nodded. "That sounds great. Golden Skillet in ten minutes?"

"We'll see you there."

Philip clasped Lauren's hand and held the car door for her.

I said, "I wonder when they got back together."

Lauren and Philip stood in front of the restaurant when we pulled in. When we joined them, Philip explained, "We were out here enjoying the sunshine."

Rob nodded. “I know. The sun is such an iffy proposition. It seems like it disappears in winter, only to come back in spring.”

Smiling in agreement, Lauren and I led the way into the restaurant. The host sat us right away, and we ordered soon after.

I put my napkin on my lap. “I stopped at Tempting Treasures on my way to work the other day. I was surprised how fast the construction is going.”

Lauren gave me a strained smile. “It doesn’t seem that fast to me. The noise makes conversations with my clients difficult.” Relaxing, she sat back. “I shouldn’t complain. I can’t wait for them to be done. Ed’s cooking will drive people to my door. Right now I don’t have to give directions to my office. I just say follow the noise.”

“When are they going to be done?”

“Andy told me about three more weeks. They might have finished sooner, but the Christmas holiday will slow things down.”

I played with my silverware. “I’m surprised Andy wanted to start before Christmas. It seems like he would want to maximize sales by beginning in January.”

“I asked him about that. He said that the construction is a draw. People in this town are so nosy they’re checking out progress several times a week. He’s now keeping hard hats by the door and said this has been one of his busiest Christmases. He’s keeping one section of the store closed off from the construction that has items most likely to sell during the holidays.”

Rob said, “I guess Amanda’s death ended up being good for their business.”

Philip gasped, and Lauren rubbed his shoulder. Rob said, “I’m sorry. I didn’t think about how difficult this discussion would be for you.”

Philip sipped his coffee. “That’s okay. Everyone knows that Amanda dumped me. I’m just glad my blinders were taken off so that I could come back to this lovely lady here." He cupped Lauren's face and gave her a quick kiss on her cheek.

Beaming, Lauren kissed his hand. "That's right. I don't want to be insensitive, but Amanda's gone and I'm happy to see people moving on with their lives. Especially this handsome fellow." She leaned closer to Philip.

I smiled. "So what have you two been up to lately?"

Lauren said, "Philip had a dental emergency Friday night. I just love hearing him talk about work. It's so fascinating."

I started to raise my eyebrows. I quickly lowered them when I realized she was serious. *Yuck.*

Rob stirred his coffee. "Really? Who had the emergency?"

"I can't say. Patient confidentiality rules, you know."

Rob nodded. "So you were gone all night?"

"Till the wee hours anyway. Why?"

"No reason. I just thought I saw you over by the supermarket around ten."

Philip's head popped up as if the crank had been turned on a jack-in-the-box. "Couldn't have been me."

Lauren stroked his hand. "Anyway, I was home alone. It gave me a chance to watch *Casablanca*. Have you ever seen it?"

I smiled, and Rob said, "It's one of our favorites." I blushed and knocked over my coffee cup while reaching for the salt.

The coffee traveled quickly toward Lauren. Rob and I grabbed extra napkins from the waiter station, dumping them in the coffee's path. "I'm so sorry, Lauren. I think the adrenaline is kicking in, what with Susan's death."

Lauren jumped up. "Susan is dead?"

I nodded. "You didn't hear? It happened sometime Friday night."

Philip frowned. "Such a shame. She works for you, right?"

I shook my head. "No. Not now. She did in the past."

Lauren sank back onto her chair. "It's just such a shock. I spoke with her Thursday. She was so excited about moving in with Drew." She clapped her hand over her mouth. "I'm sorry, Merry. That's probably a sore subject for you."

I waved my hand to reassure her. "Water under the bridge."

"Do the police know who did it?" Lauren asked.

"They've arrested Drew."

Philip leaned back in his chair with a slight smile on his face. Rob cocked his head. "What's so funny?"

"Not funny, ironic. The police released him after he killed Amanda. Now they have to believe he is the murderer." He frowned. "It's just too bad that it took another killing for them to do the right thing and keep him in jail."

I said, "They released him on bail. He was still going to have to stand trial. No one else needed to be killed."

Philip grimaced. "That's not exactly what I said."

Lauren rubbed his back. "It's just such a surprise for all of us. Let's change the subject."

Philip's face relaxed. "Good idea." He picked up the salt shaker. "How's the tooth doing? Did Dr. Malcolm do a good job?"

Still bothered by Philip's accusation, I tried to smile but only got halfway there. "He's a great dentist. I was lucky he was able to fit me in on such short notice." I tapped the side of my mouth. "See? No pain."

"I'm glad he was able to help. I'm sorry I was so slammed that day or I would have seen you."

"I appreciate your concern, but everything turned out fine."

Philip said, "This has been fun, but I promised Lauren a trip to the movies today."

I dabbed my lips with the napkin and stood. "We need to get moving too."

Rob and Philip haggled over the check. Rob said, "I'll let you pay next time when we're going somewhere more expensive."

Philip laughed and handed Rob the check. "Let's go shooting again sometime soon." Hands clasped, Philip and Lauren left the restaurant.

I moved closer to Rob. "No alibi."

He rolled his eyes. "That we know about. He could have had a real dental emergency."

"That's something I'm going to find out."

CHAPTER 24

Returning home, I put a load of laundry in the wash and settled down to do some work in my office. My hand kept reaching for the phone. Finally, I picked it up and punched in Pam Gruber's number.

"Hi, Merry. How are you? I was just thinking about that sour cream pound cake you made for the church bake sale. Would you send me the recipe?" She laughed. "I'm sorry. You called me. What's up?"

"First, I'd be happy to send you the recipe. I'll e-mail it to you as soon as we get off the phone. Second, the reason for my call was to understand the timing of your billing system."

"Our billing system?"

"Yes. I saw Dr. Malcolm last week. How long would it take for you to get the information to send out a bill?"

"Is money tight? We can set up a payment plan for you if this is a bad time. I sure know it's tight in our house, what with Christmas and all. I'm glad you're reaching out. Some people don't for too long, and then we have to turn debts over to creditors. I hate that."

My face burned. "No, it's not that, although I probably did overspend on Jenny. I need to move some money around and wanted to get an idea of how much time I had."

"Oh. Well, everything's computerized these days. As soon as the service is provided, it's uploaded to the insurance company. Once we hear back from them, we send you a bill. Let me see here. Yes. You saw Dr. Malcolm last week, so you should get the bill from us sometime in early January."

"Thanks. That's really helpful." Doodling with my pencil, I drew the beginnings of a noose. "Hey, one more thing while I'm on the phone. Do you have a moment?"

"Sure. The kids won't be back for another hour. I love Sundays."

I smiled. "What would happen if there were some type of dental emergency?"

"Same thing, but we'd tack on a fee for the emergency visit."

"So the dentist would always log it in even if it happened outside business hours?"

"I've trained them well. They know how important it is to keep good records so that they get paid." She laughed. "And like us, they do like to get paid."

"Let's test it."

"What did you have in mind?"

"Rob and I had breakfast with Dr. Philip this morning. He told us he had a dental emergency on Friday night."

"Merry, you know I can't disclose patient information."

"I don't need to know who the patient was." I mimed the word *yet*. "I'm just curious to see if he actually entered it in the system. Let's see how good your training is."

She chuckled. "I'm up for the challenge. It would be easier if I knew who the patient was, but I can look for procedures done Friday night. Huh. I'm not seeing anything. The last entry for Dr. Philip was Friday at four thirty." She typed furiously. "Nope. Nothing there. I'm sure he'll input it on Monday. And if it's not there by Wednesday, he'll get a follow-up from me." She typed some more. "There. I've set a follow-up for myself. Anything else? It appears I still have some training to do."

"Thanks for the lesson. I appreciate it. I'll make sure to move some money around by early January."

"While you're at it, you could send some to my account as a late Christmas present. Take care."

Moving the laundry from the washing machine to the dryer on autopilot, I texted Rob, "Philip lied."

A few minutes later, I received back, "????" My phone rang. Rob asked, "How did you find that out? Are you sure?"

"Pretty sure."

"I'm just wrapping up a story. I'll be there in about a half hour."

Deciding to wipe down my kitchen cupboards, I filled a small bucket with water and vinegar. I pulled a chair over, climbing onto the counter. I cleaned several upper cabinets before stretching for one of the tall ones just as Rob came in.

"Merry, what are you doing?"

"What does it look like I'm doing?"

"Trying to kill yourself. Don't you have a ladder?"

"This is easier."

He helped me down and kissed my forehead. "Broken bones would be bad."

I twirled in a circle, my arms out. "See? Nothing broken." I poured out the dirty water and rinsed the bucket.

Sitting at the counter, he patted the seat next to him. "Tell me how you know that Philip has no alibi."

I told him about my conversation with Pam.

Rob poured two cups of coffee and handed me one. "Philip could just be a sloppy bookkeeper."

"I don't think Philip has a sloppy bone in his body."

"True. Everything in his life is pretty orderly. But, from what he said this morning, he didn't finish till late. Maybe he just hasn't entered the procedure. It's only Sunday."

"Pam seemed so sure that he would have. Plus, you thought you saw him at the supermarket. Susan's apartment building is adjacent to that lot."

"It is suspicious. I'll give you that."

"Do you think we should call Jay?"

"Not yet. He's pretty set on Drew, and I'm not sure that a bookkeeping lag would make him change his mind. I'll text Philip and see if he wants to go to the range with me sometime this week." Finishing his coffee, Rob rinsed his mug and put it in the dishwasher. "I hate to listen and run, but I have a few more things to do before I put the paper to bed." He kissed me and left.

Picking up the vacuum cleaner, I decided to do the vents. As I bent over and stuck the attachment in one as far as I could reach, Andy grabbed me by the waist. I jumped and glowered at him. "Why did you sneak up on me?"

He laughed. "You really do need to invest in a new vacuum cleaner." He lifted the canister to check it out. "One from this century. Yours sounds like a jet engine." Since he was still laughing, I gave him the fish eye. He cleared his throat. "I even knocked."

"That's something new."

"I saw Rob leave and figured I may as well, as there was no chance to catch you in a compromising position." Laughing again, he playfully hit my shoulder. "Lighten up, Merry."

Giving him a half smile, I edged around him to sit on the sofa. He sat in the chair opposite me. "What's new?"

"I can't wait for the construction to be done. Either I'm there at the shop stumbling over things, or Ed's staying late. One of us has to be there to make sure things get done the way we want. Ed didn't get home Friday night till nearly eleven."

I raised one eyebrow. "Your construction crew works that late?"

"No, silly. They did work till five, though. We offered them a bonus if they finish the job early. Ed was cleaning up so that I didn't have to get there at the crack of dawn Saturday to get things ready to open."

"Good. Because I was thinking you needed to be asking Ed some pretty tough questions."

Laughing, Andy sat back on the sofa and crossed his legs. "No worries on that score. So dish. I saw the police drag your no-good ex out of his house yesterday morning." Standing up, he wandered to the tree to play with my octopus ornament. Shaking its legs and turning it in his hand he said, "Shame about Susan."

"It is. We had our differences, but I'm sorry she was killed."

"Have you spoken with Drew?"

"No."

He held the ornament up. "Who puts an octopus on their tree? Who would even make an octopus ornament for a tree?" Frowning, he rehung it.

"Me. I put odd ornaments on trees. They remind me of trips. Jenny and I bought the octopus in Bar Harbor, Maine, when we went to Acadia National Park last year."

"Does Maine even have octopuses? Isn't it too cold for them?"

"Nope. I checked."

He gave me a severe eye roll. "Whatever. I stand by my original observation: trees are for things like berries, icicles, and such."

"Prude."

"Definitely not. You and Jenny should come over for dinner tonight. Ed's making pizza."

I rose. "In the pizza oven?"

He tsked. "Is there any other way?"

"We'll be there. I'll bring wine."

He kissed my cheek. "I thought you might. Six fifteen, please. You know Ed gets cranky when people aren't on time."

Jenny and I arrived five minutes early. Andy nodded approvingly. He took the wine and uncorked it, then poured lemonade for Jenny.

She smiled. "This is great. Fresh squeezed, just like Mom makes."

Ed huffed. "I'm sure it's better than that."

I put my hands on my hips. "Hey, I make darn good lemonade. You don't have the corner on that market."

He laughed. "You're right. I mean, how hard is it to squeeze a few lemons?" Andy poked him. Ed cleared his throat. "I'm sure it's a talent you have."

I gave him a dirty look. "Isn't it too cold out for the pizza oven?"

"Nope. You just have to get the fire started earlier and let it burn a bit hotter. Jenny, what toppings would you like?"

Jenny picked mushrooms, pepperoni, and sausage. I chose mushrooms, peppers, and garlic. Jenny said, "Good thing Mr. Jenson's not here."

I elbowed her. "It's going to be delicious." Sitting back down, I sipped my wine. "Andy told me that you've both been working around the clock."

Ed dotted the dough with the toppings. "It's been exhausting, but I think I'm starting to see the end of the tunnel."

"When are they finishing up?"

"Just after New Year's, thank goodness." He picked up the baking sheet holding the pizzas, grabbed the pizza peel, and scooted out the door to the backyard.

Jenny shivered as the air hit her. "Brr. I'm glad I'm not cooking. Doesn't he need a coat?"

Andy laughed. "Believe me, it's plenty hot by the oven. And that means they'll only take a few minutes to cook. Speaking of which, I better get the salad on the table."

I jumped up to help him. The salad bowl landed on the table just as Ed banged on the door. Andy stood quickly to open it. Steam rose from the pizzas on the peel. Andy slid them off onto a wooden board, and Ed went to get the remaining two. He returned and shut the door, then quickly sliced the pies.

The fresh oregano made it smell like a trattoria in Rome. Ed handed Jenny hers. She said, "Look how puffy the dough is. I love the crispy edges." She took a bite and closed her eyes. "Yum."

Ed smiled. "I'm glad you like it."

We all dug in, and appreciative moaning ensued around the table. I said, "I'm surprised that you were able to make the dough, what with all the midnight oil you've been burning. Andy said you were out past eleven Friday night."

He chuckled. "Saturday gave me a chance to recover. And anyway, I threw it together this morning. Plus, I wasn't out that late. I'm sure I came in around nine. Andy's exaggerating."

Andy's eyes were huge. He started to object, and Ed gave him a look.

Andy coughed. "Maybe I was confused." Ed nodded slowly. "I fell asleep watching a show. I guess I was groggy when Ed woke me up."

I turned to Andy. "So you were home all Friday night?"

"Didn't I just say that?"

Jenny asked, "What's for dessert?"

Ed stood. "I hope you don't mind me testing out one of my recipes on you, but I made a cherry tart."

Jenny grinned. "Feel free to use me as a guinea pig anytime."

She and I cleared the table while Ed cut the tart. I savored every bite. "This is so good. Is there pastry cream lining the shell?

His mouth full, he smiled and nodded.

"I can't wait till your shop opens."

Later that night, as I got ready for bed, my phone dinged with a text from Rob: "Paper to bed. Dinner tomorrow?"

"Sounds good. I'll cook."

He sent a smiley face in return.

"Ed's and Andy's alibis for Friday are shaky too."

"What? Let's talk tomorrow." He appended a heart emoji.

A light snow was falling when I rose the following morning. Beginning to frost the edges of the evergreens, the flakes wandered about, glistening in the waning moon's light. Shivering, I dressed quickly.

Work was busy, and the morning passed in a rush. At lunch, I ran home to put stew in the crockpot. I had just enough time to make myself a quick sandwich to bring back to my desk. At five, I gathered up some things I wanted to look at overnight and left.

Rob was setting the table when I returned to the house. I hugged him. "Thanks for getting a head start on things, but we won't be eating for another half hour or so. Is Jenny home?"

"She's upstairs studying."

Pouring us both a glass of wine, I handed him one. "Let's go in the living room."

I plugged in the tree and flicked on the fire. Putting on some Christmas music in the background, I dimmed the lights and sat next to him on the couch. Rob put his arm around me, and I snuggled against his chest.

I said, "Mmm. This is so cozy." The snow continued to dance past the living room window, settling into a slender line at the bottom of the sash. "This would be perfect if we didn't have two murders to solve."

Rob groaned as I pushed myself away and took a sip of the wine. "Do we have to talk about that?"

I kissed his cheek. "Sorry, but yes."

He sat up. "Philip and I are going shooting again Wednesday night."

"Do you think I could come with you?"

A slight frown creased his brow. "I thought you didn't like to shoot."

"I don't. But I don't like the idea of you meeting with him alone."

"It's a shooting range. I won't be alone."

"That's right. You won't be. I'll be there." Smiling, I leaned back against him.

He sighed as he took out his phone and tapped in, "Okay if Merry comes with us on Wednesday?"

"Fine. I'll see if Lauren can come, and we'll go to dinner after."

Rob put his arm around me. "Looks like we are going to make a night of it."

CHAPTER 25

Rob pulled into the parking lot of the range just behind Philip and Lauren. He turned off the engine. “How do you want to play this?”

I shrugged. “By ear, I guess. Let’s see what happens.”

We joined them just as they checked in. Philip said, “Good, we’re all here.”

The range manager opened the two gun cases Philip brought to check that the ammo was compatible with the targets used. Passing muster, he returned the guns to him. Philip took one case, handing the other to Lauren. They also had their own eye and ear protection.

I frowned at Rob. He said, “No worries. I’ll rent what we need.”

He had a short conversation with the manager, who disappeared into the storeroom and came back laden with everything. Weighing the case containing the gun, I raised an eyebrow.

Rob smiled. “Don’t worry. You’ll do fine.”

After watching a short video on gun safety as well as getting some instruction from Rob and Philip, we entered the range. Nervous, I took the gun from its case and loaded it. Putting on my eye and ear protection, I stepped to the firing line, gauging the distance to the target. Philip took up his stance, shot, and hit the center of the target. *He’s good. This could be embarrassing.*

Aiming, I fought to keep both eyes open as I squeezed the trigger. The slight recoil surprised me, and I staggered back. I looked at the target, surprised to see that I winged it. I grinned at Rob. He gave me a thumbs-up.

Twenty minutes later, I was hitting closer to the center of the target. I was also ready for a break. I gave Rob a sign, and we put our guns back in the cases. Signaling to Philip that we were taking a break, we went into the observation room.

Taking off my safety goggles and hearing protection, I giggled at Rob. "This is kind of fun."

He smiled. "You were really getting close at the end. A few more times and you'll be a pro."

I watched Philip and Lauren through the glass. "I knew he was a good shot, but Lauren surprised me. I didn't know she was that good."

"Philip told me they met at the range. When they were first dating, they used to go twice a month."

I grimaced. "Not my kind of romantic."

"Not mine either, but I guess it works for them. Did you notice the caliber pistol Philip is shooting?"

I studied the gun. "To be honest, I can't tell. What is it?"

"It's a .38."

My head whipped around to face Rob. "He wouldn't."

"He might."

We turned back toward the range. Philip studied us, his eyes narrowing.

I said, "Break's over. We should get back."

We shot for another thirty minutes. Philip signaled Rob that we should wrap it up.

As we walked out together, Philip said, "Merry, I do believe we will make a marksperson out of you."

I grinned. "This was a lot of fun."

Rob held open the car door for me, speaking over it to Philip, "Meet you at Fiorella's?"

"Sounds good."

I put my seat belt on. "It would have been even more fun if I knew Philip wasn't the killer."

"Let's just get through dinner."

We all ordered drinks. I asked Lauren, "How did you two meet?"

"At the range. Philip was already there. I was admiring how well he shot. Then I admired how well he looked. I still admire him." She blushed, looking down at her lap. Philip beamed at her. "From then until Amanda wiggled onto the scene, we were together." She frowned at her drink and took a swig.

Philip held her hand. "In the grand scheme of time, it was a momentary aberration. And one for which I continue to feel deep shame." He kissed her hand and stared deeply into her eyes. "Let's focus on the future, not the past."

Raising my menu, I gave Rob a heavy eye roll. He shot me a quick smile and asked Philip, "Any plans for Christmas?"

"We've rented a cabin in Tennessee through New Year's. It has a private hot tub on a deck outside the cabin. Even if the temperature is below freezing, your body warms the second it hits the water. Plus, the night sky is breathtaking. They do all of the decorating and stock it with food, so all we have to do is show up. They'll even supply a chef, but Lauren wants to cook." He kissed her hand again. "We deserve some alone time." Lauren looked at him like he was the Christmas present she'd waited her whole life for.

I said, "That sounds romantic. I'm sure you'll have a great time."

"What about you two?"

I twisted my napkin and looked at the floor. Rob said, "With everything that's been going on, we really haven't had a chance to discuss it."

Lauren rubbed my shoulder. "That's right. How's your daughter holding up? This has to be rough on her."

"She's a trooper."

Our dinners came. I dove into my risotto as if I hadn't eaten in days. It was creamy, soft, and comforting. The mushrooms added a nice, earthy flavor. Philip reached for the salt and knocked over his glass of wine. It bounced off the bread basket, and as he stood to right it, his cell phone sailed under the table.

"I'll get it." I dove under the table as waiters rushed over with towels to wipe up the mess.

I handed the phone to Philip. He said, "Thanks. I'm sorry about all the commotion. Usually I'm so good with my hands."

Table cleaned, we resumed eating and chatting. Putting some more risotto into my mouth, I bit down with a resounding crunch.

Rob's eyes widened. "What was that?"

I held my napkin in front of my mouth. "There was something hard in the risotto."

I stood and ran, napkin still over my mouth, to the ladies' room. Lauren was right behind me. I shut the door after her and spit what was left in my mouth into the napkin. Among the Arborio rice grains was a small piece of chicken bone. And next to that was a large piece of tooth.

Lauren and I stared at each other in stunned silence. Then she said, "I guess it's a good thing you're having dinner with a dentist."

I put the piece of tooth in a paper towel, throwing the napkin and its contents into the trash.

Rob knocked on the door. "Merry, are you okay?"

"Yes. I'll be out in a minute."

As I leaned over to splash my face with water, pain radiated from the injured tooth. "It's starting to hurt now. And it's bad."

"You look pale. Let me get Rob in here."

She opened the door, and Rob rushed in. "Are you okay?"

I held my throbbing jaw. "No."

"Can you walk?"

Grimacing, I nodded. He half carried me out to the car.

Philip dashed after us. "Lauren told me you broke a tooth."

Moaning, I nodded and handed him the paper towel. He said, "That's a large piece." I sank into the car seat. Philip told Rob, "Bring her to my office. I'll be right behind you."

Tires squealing, Rob made it to Philip's office in record time. True to his word, Philip pulled in right behind us. Rob carried me inside. Philip pointed to an examining room, and Rob put me down in the chair.

After washing his hands, Philip clipped on my bib. "I know it hurts, but you'll need to open your mouth for me."

Tears streamed down my face. I opened my mouth.

He probed the area. "You're going to need a cap. Hopefully you won't need a root canal."

The air hit my tooth, and I screamed. Rob grabbed Philip's shoulder. "Can't you give her something for the pain?"

"I don't like to give sedatives to patients who have been drinking."

I gave him a pleading look. Rob said, "She didn't have more than a few sips."

"Okay, I'll give her something. Merry, you may have a bad hangover tomorrow, so I don't want you to blame me." He chuckled.

Writhing in the chair, I groaned again, nodding that I understood. He said, "Let me get an IV set up. This is going to take a while, and I don't want you to feel any pain. You'll be in a kind of twilight state." Philip nodded at Lauren. "Lauren, would you please take Rob to the waiting room?"

Rob frowned. "I'd rather stay here."

"I don't need anxious boyfriends pulling at me while I'm working. The sooner you leave, the sooner I can get Merry more comfortable." Philip folded his arms and leaned back against the counter.

Rob rubbed my shoulder. "Okay. But I'll be right outside." Lauren took Rob's arm, and they left.

"Merry, I'm setting up the IV now. At first, it will be just a saline solution, but then I'll put in something to take care of the pain."

I nodded. He found a vein and inserted the needle, then hung the bag from the holder. He injected the pain medication into the tube.

My body immediately started to relax. The pain went away. I felt like I was floating. Philip appeared above me, and I obediently opened my mouth.

He patted my arm. "That won't be necessary. Unfortunately, you're going to have a very bad reaction to the painkiller. I tried to help, but it happens sometimes."

My eyes bulging, I tried to speak, slurring my words. "What do you mean?"

"Pam followed up with me today. She told me you called with questions and asked why I hadn't entered my emergency patient information from Friday night. I told her it was for a poker buddy, so I wasn't charging him. That satisfied her, but I knew it wasn't going to satisfy you. I saw the way you and Rob looked at me at the gun range tonight. You knew I killed Amanda." His face reddened. "She was mine, but all Drew had to do was crook his little finger and she came running like the hussy that she was." His fists clenched. "She had it made dating a respectable dentist like me, but she threw it all away over a no-good thief." Philip straightened his shirt and smiled, a faraway look in his eyes. "Well, she can't embarrass me anymore."

My eyes began to close. "Susan."

He sighed. "Yes, Susan too. I figured that would be the nail in the coffin for Drew." He smiled, leaning back on the stool. "And it was."

"How?"

"How what?"

Eyes half open, I barely got the word out. "Tooth."

"I created a distraction. It worked perfectly, and I was able to slip that bit of chicken bone into your risotto." He tilted his head. "I'll probably have to think of some way to make it up to Fiorella's. This won't be good for their business, and I like that restaurant."

"And now, Merry, it's time." He held the needle to the IV tube and began to insert it.

Rob charged around the corner and Philip turned toward him. A small gun stuck out of Philip's waistband. I mouthed the word, "Gun," but what came out of my mouth was more of a grunt.

My eyes fluttered. I fought to hold them open. Rob smacked the hypodermic from Philip's hand. Philip punched him and he went down. Rob yanked Philip's leg out from under him and Philip fell, hitting the instrument tray as he went down. Dental implements began what appeared to be a slow motion descent around me.

I felt like I was looking through a kaleidoscope; everything seemed off kilter. Rob and Philip skirmished on the floor. Then Rob grabbed a scalpel that had landed near him. Philip attempted to hold onto Rob's arms, but the scalpel inched closer and closer to Philip's face. With a mighty shove, Philip drove Rob back, pulled his gun from his waistband, and shot him. The sound reverberated in the tiny examining room.

Tears rolled down my face.

Rob laid there motionless. Philip got to his feet and kicked him in the stomach. He smoothed his clothes and wiped the blood from his nose. Then, casting about, he found the syringe he dropped. "Oh good. It didn't break." He turned to the IV and again inserted the needle.

Lauren loomed behind him. Another blast tore through the examining room.

Philip's mouth formed a perfect circle as he fell forward.

My eyes rolled back and I felt myself sliding down the chair.

CHAPTER 26

I woke with a raging headache and a dry mouth that rivaled the Sahara. Moaning, I opened my eyes. As the bright lights assailed me, I yelped, reflexively shutting my eyes. I slowly opened them just a crack to scan the room. *I'm in a hospital. What happened?* I sat bolt upright. "Where's Rob. Rob was shot!" My head splitting, I fell back down on the pillows.

Patty popped into my line of sight. "Good. You're awake."

I croaked. "Rob? Is he dead?"

She rubbed my arm. "No. Philip got him in the shoulder. He's in surgery now, but they expect him to be okay."

"Thank God." I shaded my eyes from the relentless overhead lights. "My head hurts."

She nodded. "They said it would. Let me call the nurse so she can give you something." Patty pressed the call button.

"Thirsty."

Putting some ice chips on a spoon, Patty fed them to me.

The nurse put some type of magic solution in my IV. Within minutes, my headache level went from a loud roar to something far more manageable. Rubbing my eyes, I thanked her.

Patty hovered.

"When will Rob be out of surgery?"

She looked at her watch. "Any minute now. They said two hours."

I gripped her hand. "What if he doesn't make it."

She touched my face. "He'll make it."

Jenny ran in. "The nurse told me you were awake. I was just getting some hot chocolate in the cafeteria." She looked down at my face. "Are you okay? You scared me."

"I scared me too." I motioned her to come closer for a kiss.

She held my hand. "How's Mr. Jenson?"

I glared at the clock. "We haven't heard yet."

There was a quick rap at the door and the surgeon strode in. "Your friend was very lucky. The bullet just missed a major artery. He had some tendon damage but that should heal. He's going to need some help over the next few weeks. Does he have someplace to stay?"

Jenny said, "Of course. He'll stay with us."

I squeezed her hand. "When can I see him?"

He's in recovery right now. He checked his watch. "Probably about another forty-five minutes. Just one of you at a time." He smiled at me. "And that all depends on how you are feeling."

Patty rubbed my arm. "If you'll bend the rules a bit, Jenny can wheel her mom in if the nurses clear her."

He nodded. "I think we can arrange that."

The door shut behind him.

I chewed more ice chips and frowned. "How did Rob know I needed help?"

Patty moved the ice closer to my hand. "Would you mind a visitor? She can tell the story better than I." She stuck her head out the door to motion someone in.

Lauren trudged to the bed. Her fine porcelain complexion looked pallid and mascara marred her cheeks. "Merry. Are you okay? How's Rob? I've been so worried."

"I'm fine and Rob's out of surgery. Philip gave me some type of drug, so I was in and out when all the fighting was going on. Do you know what happened? Am I remembering correctly—did you shoot Philip?

She sobbed quietly. "I shot him. He was going to hurt you."

I touched her arm. "Thank you."

Patty handed Lauren a tissue and she wiped her eyes. "We were in the waiting room. Rob was pacing. I was replaying what happened at dinner in my mind. Philip slipped something onto your plate. At first I thought I imagined it. But then I realized I hadn't. I must have gasped, because Rob came to a stop right in front of me. I told him what I saw. He raced back to the examining room and I called 911.

"They told me to stay on the line, but then I heard the shot. My heart was in my throat. I pulled my gun out of my purse and crept along the corridor. Philip had the hypodermic needle in the IV tube and was pressing the plunger."

She looked at the ceiling as tears dripped down her face. "I couldn't let him kill you, Merry, so I shot him. God help me, I shot him dead." Sobs racked her body.

Patty retrieved water from the nurses' station. Lauren drank it and regained control.

"You looked so lifeless and Rob was bleeding on the floor. I didn't know if Philip had gotten anything into your IV so I ripped it out." She looked down at my bruised and bandaged arm. "I'm sorry if I hurt you."

The nurse came in with a wheelchair. "Anyone up for seeing the other patient?"

Rob looked so pale and his shoulder was heavily bandaged. I gently stroked his face. His eyes opened and he smiled. "There's my girl." I kissed him.

The nurse strode in. "He needs his rest, and so do you. You can visit together later."

Jenny kissed his cheek.

Patty poured a lemon-lime soda for me and unwrapped saltines.

“I could do this myself you know.”

“I know. I guess it’s just the mom in me.”

I smiled and sipped the soda.

The door opened, and Jay stuck his head in. “The hospital called to tell me you were awake. I haven’t been able to talk to Rob yet. How’s he doing?”

“Things went well in surgery and they expect him to make a full recovery.”

“That’s great news.” He smiled at me. “I’m here to get your statement.” He looked at Patty, and Jenny. “You’ll have to excuse us.”

Patty said, “No way.” Jenny shook her head too.

Jay sighed. “I figured as much.” He sat in a chair and took out his notepad. “What happened, Merry?”

I chewed my saltines and told him.

Jay nodded. “We found the murder weapon in his car. I can’t believe he still had it. He has a lot of chutzpah.”

“He had the gun at the range last night. Rob noticed it. Rob was right. He said he didn’t think Philip would be able to part with it.” I rubbed my jaw. “There’s just one thing I don’t understand: Why do I have a tooth? Philip didn’t fix it.”

Patty smiled. “When Lauren got to the hospital, she called Dr. Malcolm. He was able to put a temporary crown on here in the hospital while you were still out of it. You have to make an appointment to come back in about two weeks to get the permanent one. And he said no hard objects till then.”

I shivered. Patty rubbed my arm. “One good thing. Dr. Malcolm said that in view of what happened, he’s not going to charge you for it.”

I nodded. “It’s the least he could do.”

CHAPTER 27

The Christmas party at Patty's house was in full swing. The kitchen was food central. Pies lined the back counter near the sink, and the island groaned under its buffet of turkey and beef. Mashed potatoes and gravy joined them along with casseroles of green beans, Brussels sprouts, and broccoli. And if that wasn't enough, the kitchen table boasted coleslaw, an immense green salad, and carrots in gelatin.

Patty and I huddled near the impromptu bar Patrick erected in the living room. I savored my eggnog. "This is even better than last year. And I thought last year was phenomenal."

She smiled and hugged me. "It is fun, isn't it? Do you think we have enough food?"

I laughed. "It's a good thing you invited so many people, but I still think we're only going to put a dent in it."

Rob smiled at me from across the room, raising his glass in a silent toast, his other arm in a sling. I lifted mine to him and grinned back. Drew and Jenny played a board game with Cindy and one of her brothers on the floor in the parlor.

I hugged Patty. "Thanks for asking Drew. It's awkward, but it also makes it easier for us both to spend time with Jenny."

"How are you feeling about her going away for New Year's?"

"I'll miss her, but it will be good for her to get some alone time with her dad." I wiggled my eyebrows. "At least that's what I'm telling myself." I sipped the eggnog. "Rob and I are going away too but just for the weekend. We're going to go out to the lake house. It's nice and quiet this time of year, and I think he needs some pampering after everything he's been through."

Patty smiled wickedly. "I just bet you do."

Ed and Andy poured more champagne. Andy said, "Great party, Patty." He frowned at me. "I'm almost talking to you again. I can't believe you suspected me." Laughing, he and Ed went to talk with Rob and Patrick.

I blushed. "You don't think he's serious, do you?"

"Well, you did try to throw suspicion on him."

"Not really."

Her eyebrows arched. "Uh-huh. Like you didn't sic the police on him?"

I gulped. "That was you!"

She laughed and rang a small bell. "Everyone grab a plate, and let's eat."

Piled down with leftovers, Rob, Jenny, and I made our way back to the house after helping Patrick and Patty clean up. I shoved everything into the refrigerator. "I'll deal with that later."

Jenny kissed me. "Best Christmas ever." Then she carefully hugged Rob. "Thanks for trying to save my mom. You're the best." As she ran up the stairs, she called back, "Don't forget, Mom. You're taking me swimsuit shopping tomorrow."

I laughed. I uncorked a bottle of wine and took down two glasses. Rob took my hand and led me into the living room. He poured the wine while I plugged in the tree and clicked on the fire.

Sitting down, he put his good arm around me. "I agree with Jenny. Best Christmas ever." He gave me a long kiss, and I relaxed against his chest. He gazed into my eyes. "I love you, Meredith March. And I think it's time you made that appointment with Father Tom to talk about an annulment."

ABOUT THE AUTHOR

Eileen Hammond is an author who recently retired from a successful marketing career in the insurance industry. She and her husband share the house with two cats that are determined to train them. Rounding out the household are two koi, Daisy and Rose, as well as assorted shubunkins and minnows. Tending to this menagerie, writing, and rescuing the frog population from certain death in the pool keep her busy.

ALSO BY EILEEN CURLEY HAMMOND

Murder So Sinful

Made in the USA
Las Vegas, NV
24 October 2024

10226655R00142